Last Reels

Ben Dowell

Copyright © 2019 Ben Dowell

This is a work of fiction, although based on the author's recollection of actual events. Names, characters, businesses, places, events and incidents are either the products of the author's imagination or have been used in a fictitious manner. Any resemblance to actual persons, living or dead, is purely coincidental.

Cover photo of film and spools © 2019 Chris Swindells

Visit my website at www.mawgrim.co.uk
Email:bdowell@mawgrim.co.uk

ISBN: 978-1-09348-717-6

Dedicated to the memory of Barry
Diamondstone
1936 -1999

Reel 1

The Looming Iceberg

Bill: 2010

Imagine you are sitting in the steeply raked auditorium of a suburban super cinema, built sometime in the nineteen-thirties. Back then, cinemas like this brought a touch of Hollywood glamour into ordinary people's lives, but time has moved on and audiences have declined, pulled away by other forms of entertainment. The seat you are sitting on is well worn. The decorative lighting is kept deliberately dim, to hide the peeling paint on the side walls and the badly patched holes in the ceiling where an electrician accidentally put his boot through. The screen curtains tremble slightly, as if in anticipation of the coming film. The more prosaic reason is that there's a hell of a draught coming in from backstage where local youths lobbed a brick through the windows yet again.

Both lights and background music begin to slowly fade. The curtains swish open and a piercing beam of light is released from the small rectangular porthole behind you. A picture comes to life on the screen.

Grainy black and white footage indicates that this is the past; a caption reads AUGUST 1963. A young man strolls down the street, past the imposing frontage of this very cinema.

A voiceover begins. 'That summer, I'd just left school and didn't really know what I wanted to do. There'd been talk of going as an apprentice plumber with one of my dad's mates, but so far, it hadn't come to anything. The local factory was always after production line workers, but the work was so boring, no-one lasted long. Or if they did, they became brain dead, like those zombies you saw in films.'

Something catches his eye. He climbs the steps and peers at a notice, hand lettered.

Wanted. Part time ushers and usherettes. Full time rewind boy. Apply within.

'I'd always enjoyed going to the cinema, but I'd never thought about working in one. It seemed a bit exotic, like going off to join the circus or something.'

The door opens and he steps into the foyer. It's much grander than it appears today, with an imposing central pay box like a pulpit. There's a small queue of people waiting in front of this. We hear the chink of the ticket machine as it dispenses small, cardboard rectangles. Posters advertising forthcoming attractions are dotted around in freestanding frames. Smartly uniformed staff stand beside the inner doors, guiding people through to the stalls. The slightly better off patrons climb the stairs towards the circle.

'This was show business, not an everyday sort of job like most folk had.'

He meets the manager inside the general office, followed by a brief conversation.

'I was a practical sort of lad and I wanted full time work. He said I'd be best off talking to the chief projectionist.'

Another man comes in, wearing a long brown coat over his suit. They shake hands. A door labelled *Projection Box* opens onto a room where two large machines point towards the portholes. There is the unmistakeable sound of film running through a projector.

'And that was how my career in the cinema business began…'

The frame judders; stops, then the film begins to melt and curl as a bright white light burns through the centre. Another voice comes in, in the style of a news reporter.

'But now, in two thousand and ten, it looks as if Bill's long service to the industry is about to come to an abrupt end.'

The white screen wipes to modern day footage, in colour, showing a very different style of projection room; a wide, shiny corridor with projectors arrayed each side. Some of these are running film, served from large rotating platters to one side of them. Others are squat black boxes, only identifiable as projectors from the lenses facing the portholes.

'The cinema industry is about to go digital. And in this brave new world, is there a place for the projectionist?'

The camera swoops through an open doorway into a comfortably furnished staff room. Two middle-aged men are sitting at a table. Half-finished mugs of tea and an open tin of biscuits lie between them.

'Listen, Bill, they've wanted to get rid of projectionists for years and digital will give them the perfect opportunity.' The younger of the two men taps a finger pointedly on a printed document. The surface of his tea shivers, as if a monster stalked the projection room with a heavy, ominous tread.

Bill sighs. 'I've heard all that before. So have you, Jim. It'll be the same this time. A few jobs will go, granted, but that's always been the way with progress.'

'"We won't make anyone redundant unless we have to." That's what it says in here.' Jim picks up the document and waves it in the air, scattering biscuit crumbs. 'Maybe not, but they'll make our lives so bloody difficult that anyone who can will go and get another job and save them paying out redundancy. It's all right for the young ones – they can find other work.'

'You're only fifty-four.'

'And I've been working in projection since I left school. Who's going to take me on, at my age? At least you'll be safely retired before it all kicks off.'

'Not necessarily,' Bill points out. 'I don't intend to retire at sixty-five if I'm still healthy and enjoying the work. I know where you're coming from, Jim. I've seen it all before. Back in the sixties, when automation first came along, they cut the number of men in the box. Then they started tripling the old cinemas and had to take on extra people again. Single manning cut the numbers, multiplexes put them up. It's the way the business goes.' He's warming to the theme. 'Now look, we've had a couple of digital projectors for a while now. We know the problems. They're not reliable, are they? Think how often they crash on start up.'

Jim nods reluctantly. 'Yeah, I know…'

'Of course, there won't need to be as many projectionists because there won't be the volume of film to make up any more. But customers aren't going to tolerate it if they have to sit looking at a blank screen, or a picture with no sound. Good presentation will still be important. The company won't want to refund money all the time because something's gone wrong, will they? And that means having technical people on site. People like us, with experience and knowledge. It's common sense.'

Jim drains the last of his tea and stands up. 'I hope you're right, I really do.' He glances at the clock on the wall. 'Better go and start screen eight.'

Bill sits there alone with the distant sound of film running through projectors in the background. The picture slowly fades to black.

Graham: 2010

All day Graham had wondered how he was going to tell Maria. She must know about the vacancy by now; they worked for the same company and read the same internal bulletin published each week. And he'd mentioned often enough that if the chance came, he'd like to become a Projection Engineer.

Maria's career in the cinema had started in a similar way to his - working front of house during her time studying at university. Like him, she'd enjoyed the cinema business sufficiently to make it a career once she'd passed her degree. Except that she had chosen to become a manager, which made all the difference. Maria looked on her position as a stepping stone which suited her plans and ambition for the time being. She'd said often enough she couldn't understand why the General Manager at her site had worked for the same company all his life and demonstrated a degree of loyalty that would never be repaid.

Graham could understand it perfectly. He felt the same about cinema; to him, it wasn't just a job, but a way of life. Like Maria, he had a degree and transferable skills that would allow him to change his career if he wanted to. He just didn't want to.

'Once this digital revolution happens, you may not have a choice,' she'd pointed out often enough. Of course, she was right. He knew that the projectionist's role was bound to change when there was no more film to show on a regular basis. There would be job losses and no one could say for sure how many. Practical considerations said that there would always be a need for at least one technical person per cinema, yet digital cinema articles and adverts trumpeted the proud fact that at long last new technology would make the totally automated and unmanned projection room possible. Self-preservation made it necessary to think of a way that he could continue working in the industry.

He'd always been good at the technical side of the job, which was the reason he'd risen from Trainee to Chief Technician in just three years. The natural career progression was from Chief to Engineer. Normally, jobs only came up when people retired, but all the installation work necessary for the digital roll out meant that there were now four new vacancies. It was a no brainer.

How to explain his reasons to Maria, though? He could stress the positives - better salary, company car, and promotion - but he knew that deep down, she'd prefer him to put his IT qualifications to their appropriate use and change industry while he was still young.

So while he drove home, he played and replayed the possible conversations in his head, trying to counter all the arguments she might muster against his decision.

'Of course, I might not even get the job,' he pointed out, some hours later. 'There's bound to be a lot of applications. But I need to try, if only to prove to myself that I can do it. It doesn't mean I'll do it forever.'

Maria poured herself another glass of wine. 'But you will, Graham. If you get this job, you'll think it's saved you the effort of moving on and stay too long. You'll get happily stuck in a rut. Then when it all falls apart ten or fifteen years down the line, you'll have nowhere to move to.'

'Cinemas will always need engineers.'

'Will they, though? Ten years ago, you could have said the same about projectionists. At least if they decide to cut the number of managers I have a load of transferable skills I can take to another industry. Cinema projection is just too specialised.'

'Digital cinema is about servers and networks. It's totally different to film.'

Maria didn't listen, but carried on with her theme. 'Who's to say there'll even be cinemas in ten or fifteen years? Look at what happened to the music industry once everyone started downloading instead of buying a physical product. What happens if people don't want to go to cinemas anymore?'

'People will always go to the cinema. I heard my dad and uncle have that very same argument back in the eighties. Dad was convinced video players would kill the industry. But it didn't. And way before that, they said the same about TV.'

'But we're not living back then. Things are changing even more quickly. Our generation won't have jobs for life. We need to cover our backs and try to think ahead of the game.'

He opened the fridge and took out another can of beer. Best to go along with her, for a bit. After the best part of a bottle of wine, she could be really stubborn. 'I know what you're trying to say. I just need to prove I can get this job, on my own merits. In any case, I've heard it might just be temporary, while they're installing the kit. And it would look good on my CV.'

She took a drink. 'It's not that I don't want you to apply,' she said slowly. 'I just don't want to see you stuck in a dead end. Maybe if you took the redundancy...'

'Oh, come on. We've talked about that before and done the maths. It's not worth it for someone like me with just a couple of years' service. And what if I don't find another job right away? We couldn't afford the rent for this place on just one wage.' He saw her face change and realised he was on the right track. She liked living here and wouldn't want to trade down.

She drank some wine. 'You've got a point there. And you're right; it did say some of the vacancies were temporary...'

He drove it home. 'Plus the wage is better, so I can put away a bit more for a deposit.' It would be years before they were able to buy a place, but they were both saving what they could and tried not to be too extravagant.

'What if you don't get the job?'

That didn't bear thinking about, but he wasn't going to admit it to Maria. 'Then I'll start looking around, get my CV updated and register on a few job sites.'

'Sounds like a plan.'

'Indeed.' Together, they drank a toast to the future.

Cat: 2010

Cinemas didn't have staff Christmas parties in the way other industries did. It was too difficult to fit them in given the unsociable hours of cinema opening, especially during school holidays when the first film started at around nine thirty in the morning and the last shows ended close to midnight. Also where most businesses shut down for at least a few days, having realised the staff would all be hungover and unable to work productively, cinemas only closed for the day itself, December 25th.

During the twenty-five years Cat had worked in the business, she had never felt hard done by due to this. Christmas, in her opinion, was overrated for everyone older than ten; a day of stuffing yourself silly and putting up with your most annoying relatives in winter weather that forced everyone to stay indoors and get on each other's nerves.

The highlight of her December celebrations was the annual Projectionists' Party up in London, usually held at the Odeon Leicester Square in the grandly titled *Royal Retiring Room*, an overheated little cubby-hole in the bowels of the cinema. The lime green walls were festooned with black and white pictures of stars and Royalty shaking hands during the many premieres held since the cinema had first opened in the nineteen-thirties. It would be a fascinating place to browse for many a film buff, but most of the guests at the party didn't give a second glance at these historic records. Not when there was the far more important task of drinking as much free booze as possible and catching up on gossip with people you only saw once a year.

There were the award ceremonies too; Projection Team of the Year and the Frank Littlejohn award. During these presentations, Cat often felt that people were keeping quiet more from politeness than any real interest in the proceedings, itching to carry on with their rounds of the room as soon as decently possible. This year, even more so.

This year, they had been upgraded from the 'dungeon' to the grander surroundings of the circle foyer, whose full length windows framed a view of the frosty Square. And all the talk was of the looming iceberg ahead - the impending change from film to digital.

Even as she arrived to see the smokers gathered in groups beneath the famous canopy, the conversation had steered toward the first casualties of the digital programme.

'Did you know Phil's taking voluntary redundancy? He's only fifty-something, but he's had enough. His last day's Christmas Eve.'

She'd met Phil a few times before. Like many of his generation, he'd always kept to the high standards drummed into him as a trainee. 'Is he here?' She asked. 'I'd like to say goodbye.'

A gesture of the head toward the stairs. 'Up there. You'll find there's a lot going and some already gone.' He mentioned another well-known character. 'Mike went two weeks ago. The company made him an offer he couldn't refuse. Another union man out of the way, that's how they see it. Less resistance from whoever's left.'

'"Resistance is futile",' she quoted.

'Exactly. I'll give you a bit of advice. Don't wait too long. The best deals are going fast.'

'But I don't want to leave.'

An exhalation of smoke punctuates the air. 'Listen, love, it ain't about what the likes of you and me want. We're like those poor sods clinging on to the Titanic as it sank. No one wants to jump off, but if you don't you'll go down with the ship for sure.'

On the train going home, her thoughts still slightly hazy from the afternoon's alcohol, they suddenly pulled to a sharp focus. She remembered other events with a similar atmosphere - people drinking to numb the pain of something about to come to an end. It had reminded her of the closing parties of the early eighties; the time when her first job in the cinema had been cut short.

Reel 2

A Slow Decline

Bill: 1963-1973

Bill mopped the vast expanse of the projection box floor. He reflected that although the job had seemed faintly exotic, like joining the circus, even there someone had to muck out the elephants. After ten weeks in the cinema business, his working days followed a long standing tradition of drudgery; cleaning, mopping, polishing, making tea and coffee, washing up dirty mugs and taking the rubbish out to the bins. The nearest he'd been allowed to get to a film was carrying the heavy metal transit cases from the film dump downstairs to the lofty heights of the projection box. It was one hundred and eleven steps. He'd counted them often enough.

He was the newest and lowliest of the five men working in projection. Harold, the Chief, spent most of the morning in his office at the far end of the box, then just after eleven o'clock, went for a meeting with the General Manager to the 'other office' – the Rose and Crown pub next door. He would return before the first show was due on to make sure everyone had carried out their allotted duties correctly. In his absence, the Co-Chief, Charlie, was supposed to be in charge. In actual fact, he sat in the staff room reading the newspaper and smoking. Most of his fag ash was flicked onto the floor; it was one of Bill's jobs to clean it up and empty the stinking ashtray.

The real work was done by the rest of them. Bill did all the menial tasks while Brian, the Second Operator, maintained the projection equipment and prepared for the day's shows. John, the unlucky Third, who was just a few years older than Bill, never quite managed to achieve the high standards Brian insisted upon. It didn't help that he was slightly clumsy and got flustered under pressure.

'I hate this job,' he told Bill, just a few days after he started. 'Soon as I can, I'm getting out. This is a mug's game, anyway. My old man says as soon as everyone's got a telly, cinemas will be done for.'

Bill thought of the queues the previous night. *Cleopatra* was really doing the business. The front of house staff had to turn people away, but many of them would be back to try again. He'd managed to catch a few tantalising glimpses of the film through a viewing port when he wasn't being told to do something else. Who would want to watch something that spectacular on an eighteen inch screen in black and white?

'Besides,' John went on, 'It's no good for your love life. Girls want to go out of an evening, but when you're stuck here five nights a week, there's no chance of that.'

Both Harold and Charlie had ended up marrying women who worked in the cinema. 'It doesn't work, going out with someone who isn't in the business,' Charlie said one afternoon. 'They'll moan about you never being around. They don't understand. My first wife kept trying to get me to leave the trade. When I wouldn't, she buggered off with a plumber.'

He was right. Bill kept in contact with friends from school, but soon lost touch with who was seeing who, where they'd been and where they were planning on going. After just a few months, they had little in common any more. It was almost inevitable that he ended up on a date with the prettiest ice-cream sales girl.

'That afternoon when you came down to the ice room to fix the light on my tray, I knew there was something between us,' Maureen said later.

'Yes, five raspberry ripples and a choc and nut sundae,' he joked.

By then, he'd been at the cinema nearly a year and in addition to his menial duties, was finally allowed to rewind film, as his job title implied. His fingers had hardened up so they no longer burned when he built up a bit of speed. He'd passed Brian's scrutiny before he was permitted to progress from scrap film to adverts, trailers and finally, the feature itself.

He'd also learned how to lace up a film through the projector and how to start it up, although only on the quieter afternoon performances. Harold or Charlie always started the main show of the evening, to ensure good presentation. They also took the changeovers between reels, as inexperienced trainees couldn't be trusted to do it correctly.

'If it's smooth, the audience shouldn't even know we've changed over from one machine to the other,' Charlie said. 'Back when I started, if you messed up a changeover, you were fined sixpence from your wages.'

There was something about getting everything just right that gave him a great deal of job satisfaction. Even the never-ending cleaning had a purpose – tiny specks of dust on the film were magnified into huge black spots on screen and could cause scratching too.

Bill and Maureen 'went out' for nearly two years, although actually going anywhere was made difficult by their shift patterns. Sometimes, on a quiet afternoon when they managed to wangle their breaks together, they would sneak into the darkened auditorium and cuddle in the back row or go and explore the vast and empty backstage area, which often ended in other kinds of exploration. Maureen was a kindred spirit. She was a real film buff and kept up with all the gossip about the stars. Soon, everyone knew they were an 'item' and proposing to her was just the next logical step. They married in nineteen sixty-seven. The wedding was attended by as many of the cinema staff as could get the day off. There was more popcorn than confetti thrown as they came out of the registry office.

When John finally left, Bill was promoted to Third. He would still be the lowliest member of the crew though; the company had started to reduce staff numbers due to steadily declining admissions.

Harold had protested this vehemently. 'How can they expect us to keep up standards if there aren't enough men to do the work?' He was even more opposed to the introduction of automation, which was gradually being installed around the circuit. 'Listen to this rubbish,' he said, reading from an advertising brochure. '"Runs the show perfectly every single time." What do they think we do all day?'

Electricians came in and installed a new isolator for the Projectomatic system. Then the company engineers arrived and within two days had it assembled, connected and ready to run. It worked along the lines of a musical box; a rotating drum with removable pins, one for each function such as projector start, tabs open, non-sync and film sound. You pinned up the shows for the day and then left everything in the charge of the machine. And it was clever, no doubt about that, but never one hundred percent reliable. You couldn't deny it did a perfectly good job of running shows nine times out of ten, but something was lost; that individual touch and the feeling of pride in good presentation that had always been an integral part of the job.

The cinema union representative visited every couple of months. He provided a useful source of information about what the company intended to do. Projectionists were rarely informed about what was planned by those whose days ranged between high level meetings and all expenses paid lunches, so they had to rely on the 'grapevine'.

'We've had some talks with the company about what's going to happen once the installations have finished. They don't spell it out, of course, but we know they've been over in the States, finding out how they run things over there.'

'And how do they run things over there?' Harold asked.

'With a lot fewer projectionists than we do. Most cinemas only have one man on duty at a time. It's only a matter of time before it happens here as well.'

'So do you think there'll be redundancies?' Bill asked. The tea left an acid taste behind in his mouth. Now he was a married man, he couldn't afford to be out of work, and the usual rule was 'last in, first out'.

'As far as we can tell, it's not going to be that drastic. If someone leaves, it's unlikely they'll be replaced. Mind you, the business hasn't been great these past few years, as you know. And it doesn't look as if it's going to improve.'

'Bloody television,' said Harold. 'It rots the brain. My grandkids sit in front of the goggle-box for hours, when they should be out playing.'

'I know, I know. But we can't do anything to stop that. We've just got to limit the damage. There's still a place for cinema. People will always want to see a big film on the big screen.'

Charlie retired. Brian kept writing to the Zone Engineer, asking to be promoted to Co-Chief. When it was obvious nothing was going to happen, he applied for a Chief's job elsewhere. He seemed as surprised as anyone when he was successful. 'Just goes to show you don't have to be over fifty to be a chief these days. Times are changing.'

When he left, Bill was promoted again, but no-one else was taken on, so despite the title of Second Projectionist, he wasn't actually in charge of anyone. With just the two of them left, there was no choice but to 'single man' the cinema. Bill was earning good money from all the overtime. He wasn't going to complain; especially now there was a baby on the way.

His early years in the cinema trade were marked out by notable film releases; the Carry On films, slightly risqué and good fun. The inevitable Bond movies; *Goldfinger, Thunderball, You Only Live Twice* and *On Her Majesty's Secret Service.* Spaghetti Westerns, such as *The Good, The Bad and the Ugly* and *Once Upon a Time In The West. The Sound of Music;* destined to become a Christmas TV classic long after its last showing on the big screen. There was Disney for the family audience and Hammer Horror for the adults.

He'd got himself a reputation for being reliable, dependable and conscientious. Whenever the Sound Engineer came in, he always made sure to be there, finding out as much as he could, asking questions and helping out as much as possible without being in the way.

'You should put in for a chief's job yourself,' Bertie Arkwright, the engineer, said one afternoon as he slurped his black coffee and chain smoked his way through a pack of ten cigarettes.

'I don't have the experience yet. I've only been a projectionist for six years.'

Bertie made a disparaging gesture, punctuated with a snort that sent ash flying in all directions. 'And you've already learned more than some of these idiots will ever know. You must have heard about the plans for tripling cinemas?'

Bill nodded. '"More screens, more choice," so they say.'

'Well, it's going to be a whole different operation. Xenon lamps, cakestands. Two or three separate boxes. Lots of opportunities for young blokes like you.'

Harold was due to retire in eight years' time. Bill could wait it out. He was content enough here. Besides, he and Maureen had settled down in the area. Neither of them wanted to up sticks and move and it was a good place to bring up a family. Still, Bertie wasn't one to mince his words and if he thought Bill was fit for a chief's job, it meant a lot.

In the early part of nineteen seventy-two, they were given a date for the work to begin on the conversion to three screens. The Circle would become Screen One, and the rear stalls area Screens Two and Three. Another cinema in a nearby town had already been tripled, so Bill caught the train over on a day off to have a look and get a feel for the changes that were about to happen.

As he walked along the suburban street, daffodils in the front gardens were just beginning to bud and the sun shone bravely as it broke through a bank of dark cloud. Like his own site, the cinema he was visiting dated from the nineteen-thirties and was one of those tiled and curvy examples of Art Deco which had once been thought shockingly modern. To the left was a shopping parade dating from the same era. On the right, a newly built office block with big windows and bright orange panelling made everything else seem slightly out-dated and grubby.

As he drew closer, he could see that attempts had been made to bring the cinema into the seventies. The original entrance doors had been replaced by up-to-date aluminium frames with large glass panes. Above the canopy an illuminated Readograph covered the grimy Art Deco windows. All the film titles were displayed along its length in large red letters, legible not just to pedestrians, but also the bus passengers and car drivers who passed by. The canopy itself had been repainted and proclaimed the building to be a Film Centre rather than just another boring old cinema.

The refurbishment continued inside the foyer. A suspended ceiling hid all traces of the original architecture. Fluorescent lights hung over the large kiosk and a new carpet covered the floor, springy and soft beneath his feet.

'Lovely, isn't it?' said the manageress, who had let him in. 'We've got a double hot dog steamer so we can cook twice as many sausages at once and extra popcorn warmers too. And now that they've integrated the ticket office and kiosk together, you only need one person on duty to sell tickets and sweets during quiet times.'

More staff cuts, naturally. He wondered how the cashiers felt about it. Among front of house staff, selling the tickets had always been seen as the most responsible position, occupied by those who had worked their way up to it over the years. Very similar to the hierarchy of projection really. Now those same cashiers who'd thought their days of selling Maltesers were long past had to do both jobs.

The chief arrived. Bill noticed that he was quite a young man, probably only in his late thirties. He led the way to the main projection box upstairs. Once out of the public areas, the facade of modernity vanished. Painted brick walls that hadn't been touched since the place first opened and concrete steps in the traditional red tile paint with white nosings. Varnished wooden doors bore faded lettering; Rectifier Room, Battery Room, Rewind Room.

'You'll find you get plenty of exercise carrying films up and down all the stairs,' he said. 'During the school holidays we had the Disney release playing up here all afternoon - and to packed houses - then swapped it with screen two for the evening show. A right pain it was, pushing your way through the crowds carrying the film. They don't always wind on tight, so you have to be a bit careful.'

He opened the projection room door. At first sight, not much was different. A pair of Victoria 8 projectors raked steeply towards the portholes, with old carbon arc lamp houses converted to take xenons. The most obvious change was the Philips cakestand standing next to 'A' machine. Bill had only seen pictures of them before and was surprised at the diameter of the three horizontal platters and the size of the film which lay on the top plate like a huge Liquorice Allsort.

The chief patted it fondly. 'That's the whole programme there; adverts, short, trailers and the feature. No more changeovers nowadays. Once you start this, it runs right through to the finish.'

There was a multitude of rollers to transport film between the cakestand and projector. 'It looks complicated,' Bill said.

'No more than lacing up the projector, once you've done it a few times. Mind you, you need to double check it's sitting on all those rollers properly. When you're running reel to reel, if you've made a mistake you'll damage twenty minutes of film at worst. With this set up, you can wreck a whole print if you aren't careful.'

Bill looked through the viewing port to the former circle, starkly lit by cleaner's lights at this time of the morning. 'They've not done anything out there, then?'

'All the money was spent on the new screens downstairs. Come on, you can have a look yourself. But let's have a brew first, eh?'

While they drank their tea, the chief talked enthusiastically about the new procedures he'd had to learn. 'To be honest, it wasn't that hard for me, but some of the older guys who've got set in their ways haven't made the change easily. And even though there's two of us on for most of the day, you'll find you're up and down those stairs a good few times.'

Afterwards, they went downstairs to see the new boxes, one for each of the screens that had been constructed underneath the Circle. Bill's first impression was that they were tiny. You had to squeeze past the rear of the single Victoria 4 projector. The cakestand and a tiny rewind bench filled the rest of the room.

'I know what you're thinking. It's not much space, but you get used to it.' He showed Bill into the auditorium. It had a surprisingly small picture; no more than about fifteen feet from one edge of the masking to the other. The auditorium was an odd shape, too. The outer wall, unaltered in any way save for a repaint, was still as ornate as it had always been, but the decoration stopped abruptly where a plainly constructed partition cut the stalls straight down the middle. The old ceiling light fittings had been removed, leaving empty recesses behind. Two pageant lights mounted on the side walls provided all the decorative illumination. Bill couldn't help but think that something was missing; the sense of occasion you got in a single screen cinema, whether sitting in the circle or stalls. Yes, you needed to offer choice, and at least with three screens you wouldn't be stuck with empty houses all week if the film wasn't a hit, but would people really pay good money for this? He asked the question.

'They say we've doubled our takings since the conversion. Personally, I still prefer to watch a film upstairs on the big screen, but if it's a choice between this, or becoming a bingo hall, I'd rather stay open.'

You couldn't argue with that. Over the past decade, so many cinemas had closed, some turned to other uses; bingo, churches and car showrooms, while the less fortunate had simply been demolished.

He reported back to Harold, who was becoming more worried about the conversion the closer it came. Bill found himself glossing over the less-than-ideal parts. He didn't mention the tiny projection boxes or the picture size in the new auditoria.

'I don't know…' Harold shook his head. 'When you're my age, you don't like things to change. At least, not all at once, like this. I didn't want them to take out my good old B.T.H. projectors, but I know what I'm doing on these ones now. I coped with the change from Academy to Widescreen and all the different sound systems we've had through the years.' He paused for a moment. 'When I was just starting out, I remember some of the old boys saying it wasn't the same since talking pictures came in. A few of them didn't want to learn about sound, amplification and all the new kit as it was then. Some of them left the business…'

He fell silent. Bill felt as if he should say something to reassure him. Harold was a good chief, after all, not like some of the idiots Bertie talked about. 'Listen, it'll be fine. We'll be back to multi-manning again. And we get a pay rise for more screens too.'

Harold nodded. 'I suppose so.' He glanced at his watch. 'Ah well, time to get the old place open.'

'Is everything okay, love?' Maureen asked him the next day.

He knew he had been quieter than usual, mulling over the coming conversion and what it might mean. 'Fine. Just thinking about work.'

'You said it was going to be fine after you visited that place. What's happened?'

'Well, it's Harold. He seems to think he's too old to cope with the changes.'

'And what if he is? It might be your chance at a chief's job.' She spooned mashed potato into Neil's mouth as he sat in his high chair. 'I know you'd make a good job of it. And the extra money would come in useful.' She glanced down and patted her stomach. 'I've got some news too.'

'Oh, Maureen, you're not?'

'I am. We're having an addition to the family.'

A few weeks before the conversion began, Bill helped bring the new equipment in. The cakestands came in separate pieces, so they were fairly easy, but it took four of them to carry the new rectifiers up the hundred and eleven steps, one at each corner, moving slowly up one stair at a time. The existing mercury arc rectifiers didn't provide smooth enough DC current for xenon lamps, so would be rendered obsolete.

'But we won't be taking them away – too bloody heavy!' one of the engineers said. 'Only good for the scrap heap anyway.'

It had been decided that it wasn't necessary for the cinema to close fully while the work was carried out. They would open each day at five o'clock, making two evening shows possible.

The first night's work entailed ripping out all the stalls seats. These were left stacked untidily against the stage, fully visible to patrons in the Circle, along with various building materials. Bill was on shift that night and went down to the office as soon as he saw it.

'Look at the mess they've left,' he told the assistant manager. 'We can't charge people to watch films in a tip like that. Come and have a look yourself.'

He was reluctant to leave the office, but eventually agreed. 'It's not too bad,' he said. 'Anyway, we were told us that if anyone complains we're to give them free tickets.'

'If that's their attitude, they'll be lucky if there are any patrons left by the time this thing's done,' he said to Maureen as they had tea and toast before bed.

'Well, there's always a bit of a mess when builders are in,' she said. 'As long as people know what's going on, they'll put up with it.'

Next stage was the construction of a drop wall down from the front of the circle, closing off the area that would become the two new auditoria. The dust was appalling. It travelled far beyond the building works. The workmen were supposed to clean up at the end of each shift, but their idea of cleanliness left much to be desired. It was a miserable experience putting on a show each evening when half the lights no longer worked and the power had been turned off at the stage end, meaning the curtains couldn't be used.

Gradually though, the conversion began to take shape. Bill helped install the new equipment in the boxes for Screens Two and Three. Thankfully they were larger than those he had seen on his visit, as there was more space to work with here. The picture size was also slightly larger, although Harold shook his head sadly when the screens were put up. 'Whatever happened to big screen entertainment? People will laugh when the tabs open to reveal that… postage stamp.'

They both worked hard to get the new boxes cleaned and ready for action. By then Pete, one of the new projectionists, had started, so there was another pair of hands to help with the extra film make-up. On opening night, Bill felt quite proud and excited as the Mayor cut through a piece of black film spacing and declared the new three screen Film Centre open for business. Soon the foyer was bustling with people, the Automaticket machine ringing and the smell of hot popcorn filling the air. He recognised familiar faces; the regular patrons, many of whom were using their free tickets given out during the building works. One of the staff told him the car park was overflowing. It looked – and felt – like a success.

They became used to the routine of moving films around between boxes and the extra workload. It wasn't just the amount of film to be made up, but all the maintenance for the new projection equipment. Plus there was Harold's problem.

Harold wouldn't go near the new boxes and always chose to run Screen One. During the first couple of months they were open, two prints were badly damaged. He blamed the cakestand, but the engineer who came in to check it said it was working perfectly. The scratching had been caused by the film coming off one of the rollers returning the film from the projector to the take-up plate.

After that, Harold decided he wouldn't use the cakestand anymore.

'This new equipment's no good,' he stated. 'I'm going back to running changeovers. That way, we can be sure there won't be any damage.'

Bill didn't like to point out that they also had cakestands downstairs, but no damage had occurred in the smaller screens. Harold was the chief, and if he wanted to run Screen One his way, that was his prerogative. It made for a lot more work when the film needed to move from the main screen to a smaller auditorium on its second or third week, though.

It was during the school holidays that everything went wrong. Booking department insisted on *Dumbo* being shown in Screen One for two afternoon performances, then moving to Screen Three for the

26

less busy evening show, when *Young Winston* would take its place upstairs. It was obvious even to Harold that there would be insufficient time to run the kid's film onto the cakestand and to put *Young Winston* back onto spools so that Harold could run it in his chosen way. There was no choice but to use the cakestand in Screen One, if only for that week. He reluctantly agreed.

Bill was off the day the disaster happened. He heard about it the next day, when he arrived at work. *Young Winston* had wound on loosely. Harold had unwisely tried to move it on his own but half way across the foyer, the centre ring had come out, leaving two hours and fifty-seven minutes of film all over the carpet. He'd been so shaken up by the event, he'd had to go home early, leaving Pete to carry on alone while also trying to get the feature back into one piece. The evening show had, of course been cancelled.

All credit to Pete that he'd managed to get three reels back on a platter. 'I had to cut it loads of times, it were just so twisted up. There's carpet fluff all over it too.' Together they worked at untangling the rest and managed to get it back together for the first afternoon performance, but it was dirty and damaged from the experience.

Harold called in sick before his next shift. He came back just over a week later, but his confidence had been shaken. In his entire career, he'd never lost a show for anything less than total mechanical failure and it had hit him hard. He began to take more time off for a variety of health problems, until finally, after consultation with the Personnel Department, he took an early retirement package.

Bill became Chief Projectionist just ten years into his career. He felt proud, yet sad that Harold hadn't felt able to see out his time. Now it was his responsibility to look after the place and ensure that the presentation standards were maintained. You couldn't bring back the old days and the old ways of working, but you could always do the best job possible.

Cat: 1979-1980

'Studying art? Where's that ever going to get you in life?' Cat's mum obviously didn't think much of her choices.

'She could become an art teacher.' Dad always stood up for her.

Cat didn't like to mention that being a teacher was her idea of living hell. 'Art's the only thing I'm any good at,' she mumbled.

'Well, if you're going to carry on living at home you'll have to pay your way. College isn't going to take up all your time, so you can get a job.'

She leafed through the pages of vacancies in the local paper. They were mostly full time, which was no good to her as it clashed with her course. There were supermarkets, of course; they were open late, so would have evening shifts available. But she envisioned herself trapped behind a till as the queues got longer and longer, being snapped at by irritable office workers on the way home from their own boring jobs. It didn't appeal.

A lot of employers asked for prior experience. All she'd ever done, work wise, was a paper round when she was younger, and a Saturday job in a small, independent clothes shop during her 'A' level years. She'd enjoyed it, but it hadn't paid much. Anyway, the shop had closed last Easter, driven out of business by a couple of bigger stores opening locally.

Then something caught her eye. 'Part time staff required for evening and weekend shifts. Apply to the Manager, Gaumont Cinema.' It sounded promising. Plus working in a cinema must mean you would get to see films, free of charge. She was an avid cinemagoer, when she had money to spare.

Hands trembling slightly, she dialled the number. The ringing went on and on. There's no one there, she thought, or they're too busy to answer. All the vacancies are filled by now (the paper was three days old, after all).

'Gaumont Cinema,' said a female voice, 'Can I help you?'

She was taken by surprise. Must stop daydreaming. 'Er, yes. Can I speak to the manager? Please,' she added.

'What's it about?'

'Um, the job? I saw the advert in the paper for part time staff.'

'Oh, that. Hang on, I'll put you through.'

She could hear muffled speech, as if a hand had been put over the receiver, then a man spoke. 'You're interested in the job?'

'Er, yes.' She expected to be asked all sorts of questions and took a deep breath.

'Excellent. Could you come down for an interview?'

'Of course. When?'

'Later today?'

'Yes, that would be fine.'

'What's your name?'

'Cat Taylor.'

'Cat?'

'Well, it's Caroline really, but everyone calls me Cat.'

'Can you make it for six-fifteen, Cat?'

'Yes, sure.'

'See you later. Just ask at the paybox for Mr Watkins.'

Less than a week later she got off the bus next to the Gaumont. It was her first evening at work. The cinema towered above her, each grey windowsill stained with bird droppings. She walked slowly round to the front, feeling nervous. What would her co-workers be like? Would she like them? Would they like her?

The interview had been much more casual than she'd expected. The manager had reminisced wistfully about the 'good old days' of the nineteen-sixties when *Summer Holiday* was full for every show and there had been queues around the block. All she'd done, it seemed, was to nod in the right places and mention a few recent films she had enjoyed. After about twenty minutes of this, Mr Watkins had asked her, 'So, when would you be able to start?' Landing a job so easily felt weird. Deep down inside, she wondered if maybe she'd got it because she was the only one to apply who had, as her dad put it 'more than half a brain'.

Low-angled sunlight reflected off the glass panes of the front doors. Nothing of the interior was visible until she pushed the door open. The foyer was cool and empty. The scrape of her shoes on the hard flooring broke the silence. A woman was sitting inside the island kiosk. She looked to be in her forties or fifties, Cat thought. Her hair was bleached blonde and an imposing bust strained against her striped blouse and tightly buttoned purple uniform jacket. She looked up from the magazine she had been reading as if annoyed by the intrusion.

Eye contact, thought Cat. Look her straight in the eye.

'Um...' don't hum and hah. Get on with it. She's not going to eat you. She only works here, and so do you. 'My name's Cat Taylor. I'm supposed to start work here tonight.'

'Oh, right. Another new one. Just go in the office.' She pointed at a recessed door. 'Miss Baines will sort you out.' Her eyes flicked back down to the page.

Cat knocked and went inside. Miss Baines was younger than she had imagined, with her feet up on the desk and the phone in one hand.

'I don't care if he does top himself. I want him out of that room when I get back, or there'll be trouble.' With her free hand she jabbed at the air until the ash from her smouldering cigarette threatened to fall. She flicked it quickly into the large chrome ash tray. 'He knew what the rent was, and if he can't be bothered to pay on time we'll find someone else.'

Cat stood just inside the door, feeling slightly awkward and embarrassed. Miss Baines ignored her and went on with the conversation, if it could be called that, as the person on the other end didn't seem to be saying very much.

She looked around the office while she waited. It was far more utilitarian than the one in which she had been interviewed by Mr Watkins. Miss Baines' feet rested on a solid wooden desk which looked as if it had been placed there when the cinema first opened in the nineteen thirties and would remain until the building was demolished around it. On the wall directly behind the desk was a poster of the Rank Gongman. Another wall held shelves filled with box files, below which were two safes; a large one with flaking green paint and a smaller one in a faded maroon shade with scorch marks around the locking mechanism. A battered electric kettle stood on a tray on top of the smaller safe, together with several mugs, an almost empty jar of instant coffee and a stained brown spoon.

After an interminable few minutes of threat and bluster, Miss Baines slammed the phone down. 'Useless, useless,' she muttered. 'Never share a house with blokes.' She ground the cigarette to death and stood up. 'So you're one of the new starters?'

'Er, yes. Cat Taylor.'

'Just sign in here, Cat.' She took down a large brown book off one of the shelves. 'We don't have enough uniforms for all the part timers, so you'll have to make do with an overall for now.'

While Cat signed, she left the room and returned shortly with a pink and purple striped object draped over one arm. 'Not the most fetching garment, as you can see, but at least it stops your clothes getting dirty. If you stay, then we'll get you something more permanent.'

Why wouldn't she stay, she wanted to ask. Was it that bad, working in the cinema?

Miss Baines seemed to read her thoughts. 'Lots of people think working here means they do nothing but watch films all the time. Then they find they don't like having to be at work when their friends are out enjoying themselves. Or they can't take the boredom. Cinema's like that, you see. All or nothing. Twenty people through the doors all day, or hundreds queuing up and every show packed. It just depends what's on each week.'

'So this is a quiet week?' Cat ventured.

'Dead as a dodo. We haven't been busy since *Moonraker* finished. Anyway, come on. Let's find Geoff. He'll show you what you have to do. Put your overall on first.'

Cat was glad she didn't have a mirror handy to see what she looked like. The overall felt shapeless and unflattering and was made of a cheap, synthetic material. There was a short zip at the back that was awkward to reach, and a pouch pocket on the right hand side. She wondered if some people left through the embarrassment of having to wear such a thing.

She followed Miss Baines through the foyer. It was still empty, the cashier engrossed in her magazine just as before.

'How many do you think we'll have in this evening, Elsie?' Miss Baines called across.

Elsie barely raised her eyes. 'I reckon forty-eight tonight.'

'I'll say sixty-two. Usual rules?'

Elsie nodded. 'You'll be buying me a drink later, then.'

She led the way up the steps behind the kiosk, stopping outside the heavy doors leading to the Stalls. 'Wait here. Geoff's probably inside.' She pushed open the door. Cat heard an amplified scream and dramatic music from the film's soundtrack, muted as the door swung shut behind her. After a few seconds, she re-emerged with a middle-aged man. He looked a bit like her Uncle Joe; balding, rotund and cheery.

'This is Cat. Show her the ropes.' Miss Baines returned to the office, high-heels echoing across the foyer.

'Have you got a torch?' he asked.

'Er, no. Should I have?'

'You're supposed to be issued with one, but they're probably all broken. Or those thieving buggers went off with them.'

'Who?'

'The ones who got sacked. Couple of weeks back. They were all on the fiddle together. That's why the jobs came up. Anyway, you can borrow mine for tonight. I'll tear the tickets, you can seat. Remember, don't shine it in their eyes or on the screen. Always point it at the floor.'

'Okay.' She took the torch. It was too big to fit in the tiny pocket of her overall.

'This show's ending soon. Come on.' As he held open the door for her, he put a finger to his lips. 'Mustn't talk once we're inside,' he whispered.

As she walked in, the darkness enveloped her. They were in a curved walkway at the rear of the stalls. It smelled of old wood, dust and the years of cigarette smoke that had been absorbed by the fabric of the building. Geoff leaned against the rail and they watched the last five minutes of *Phantasm*. The posters warned, 'If this one doesn't scare you, you're already dead.' It wasn't the sort of film she would normally watch, but this was work, not pleasure. And already it was far more interesting than any of the alternatives she had considered.

As the credits began to roll, Geoff propped open the doors. They stood to either side and said goodbye to the few audience members. An elderly couple came out.

'How was that?' Geoff asked them.

'Not my sort of thing, really,' said the wife. 'Too much blood and gore. Give me a good Dracula film any day.'

Her husband agreed. 'Didn't really get the plot to be honest. And these young American actors mumble so much, it's hard to hear what they're saying.'

Geoff nodded agreement. 'Oh well. See you next week?'

'I expect so, if we're spared.' The old lady sighed. 'Such a pity you don't do meals nowadays. It used to be such a lovely restaurant upstairs.'

They made their way through the foyer, stopping to chat with Elsie on their way past.

'Regulars,' Geoff said. 'Here every Monday, whatever the film. Nice couple, too.'

'I didn't know there was a restaurant.'

'I'll show you some time. Bit of a mess these days, though. It's been closed for years and the roof leaks. Anyway, we'd best check inside before the next lot come in. Just flip up any seats that are still down.'

Smoking was allowed on the left hand side of the auditorium and Geoff warned her to watch out for smouldering cigarette ends, especially last thing at night. 'Or else we might not have a cinema to come to tomorrow.' As they worked, he told her a bit more about the job. 'One of us has to stay in here all through the show, just in case something happens.'

'Like what?'

'People disturbing other patrons. Kids trying to bunk in. Fires, floods and the like. And if Clive's on duty up there,' he raised his eyes heavenwards, 'Then we need to keep an eye on the film as well.'

'Clive's the projectionist?'

'The chief, God help us. Trouble is, he's a bit of a ladies man, if you get my drift. And he's having a fling with one of the cashiers, Laura. Every time she's on a break, she goes upstairs and well, let's just say he doesn't pay much attention to what's on screen. So if the sound goes, or he forgets to change the reel, someone needs to tell him.'

Cat frowned. She didn't like the idea of bursting in on a couple in the throes of passion. It would be extremely awkward and embarrassing for all parties.

'No, you don't have to go up there,' he chuckled. 'He locks the door, anyway. There's a house phone at the back of the auditorium. You dial number three, he answers, you tell him what's up. Easy.'

When they went back out to the foyer, two couples had come in and were choosing sweets. It was beginning to get dark outside, so Geoff showed her where to turn on the canopy lights and the neon sign. Due to a fault, some of the letters didn't light up, so it read GA M NT.

'They'll get it fixed one of these days, when there's money to spare. Head office are always telling the management not to spend anything they don't have to.'

By the time the film started, there were just forty-seven people inside an auditorium with a capacity of eight hundred and thirty. Cat watched Geoff thread the torn halves of tickets onto a long curved needle, then hang the string up on a peg in the office. There were pegs labelled with each day of the week, and the halves had to be kept so the auditors could check the number of tickets torn against those sold.

'Which is how they caught the fiddlers,' Geoff told her. 'People think they're clever, but they always get caught in the end.'

Geoff opted to sit inside and watch the last show. Cat stationed herself in the kiosk, found an old magazine and finished most of the crossword. She wondered if anyone would mind if she brought in one of her college projects to work on tomorrow evening.

The hands on the foyer clock hardly seemed to move, as if time had another dimension here. At ten past ten, Miss Baines emerged from the office and Cat helped her to recount some of the sweets. At half past, Geoff emerged from the auditorium, wedged open the doors and stationed himself at the top of the stairs as people began to leave. He beckoned her to join him and together they bid goodnight to the last few patrons.

'Now we check round to make sure no one's asleep, or locked in one of the loos.'

Already the auditorium felt strangely silent; rows of empty seats stared blindly toward the red curtains that hid the screen. As Cat made her way down the side aisle, she felt as if she was being watched. The door to the ladies creaked ominously as she pushed it open. 'Anyone here,' she called, half afraid of an answer from something invisible. Thankfully, there was none and she re-joined Geoff in the foyer.

'Almost done,' he said. 'We just have to lock up the exits.' He handed her two long chains with padlocks. 'I'll do the left side, you do the right. Take your torch, though. He'll put the lights off soon.'

The houselights dimmed as she was half way down. With no reflected light from the screen such as you had when a film was showing, the auditorium was very dark. The spookiness level increased a notch. On her way back to the foyer, she had to try very hard not to break into a run, convinced that something was stalking just a couple of paces behind, about to pounce.

'It's always worse when there's been a horror film on,' Geoff said. 'Your imagination gets the better of you. Oh well, see you tomorrow.'

They went their separate ways. By the time Cat arrived home, everyone was in bed. She made a mug of tea and reflected on her first day. Now she knew that her odd interview wasn't the only thing different about working in a cinema. How many other jobs let people read magazines, make personal phone calls and conduct passionate affairs while on duty?

Over the next few days she learned more about the cinema and the people who worked there. The circle was closed to the public as it was in such a bad state of repair. The carpet was mouldy and some of the seats had collapsed, but the main reason it remained out of bounds was due to the rodent problem.

'Imagine sitting up there and having a great big rat scamper over your feet. The local papers would have a field day,' Geoff told her. They had a little tour upstairs, when he showed her the ice room. One of her duties was to carry a tray around the auditorium in the short break before the main feature. Immediately before the sales break, an advert was shown encouraging patrons to buy ice creams, popcorn and 'delicious hot dogs'. Now that Cat knew what happened to the unsold hot dogs, she had vowed never to buy another one, however hungry she might be. Having sat in the steamer all day keeping warm, any remaining sausages were put into a plastic container and taken up to the ice room fridge until the next day, when they had another chance to be sold. If it was a quiet week, they might be in and out of the fridge five or six times.

'Don't worry about it,' Elsie said, when she asked if this was strictly hygienic. 'There's so little meat in them there's nothing to go bad.'

As promised, she had been shown the old restaurant. It was a sorry sight. Its full length windows were cloudy and streaked with bird droppings. In places, the floor shone wetly. A jumble of tables and chairs were piled roughly together, as if the building had been tipped on one side. Many were broken. Glass crunched loudly underfoot. For some reason, it made her think of the restaurant on the *Titanic* as it began to sink.

The back wall was lined with rose-tinted mirrors, etched with figures of dancing girls and forest creatures in Art Deco style. She thought of all the people whose reflections had been captured here during a meal or afternoon tea. It made her shiver. Once this place had been bright, busy and full of life and now the years had brought it to this state of decay.

She left hurriedly, wanting to be back among people again.

'You all right, love?' asked Frances, the administrator, who was busy counting the drink cups. 'Did you see a ghost?'

'Ghost? Is the cinema haunted?'

Frances smiled. 'Course it is. Stands to reason, doesn't it? All the people who've come through those doors over the years, it'd be amazing if someone hadn't died. And there are all sorts of stories about the place.'

'Really? Like what?'

'Well, you know the flats at the back? They're empty now, but a few years ago this young manager who'd transferred from somewhere up north asked if he could stay in one until he found somewhere to live. He was only there two weeks. Apparently, one night he came in through the back door and heard a noise in the auditorium. Well, his first thought was that someone had been locked in and was trying to get out, so he went to help them. And when he opened the pass door, you'll never guess what he saw…' she paused for dramatic effect.

'What?' Cat found she was holding her breath.

'The whole auditorium was full of people. They were wearing old fashioned clothes and hats and looking up at the screen as if they were watching a film. He suddenly realised he could see right through them. So he dashed up to his flat, locked the door, put a heavy table against it and didn't come out till morning. He only lasted a couple more days after that.'

'What? He died?'

'No. Left the business.' She tidied up some bags of popcorn and looked sharply at Cat. 'You mean you've not felt anything yet?'

'Well…' Every time she locked up in the dimly lit auditorium, she had to force herself to walk at her usual pace, not to give in and rush back up the aisle. 'Sometimes it feels like something's watching you.'

Frances nodded. 'Yes, lots of people say that. And there've been a few times when I've been out here in the foyer and thought someone just came in through the front doors, but when I look, no-one's there. This is a funny old place if you ask me. I wouldn't spend a night in those flats if someone offered me a hundred pounds.'

Cat tried to be logical about it. It stood to reason that if you were alone in a big, echoing building, you were bound to get spooked at times. Some evenings it was worse than others and the mere thought of going up to the ice room alone filled her with trepidation.

There were always two front of house staff on duty until the last show ended. She discovered that it was quite normal for one of them to disappear for a while. Geoff often went out to get something to eat, while Phil, the other doorman, liked to go up to the circle alone and smoke a joint while he watched the film along with the rats. She decided that she might as well explore the vast and unmapped depths of the cinema, overcoming her fear of the shadowy darkness.

Armed only with a torch, she roamed the dusty passageways backstage. There were lots of dressing rooms with filthy sinks and cracked mirrors. Many of them had been used for storage once the live shows stopped. Old posters and publicity stills with curled edges littered the floor along with broken popcorn warmers, leaflets for shows that were long finished and lost property that had never been claimed.

A passage under the stage had tide marks on the wall showing where it had flooded more than once. Her feet made tracks in the dried mud. The stage itself was frightening in its vastness. Above her head, metal framework rose into the gloom. Ropes and cables dangled down. Light from the film spilled through the thousands of tiny holes in the screen, giving partial glimpses of what lay behind. A large speaker cabinet draped in tattered black cloth put her in mind of a hunchbacked giant.

Worst of all were the pigeons. She'd soon realised that pigeons can get into a building through gaps that look more like the size of a sparrow. In some of the stairwells, years of droppings covered the rails and the steps. As they heard her approach, they fled for the exit holes, their wing beats echoing down the empty passages in a terrifying staccato. By the time she turned the corner, all that remained were a few drifting grey feathers.

One night she found the flats. Most of the furniture dated from the fifties and looked its age. The walls were streaked with damp and some of the paper hung in strips. There was a smell of stale cooking and mould. Even if the young manager hadn't seen a ghost, he surely wouldn't have stayed in such depressing surroundings for very long.

She checked her watch, thinking that it was time she should get back. In the foyer, Geoff was propped up against the kiosk reading a magazine. 'All quiet in there, is it?' he asked, assuming she'd been sitting inside the auditorium all along.

She nodded. 'Nothing much happening tonight.' Clive was on duty in the projection box, but it was Laura's night off, so it was less likely anything would break down.

'Well, now you're here I'm just nipping out.'

'Okay.' As he went to get his coat, she leafed through the magazine. It was one Laura had left behind, full of stories about celebrities and their latest diets, affairs and scandals. Before working in the cinema, she'd never have read anything like that, but it helped to get through that interminable hour and a half, once the kiosk was closed and there was nothing to do but wait for the last show to finish.

The clock's hands moved slowly. Occasionally a noisy part of the film penetrated through the thick auditorium doors. After a few minutes, the phone on the cash desk rang. She answered it, knowing that Mr Watkins would be busy counting money and filling in paperwork and was not to be disturbed.

'Hello. Gaumont Cinema.' Most likely it would be someone wanting to know what was on and when. She reached for the timesheet.

A sharp, female voice said, 'Is Clive there?'

'Well, he's up in projection. Do you want me to get him for you?'

'No, don't bother. Can you just give him a message for me?'

'Okay.'

'Tell him that when he finishes tonight I'll be waiting for him in the car. I'm going to run that bastard over.' Her voice was quite calm, not at all hysterical or crazy.

'Who is this, please?' Cat thought she'd better check.

'I'm his wife.'

'Oh…' There was a click at the other end as the phone was put down.

She tried calling the box on the house phone, but there was no reply. There was nothing for it but to go up and warn him herself.

She'd never been up there before, but the route had been pointed out to her. You went through a small door just before reaching the circle foyer. This led into a dingy exit stairway, which smelled of damp and pee. She climbed up and up, past three landings before she found another door leading to a much narrower stairway. From far above, she could hear the sound of machinery and the film soundtrack playing, so it must be the right way.

Worried that she might walk in on Clive doing something she'd rather not see, she called his name as she climbed. 'Hello, Clive. Hello!'

The whirring noise grew louder. The stairs became a corridor. An open doorway on her left led into the projection box. She peered in cautiously.

'Hello, Clive. Are you there?'

Two huge projectors stood by the front wall, perched at an extreme angle. One was running, the other ready to start. She knew that each projector ran for twenty minutes at a time; Geoff had alerted her to the marks in the top right hand corner of the picture which the projectionist used as a cue to change over when a reel was about to end. 'If Clive's on, sometimes he forgets to push the button in time, and the screen goes black for a couple of seconds,' he'd warned. She wondered what on earth she would do if the film ran out now, with no sign of a projectionist anywhere.

'Hello,' she said again, stepping forward. It was warm in the box. There was a smell that reminded her a little of a tube train. Everything hummed with electricity and life. Light spilled out from the projectors, making patterns on the floor beneath.

She looked through the porthole. How tiny and distant the screen seemed from here. You wouldn't know if anyone was down there at all in the darkness of the auditorium.

'Wotcher,' said a voice behind her. 'You looking for me?'

Clive winked as she turned around. He was holding an enormous mug of tea in one hand, a doughnut in the other.

'Oh, er, yes. Your wife just phoned. She asked me to give you a message.' Cat paused. 'She said she's going to run you over when you leave tonight.'

Cat waited for some kind of reaction but Clive didn't look particularly bothered by the news. He nodded calmly, took a bite of his doughnut and washed it down with a swig of tea. 'She's always saying stuff like that. It doesn't mean nothing.'

'Are you sure? She sounded serious.'

He shrugged. 'She's just impatient for the divorce to come through, that's all. But ta for telling me, anyway. I'll make sure to look both ways.'

A bell tinkled. 'Nearly time for a changeover. You ever seen one done?'

'Only from downstairs.'

'Well, just stand there and you can see what happens.' He ate another chunk and carefully put his tea and the remains of the doughnut down on the rewind bench.

'Watch through that porthole. Look for the dots.'

She did. Nothing happened for a while. She wondered if she'd missed it just as Clive said, 'There's the motor dot.'

He started the projector, turning the bottom spool by hand a couple of times. 'Now for the over.'

She saw it flash past this time. He pushed a button. There was a loud click and suddenly the beam of light was coming from the lens of the other machine.

The tail end of the film reel rattled through the far projector. 'There you go. Nice and easy.'

If it was that easy, how come he managed to make a mess of it so often? She sensed he was just trying to impress her and wondered if that was how it had started with Laura. 'Thanks for showing me, but I'd better go before they miss me.'

'Come up any time,' he said.

Cat wanted to tell him to be careful, but decided it might be misinterpreted as showing interest in his well-being. She wondered what on earth Laura saw in Clive. He was at least forty, with a beer belly and stained teeth. What was left of his hair was greasy and unkempt and there were food stains down his T shirt. It definitely wasn't looks, and she hadn't seen much evidence of personality either. Was it the romance of the job? Projection seemed a lot more skilful than her own job in the cinema but that didn't seem like a good enough reason.

She made her way back downstairs just as Mr Watkins came out of the office. 'Oh there you are. I was looking for you,' he said.

She felt herself blush, as if she had been doing something wrong. Maybe he would assume she fancied Clive too. She decided the best course of action was to be honest and told him about the phone call. 'I thought I'd better warn him, that's all.'

'Don't worry too much. She's threatened the same thing a few times before. And Clive's still here isn't he? Mind you, I wouldn't cross the road next to him, just in case.'

Weeks passed. Clive didn't get run over. Cat started to bring in her coursework to fill in the last hour and a half of waiting time. No one seemed to mind. A couple of the staff asked if she could do portraits, so during the quiet midweek evenings, they sat under the kiosk lights while she made quick pencil sketches.

Another popular way to fill the evening was a game called 'ping the lights'. In every sleeve of popcorn there were always lots of un-popped kernels and these made the perfect missiles to throw at the frosted glass lampshades. When you scored a direct hit it made a satisfying ringing sound and sweeping up afterwards killed a bit more time.

Cat met the other projectionist, Steve. He was a quietly spoken man who seemed to care about the job a lot more than the so-called chief, Clive. Once everything was running, he wouldn't leave the box, so he sometimes asked the front of house staff to pick up a Chinese takeaway for him. Beef Chow Mein was his favourite, and Cat became used to popping out for it, then taking it up for him to eat between changeovers. One evening, she walked in to find him hitting one of the tall amplifiers with a broom handle. It reminded her of the scene in *Fawlty Towers* when Basil loses his temper with his car and starts thrashing it. She stood in the box doorway, unsure if it was safe to enter.

Steve spotted her. 'Don't worry, I haven't gone mad,' he said. 'The sound just failed again. It's a dodgy valve in the amp rack. A few sharp blows usually sorts it out. Listen.'

She could hear the soundtrack playing through the monitor speaker. 'It'll be fine now for a few days,' he said.

She liked to sit on the usherette's seat at the back of the auditorium, waiting for the moment when the lights dimmed, the music faded and the heavy curtains swept back as the picture magically appeared on screen. Watching the adverts was always boring, but the trailers provided something to look forward to. Cat soon developed theories about which films would be good or not, based on the style of the trailer. If it was all voiceover, then generally the film would be rubbish. Trailers that gave away the entire plot of the film were never a good omen and she soon learned that some so-called 'hilarious comedies' put all of their best material in the trailer to entice people to come along.

As there were no other cinemas in the area, the Gaumont played both Rank and ABC releases, but with only a single screen it was inevitable that they missed out on some films. In the first few months Cat worked there, she watched almost everything. That was the best thing about being allowed to see films as part of your job - you watched stuff you might not have gone to see if you'd had to pay. For example, she probably wouldn't have chosen the double bill of *Midnight Express* and *Taxi Driver* and would therefore have missed out on Robert de Niro's brilliant performance as Travis Bickle. She would definitely have bought a ticket for *Monty Python's Life of Brian*, but would only have been able to afford to go once. As it was, over the week it was showing, she managed to watch most of the film several times until she was able to quote chunks of dialogue.

When *Alien* was released, a group of staff went up into the circle to watch it in the scariest possible conditions. Cat had to shut her eyes some of the time, not sure whether to be more afraid of face huggers or rats. She loved the way the film had been shot; so gloomy and atmospheric. The fact that you never saw the alien in full until right at the end made it all the more frightening. Imagination can scare you much more than any special effect.

After this, she didn't dare to go into the more remote areas of the cinema for a few days. The stage was the worst; all that darkness above your head. Anything could be hiding up there, waiting for the right moment to reach out and grab you.

She was also dissuaded from exploring as the passage under the stage slowly filled up with water throughout the wet winter. Because of this, the auditorium started to smell like a river at low tide. The heating wasn't very efficient either, and patrons often complained about chilly draughts. It was a good job they didn't know the projectionists had to paddle through the flooded boiler house in a dinghy to get the heating going each morning.

'Those boilers are on their last legs,' Mr Watkins said. 'With the price of oil these days we hardly make enough money to heat a building this big. And I've been told not to spend any money on repairs.'

'Do you think they'll close us down?' She had heard rumours almost since the day she started.

'One day. But the threat's been hanging over us for years and we're still here so far. There are some good films coming along soon that should put a few more bums on seats. We'll get by.'

Every few weeks the gloomy union representative dropped in with news of how many cinemas were facing the axe, making it seem impossible that such a huge white elephant had survived so long. Now that she was in the business she knew how it worked. The company had a lot of cinemas in the suburbs and many of them had already been twinned or tripled, offering more variety. The cinema in Fairham she'd always gone to as a child had been modernised with two smaller screens built underneath the circle. And it was only twenty minutes' drive away. People often came in to the Gaumont, found that the film they wanted to see was on 'up the road' and drove off again to the superior comfort of Fairham Film Centre.

Spring came at last, and the tide under the stage slowly receded. Once the clocks went forward, admissions dwindled even further. It was depressing being stuck inside the empty foyer while people sat outside the pub on the other side of the road, enjoying the evening sunshine.

Even though Cat only worked a few evenings each week, it was obvious that breakdowns were happening more frequently. She didn't count the late night Kung Fu shows; the poor state of them meant that there would always be some stops when the joins snapped. But even during regular shows the sound would fail, or the light dim and flicker all too often.

It was embarrassing trying to placate annoyed patrons whose enjoyment of the film had been spoilt, especially when she had no idea why. Her excuses became more creative as the weeks went on. She tried to learn a little about projection, but it was difficult. Asking Clive questions gave him the idea she fancied him, when nothing could be further from the truth. Steve was approachable but didn't give much away, as if he was worried he might be imparting some trade secret. He did say, however, that Clive had called the Service Engineer to take a look at the equipment.

'And that's desperation. He's a funny bugger, is Bertie Arkwright and Clive's dead scared of him. I heard he once threw a chief down the stairs for not looking after the kit properly and I wouldn't be surprised if it's true.'

Following the visit, Clive was very subdued and the projectors behaved themselves as if they too had been frightened into running more reliably.

The summer holidays arrived. Free from college, Cat took on some extra overtime each week.

'Good job the summer's here,' Mr Watkins said. 'Those boilers won't make it through another winter. I'm expecting a call from head office any time to tell us our days are numbered. Just so long as I have the time to finish fitting out my boat first.'

It was a standing joke that whenever he was on duty, if he wasn't in the office, then he'd be in the old scene dock at the back of the cinema where his boat was currently up on blocks, busily trimming carpet or varnishing wood.

'What will you do, if it happens?' She couldn't bring herself to say 'when'.

'Take the redundancy, I expect. Then I can go back to the coast and spend a year sailing before I find something else.'

'Won't you miss the cinema business?'

'Of course I will. But it's not what it was. Even back when I started, fifteen years ago, it was very different. I remember queues around the block and the "House Full" signs out every night. We played *The Sound of Music* for ten weeks to packed houses. They made films people actually wanted to see back then. Now it's all sex and violence, and not everyone wants to see that kind of stuff.'

'My dad says home video will kill off cinemas for good.'

'Well, they said the same about television and we're still around. Mind you, a lot of places closed back then. And a lot more will close over the next few years, because no-one's spent any money on them and they're falling to pieces. But I reckon cinema still has a future, as long as they show films that people want to see.'

And as long as the circle isn't full of rats, the heating still works and the projectionist knows what he's supposed to be doing, she added silently.

There was a great deal of excitement about *The Empire Strikes Back*. They hadn't shown it on first release as Fairham was considered the preferred site, but now, at last, it was here.

This was how the 'old days' must have been, Cat thought, as she had a brief rest between houses. It was packed out; not an empty seat. Elsie and Laura were busy re-stocking the kiosk shelves, Geoff was outside making sure the queue of people made an orderly snake around the building rather than rambling into the road. Mr Watkins had just brought out more bags of change and was having an impromptu light-sabre duel with Phil, using old poster tubes.

Frances poked her head around the office door. 'Mr Watkins. Can you come over? The area manager wants a word on the phone.'

'Never a quiet moment to enjoy yourself,' he grumbled, and walked across with his light-sabre over his shoulder. 'Back shortly, folks.'

Cat went to check inside the auditorium. The audiences were generally well behaved, but they'd had a problem with kids who had bought tickets sneaking their friends in through the exit doors. As there were no spare seats, they were easy to spot sitting on the floor in the aisles. So far today, she had evicted fourteen of them, some more than once.

Having had a look around and found nothing amiss, she'd just sat down on the usherettes' seat at the back when Geoff pushed open the entrance door and beckoned her over. 'Best come out here,' he said.

'Why? What's happened?' As she reached the doors, she saw the little group of staff clustered around the island kiosk and Mr Watkins, bereft of his light-sabre standing to one side. He looked tired and sad.

'Now that everyone's here, I'll give you the bad news. I've just been told we're closing on October the sixteenth.'
Fewer than two months, she thought. That's all the time we have left. She wished the news could have come when they were bored and throwing popcorn at the lights instead of working their guts out and turning customers away.

'They'll be sending out redundancy notices in the next week or so.'

Laura sniffed. 'It'll be peanuts, Clive says.'

'And for those who don't fancy blowing their redundancy on a weekend in Clacton, I've been told there'll be some jobs available up at Fairham.'

Cat thought about the options. She didn't want to leave the cinema business right now. But maybe the shabby grandeur of the Gaumont, with all its quirks and characters couldn't be replicated elsewhere. Maybe it was truly unique. Still, she'd need a job to pay board to her mum and cinema was still better than most other options, even if it wasn't as much fun as working here. After finishing college next year with some qualifications, she'd be able to look around for something else.

Once *The Empire Strikes Back* had finished its run, the cinema returned to its usual lacklustre performance. Many an evening was spent playing 'ping the lights' and trying to fill the gaps in the display of sweets. It was surprising how quickly the more popular lines ran out. Miss Baines had said they weren't allowed to order any more stock as they were due to close so soon.

'Sorry, we don't have any chocolate raisins,' became the refrain each night.

'What about sherbet lemons?'

'None of those either.'

'Fruit gums?'

'Sorry, but if it's not on display, we don't have it in stock.' Cat became fed up apologising for the lack of variety. 'We're shutting in a few weeks, you see.'

'Really? But I've always come to this cinema.'

'Yes, a lot of people say that.' And if they'd all come here a bit more often, then maybe we'd be staying open, she thought.

Late one afternoon, she heard the sound of sawing from the stairs leading to the closed circle and went to investigate. It was Mr Watkins, taking a hacksaw to the banisters.

'Don't look so surprised,' he said. 'These are solid brass underneath. It'll go towards my pension fund.'

The second week of September brought cooler evenings, and the inevitable happened when Steve went to fire up the boilers after the summer break; they wouldn't work. Cat arrived at six one evening to find large notices advising patrons that the heating had broken down.

'They won't let us get it repaired,' Mr Watkins said. 'It'd be a waste of money as there's only four weeks till doomsday.'

Each day, the auditorium became noticeably chillier. Elsie brought in a fan heater and sat behind the pay desk with her feet on it. People came in, saw the signs and asked if it was warmer inside the auditorium than in the foyer.

'A little bit,' Cat lied. 'Actually, you'll find it adds to the atmosphere of the film.' They were showing *The Shining* that week, and there was no doubt that sitting in a cold auditorium really helped to make you believe you were trapped in the snowbound Overlook Hotel. However, most people decided to get back in their warm cars and drive the five miles up to Fairham instead.

Suddenly it was the last week; the last few shifts before the Gaumont became history. Signs outside advertised a double bill for the final late show; *The Last Picture Show* and *Monty Python's And Now for Something Completely Different*. A local reporter came in and wrote a story on the topic. Following the publication, there were even more phone calls from people who couldn't believe the news. Some of them said they would write to Head Office and start a campaign to save their local cinema.

'They can try,' Mr Watkins said. 'It won't make the slightest difference.'

With just four days to go the tab cable snapped. Clive and Steve had to drag yards of heavy material open by hand.

'There goes the dramatic last closing of the curtains,' Steve said gloomily. 'Let's hope the projectors keep going or we'll be in real trouble.'

Cat hated the sight of the stark, grey screen as she locked up each night in the freezing auditorium. Due to a mild spell, it now felt warmer outside the building than inside. It was as if the cinema already knew of its fate and had decided to die slowly, piece by piece.

The last day came. Only a few hardy souls turned up for the regular evening performance.

'What's showing next week?' someone asked.

Mr Watkins smiled wryly. 'Rubble and redundancy.'

'I've not heard of that one. Is it any good?'

'I doubt it.'

The remaining staff clustered around the small island of warmth surrounding the kiosk. The last three hot dogs stewed in the steamer. They had been in and out of the fridge all week due to the lack of patrons and were in a sorry state. There was no point in taking them back up to the ice room, as they would never have another chance to be eaten.

Elsie dared Geoff to eat one, but he refused. 'I want to survive a bit longer than this place, thanks.'

Up in the circle lounge, the traditional closing party had commenced. Managers and projectionists from other sites were the principal guests, along with former members of staff, family and friends. As the evening progressed, the sounds of revelry became increasingly louder.

Even those who were still on duty, like Cat, were invited up for a drink, all normal rules of conduct having been suspended. There seemed to be a touch of desperation in the way people were drinking. For some, it was simple determination to get through as much of the company's free booze as possible. Others were out to celebrate their own fortune in having escaped closure so far.

'Got to make hay while the sun shines,' a man said. 'It might be us next.'

One of the projectionists had brought tools, and was dismantling an Art Deco light fitting, packing the pieces carefully into a holdall.

Cat almost fell over an expensive SLR camera at the top of the stairs. 'Whose is this?' she asked several people, but no one was sure.

'It might belong to the chap from the paper. He went off with a bottle of gin about an hour ago and hasn't been seen since.'

She put it to one side, in a corner where it was less likely to get trodden on and went back downstairs. People were starting to arrive for the late night double bill. Many of them had clearly been to the pub next door first and were in a similar state to the party guests.

'This lot's going to be trouble,' Geoff said grimly.

The Automaticket machine chimed merrily as it disgorged the last ever roll of tickets. The sight of so many people in the foyer brought back memories of better times. Cat and Geoff tore tickets as fast as they could. Some of the drunks looked ready to fall asleep or throw up.

Inside the auditorium, someone started shouting. Cat went inside to see what was going on. A fire extinguisher lay in the side aisle, fizzing and foaming as it rolled around under its own steam. A loud banging noise was coming from the Gents.

51

'They're running amok already,' she told Geoff. 'Letting off fire extinguishers. And it sounds as if they're vandalising the toilets too.'

He shrugged. 'Do we care? Do we hell. It'll be a bit less work for the demolition men.'

It didn't feel right to Cat. She'd grown to care about the place, even in its decline. But what could she do?

'They'll quieten down once the film starts,' he said reassuringly.

But they didn't. *The Last Picture Show* was the poignant story of the demise of a small town cinema in nineteen-fifties Texas. It was quiet, understated, and filmed in black and white. The crowd had mostly come to see Monty Python and to carry on drinking after hours somewhere a bit more comfortable than in the local park. It wasn't to their taste at all. The noise from inside the auditorium began to rival that from the party upstairs.

Phil went to use the loo and reported back. 'They've pulled the condom machine off the wall and broken into it.' He sounded impressed. 'That takes a bit of doing. Those things are built like Fort Knox.'

'Maybe we should tell Mr Watkins?' Cat suggested. She headed for the stairs. Just as she reached the foot of them, Mr Watkins himself ran down, taking two steps at a time.

'Excuse me…' she began, but he fled past her unheeding. Three other managers and Miss Baines almost knocked her down as they followed in hot pursuit. They caught him as he struggled to unlock his office door and dragged him back over to the kiosk. Two of them held him while Miss Baines pulled his trousers down, and then took a photo of him sprawled among the popcorn in just his underpants. Shrieking with laughter, they went back upstairs, leaving him to try and regain some kind of dignity.

'Sorry about that,' he said. 'Apparently it's become some sort of tradition. What were you going to say?'

'Just that the patrons are vandalising the place.'

'I've heard that's traditional too. Best leave 'em to get on with it. Enjoy yourself. Come and have another drink.'

She followed him up the stairs. Now the circle lounge looked like a scene from *The Fall of the Roman Empire*. People in various degrees of undress and unconsciousness slumped over the trestle tables. Food had been trampled into the threadbare carpet. The smell of spilled alcohol overpowered the usual damp. She poured a glass of wine and went through the open doors into the circle. Others had taken refuge there, too. She supposed that if you had drunk as much as some of them, you wouldn't feel the cold too badly.

The wine was overly sweet for her taste. She sipped it and stared across the empty seats, illuminated by the changing scenes of the film. Cinemas such as this – super cinemas of the nineteen-thirties - had been described as 'an acre of seats in a garden of dreams' in a book she'd borrowed from the library. How grand it must have been on opening night. Even now, in its final days there was still something awe inspiring about the place.

A cue dot caught her eye. She waited for the changeover. Steve was running the show and it was perfectly timed. Several anorak-clad enthusiasts had made their way up to the box earlier, and were recording every moment of this last picture show at the Gaumont.

A man stumbled toward her, nearly falling over a seat. He clutched at the arm rest for support and it came off in his hand. 'Excuse me,' he slurred, 'I seem to have lost my camera somewhere. Have you seen it?'

She recognised him as the press photographer. 'Actually, I did. Come on, I'll show you where it is.'

She had to help him to the exit doors. He was a big man and she worried that if he fell she might get squashed beneath him. But they made it, and she handed him the camera, which luckily was still where she had stashed it.

'Be careful with that. It's a nice piece of kit.'

He smiled. 'Are you into photography, then?'

'It's part of my course at college.'

'Do you want a drink.'

'No, I've had enough. I'm still on duty, officially.'

'I was going to have another, but I've mislaid… my bottle.'

That might be a good thing, she thought.

'Suppose I should be getting home anyway. Have to work tomorrow.'

'I'll give you a hand down the rest of the stairs.'

Once he was safely in the foyer he waved goodbye and carried on weaving his way toward the exit. He pushed the inner doors far too hard and hurtled through, crashing into the outer set. Cat winced. Fortunately, the glass didn't break. He stood, poised at the top of the three shallow steps onto the street and in a move Charlie Chaplin would have been proud of, tripped over his own feet then miraculously regained his balance as he reached the pavement. The last she saw of him, he was leaning against a parked car, being sick all over the driver's door.

It was one-thirty in the morning. The audience had quietened down, having passed out, fallen asleep or exhausted themselves from the earlier mayhem. An occasional ripple of laughter from the auditorium indicated that the Monty Python film had started. A couple of elderly men made their way down the stairs. From their sober appearance, their anoraks and the large bags bulging with two thousand foot spools, they had obviously spent the evening in the projection room. They nodded goodnight to Cat.

As had always been the way, the final hour was the longest, waiting for the film to end with nothing left to do. Tonight, there wasn't even any point in clearing up or wiping down the kiosk shelves. She turned off the steamer. The hot dogs had vanished. Surely no-one could have eaten them?

Cars slid past soundlessly out in the orange-lit street. The sign above the Chinese take-away went out abruptly as they shut up shop for the night. Leaves and polystyrene cups blew along the pavement like modern day tumbleweed. There was something desolate about the bright and empty foyer at this hour of the night. It reminded her of an Edward Hopper painting.

The auditorium door opened at last and a few of the staff emerged. 'That's all, folks,' Geoff said. 'Credits are rolling for the last time.'

They lined up at the top of the stairs and watched the patrons file out. Once they had left, Cat went inside to see the last few names disappear at the top of the screen and the houselights being raised. No swish of closing curtains, of course, because they were broken.

'This is the way the world ends. Not with a bang but a whimper,' she said softly, to the acres of shabby seats and the auditorium that would never dream again.

They locked the doors as usual and checked the vandalised toilets. A few more people came down from projection, carrying souvenirs and saying what a good show it had been. Steve had already got a job in another cinema. Clive was leaving the business to run a mobile disco.

Mr Watkins rounded up the last of the partygoers and told them it was time to leave. The booze had run out anyway, so there was nothing left for them here. Last to go was the union representative. 'There are three more closing tonight,' he told them. 'And another two next week. It's a bad time for the industry.'

The lights went out in the foyer. Mr Watkins switched on his torch and led the way down the centre aisle and up onto the stage, illuminated by two fly-spotted lights far above their heads.

'I've always wanted to know what that does,' Cat said, pointing to the large lever at the side of the stage. Above it was a red-lettered sign – DO NOT TOUCH.

'It's the self-destruct switch,' Mr Watkins joked. 'Want to try it?'

'It's just the safety curtain,' Steve said. 'But it's not been dropped in years. We were worried that if it was let down, it might never go up again.'

Now that it had been mentioned the temptation was there.

'Shall we?'

'Is it dangerous?'

'Mr Watkins should have the honour.'

'Yeah. Go on.'

He grinned. 'I don't know how I'm going to explain this to the area manager, but I'm leaving anyway, so why should I care?' He reached up to the lever, brushing away cobwebs. 'Stand clear, everyone.'

He pulled it firmly. For a second or two, nothing happened.

'It's broken, just like everything else,' Geoff said.

But then, far above, there was a creaking sound, followed by the panicked flurry of pigeon wings as their roost was disturbed. The safety curtain began to move, slowly at first, gathering momentum as it slid inexorably downward, sealing off the darkened auditorium like an ancient tomb.

'Ooh, er…' said Elsie.

'Awesome,' Phil muttered.

Dust and droppings fell with it, swirling in the pools of light. A heavy, grinding noise accompanied the descent. When it finally touched down the stage floor shook and even the walls shuddered. A few feathers floated down.

'Must have been the vandals,' Mr Watkins said. 'Impressive, eh?'

He pushed the panic bolt to open the exit door. They stepped out into the warm October night. Steve reached back inside and turned off the last few lights. It was over.

Bill:1982

Bill leaned down and picked up the coin from the wet pavement. It was only ten pence, not enough even to buy a bag of chips these days, but he couldn't just leave it there. He remembered the smile on his dad's face, all those years ago, when he'd spot a penny or even a halfpenny in the street.

'Life always brings you something,' dad used to say. 'However small it seems, don't ignore it.'

And these days, you needed every penny. Inflation was through the roof and the mortgage rate kept going up. Neil was at senior school now and there was always something to be bought. The other two were growing out of shoes and clothes every few months. Lots of folk were unemployed with no hope of finding a job. At least he was fairly safe. Cinemas were still closing but the attrition of the past few years had slowed, probably because the least profitable sites had already gone. Everyone struggled to keep their heads above water. Big films still pulled in the crowds, but they were few and far between. Last summer they'd had *Raiders of the Lost Ark* but that was the only film that came anywhere close to being a blockbuster.

As he neared the front doors he made a quick check of the poster frames. Despite being padlocked, there were ways to lift a corner and extract a poster. It rarely came out in one piece, but that didn't seem to be the point as the tattered remains were usually left on the steps. Why did they do that? It was senseless vandalism, almost as bad as the graffiti sprayed all over the side wall beside the fire escape stairs. He'd painted over it a few times, but paint was too expensive to waste on the outside of the building these days and he'd been told not to bother any more.

The budget for repairs and renewals was non-existent. Bill's DIY skills were as prized – perhaps more so – than his ability to put on a good show. Keeping the building from falling apart was part of the daily routine; unblocking drains, fixing leaky taps, repairing seats and patching up the kiosk shelves. Anything the manager asked, he did, because not to do so was to put his own livelihood in jeopardy. Cinemas that overspent went to the top of that list no-one wanted to be on.

There was another closure coming up this Saturday. Mr Hooper, the manager, had requested his presence. Apparently there were some decent bits and pieces to be had. He'd also drive Hooper home afterwards, as he'd be in staggering mode. Bill himself wasn't much of a drinker. A beer on a Saturday evening if he was at home was about his limit.

You always saw the same faces at those do's. The unlucky ones drinking to try and forget they would be out of work the following day, the others celebrating their own good fortune at having escaped this round of cuts. Among the drunks, a few sober people like himself, there to pick through the bones for anything useful. He often ended up in the box towards the end of the night watching the final reels turning, the last few thousand feet of film running through the doomed projectors. In most of these sites, the projection equipment wasn't considered to be worth saving. Old Westars, Supas, Kalees and the like. Once the lights went out and the front doors were boarded up they'd moulder away in the damp and darkness; sprockets slowly tarnishing, oil turning to sticky gloop. Sometimes scrap merchants smashed them, for the fun of it. Mostly they just came down with the rest of the building when the wrecking ball went through the box.

He let himself in to the cinema. The office was a mess as usual. It smelled of last night's chip supper. Unfinished paperwork had been left strewn all over the desk. How did they work in such chaos? It was a good job, he reflected, that managers didn't go near the projection box.

In the switch room, he flicked on just enough lights to see his way around. Most of the lights would stay off until nearer opening time to save electricity. As it was he'd dropped the brightness as low as he dared, replacing forty watt lamps with twenty-fives and twenty-fives with fifteen watt pygmies. It wasn't a bad thing keeping the corridors dimly lit. That way you didn't notice the damp patches and the cracks so much.

It had rained for most of the night. That determined his next job. Above the fibrous plaster ceiling of Screen One was a huge void; the roof space of the entire building. And as the roof leaked in numerous places, he had carefully placed buckets to catch the drips.

He unlocked the plain black door and climbed the wooden steps into the void, turning on the light switch with the end of a broom. Sometimes it fizzed and sparked in damp weather and he didn't want to take any chances.

There were five buckets to be emptied, which took the best part of half an hour. A few panicked starlings, disturbed by his unexpected presence, squeezed themselves out under the eaves. This time of year they'd be starting to nest. Sometimes you could hear their chirrups down in the auditorium. Patrons thought it was part of the effects on a film, not realising the cinema hadn't been kitted out for Dolby stereo. And who was he to disillusion them?

That was another symptom of the decline. Not so long ago, upgrading equipment was considered important. Dolby Stereo had been around since the mid-seventies yet only a few cinemas had it installed. Nowadays people were used to decent quality sound from their hi-fi systems at home. You couldn't fob them off with mono any more, especially with all these big action films that were made to be heard in stereo. They'd be watching it on dirty screens too. Smoking in auditoriums took a heavy toll on screens. Once they'd been replaced every three years, but now you'd only get a new one if it was vandalised. Add to that the discomfort from worn out seats and the sticky carpets that were an inevitable result of all the spilled fizzy drink and it was no wonder people were staying away.

He'd had long, serious talks with Maureen. She always knew when he was worried.

'What's up, love? I can see you've got something on your mind.'

'Just the usual stuff. More closures. Wondering if we're next for the chop.'

'Have you heard something, then?'

He shook his head. 'Nothing specific. Just rumours.'

'That Mr Hooper is a good manager, isn't he? You said he had friends in high places; that things would be all right.'

'So he always says. But sometimes I start to have my doubts. Sometimes I wish I'd got out a few years back, when there were still jobs to be had.'

'But Bill, you love the cinema.'

'I know, I know. And I don't want to leave it, not if I don't have to. Maybe I should learn a trade in my spare time. I'm not too old. Plumbing maybe?' He did enough of that in the cinema even now, patching up the ancient pipework.

'Well, if you want to. But I don't think you'd ever be really happy if you weren't in projection. We'll get by, even if the worst comes to the worst.'

It was the uncertainty that bothered him. If he was told tomorrow that the place was going to close it would be a shock, of course, but give him a couple of hours and he'd be making plans. Maureen was right – he didn't want to leave the business – but if there was no alternative then he'd retrain and start again.

If he could only keep the place running and his family happy, then things would – must – get better.

His next job was to get the kettle on. Bertie Arkwright, the Service Engineer was due for a visit. Because Bill kept the equipment well maintained, there wouldn't be much to do, which would please Bertie. He'd probably stay for most of the day, drinking gallons of black coffee, smoking his way through a pack of cigarettes and telling Bill all the gossip from round the circuit.

He took the rubbish sack from the box staff room to the car park, down the wobbly fire escape stairs. There were always a few cars parked, even when the cinema was closed. Mr Hooper had cooked up a deal with the local used car dealer, letting them store some of their vehicles on cinema land in return for cash. Rumour had it that the money didn't go through the books, but straight into the manager's pocket. Today there were a couple of Cavaliers, a Cortina and a fairly new Datsun Sunny. Bill's neighbour had recently bought a Datsun and was always boasting about all the extras that came as standard, so he took the opportunity to have a look round.

As he peered inside, someone spoke. It made him jump. He'd not spotted anyone about.

'Do you work here?' It was a youngish man, with messy hair. He didn't look like a salesman, but you could never tell these days.

'What if I do?' Surprise put him on the defensive.

'Nice car, eh? Bet you'd like one of those.' He smiled in a friendly fashion.

Now he definitely sounded like a salesman. 'I was just looking.'

'And why not, eh? So, you do work here, then?'

'As it happens, yes.'

'That's great. Does it pay well?'

Maybe he was after a job. 'It's not bad. You should wait for the manager to come in if you're looking for work.'

'Oh, so you're not the manager?'

'No, I'm a projectionist. Chief, actually.'

'Right, right. You see, what I wanted to find out was if I can hire a film.'

Bill was puzzled. 'What do you mean, exactly? You want to hire a screen for a private showing?'

'That would be it, yes.'

'Well, you'd still need to see the manager. He should be in soon.'

61

'No, mate. What I mean is to, you know, hire… a film.' He said the last words slowly, like someone trying to make a foreign language speaker understand English.

'Sorry, I don't get it.'

'Look, let's put it another way. Could you show a film for me and some friends? You'd be well paid for your trouble.'

Bill was getting tired of this. 'Just ask the manager, all right. I've got work to do.'

The man followed him. 'Don't you want to earn a bit of extra cash?'

Bill rounded on him. 'I'm not sure what you're on about.'

'All right, mate, all right.'

'And I'm not your mate.'

'Okay. If you don't want the work, someone else will.' He began to walk away.

Bill watched him, still not entirely sure what he had been implying. A car came down the track, bouncing over the uneven ground and splashing through the puddles. The man had to jump out of the way abruptly. The car pulled up next to the other parked vehicles. Smoke poured from the open driver's window.

Bill made his way over. 'Morning, Bertie.'

'Who was that bloody idiot? He's asking to get run over.'

'I'm not sure. He was asking me all sorts of odd things.'

'Like what?' Bertie got out. He slammed the door hard. The car lurched.

'Well, he said he wanted to hire the cinema – to see a film with some friends – but he didn't want to speak to the manager. And he was offering me money. "You'll be well paid," he said.'

Bertie exhaled. 'You know what that was, don't you?'

'No. I just thought it was strange.'

'He's a fucking pirate! A video pirate. One of those bastards who are killing this industry.'

All at once, the penny dropped. 'Bloody hell!'

'Bloody hell is about right. Come on. Let's get him.'

They ran along the track, towards the front of the cinema, but when they got there the pavements were empty, apart from a woman with a pushchair looking at the film times.

'He cleared off sharpish,' Bertie said. 'Can you remember what he looked like?'

'Well, he was young – early twenties I'd say. Slim. He had a London accent.' The description would fit thousands of people. Bill realised he couldn't even remember exactly what he'd been wearing; only that it was dark in colour, probably black. He wasn't even sure that he'd be able to identify him in one of those police line-ups you saw on TV cop shows.

'Not much to go on.' Bertie said.

'I just didn't think, at the time.'

'It's happened at a few sites. No-one's taken the bait yet, but it's only a matter of time.'

'They wouldn't, surely. It'd be a stupid thing to do. No projectionist worth their salt would do that.'

Bertie gave him one of his looks. 'There are a lot of stupid idiots out there. Come on in and I'll tell you about some of them. And I'll make sure this gets passed on to the right people.'

Cat: 1985 -1986

Five years had passed since the Gaumont closed. Cat reflected how strange it was that she could recall events from that year more vividly than things that happened just a few months ago. Her life had become a dull routine; there was no doubt about that.

Back then, she had been naive enough to believe that if you had genuine talent, opportunities would open up before you. Now she knew it didn't work that way. People who had left college with far worse grades had become successful through being better at self-promotion and having the knack of being in the right place at the right time. It rankled sometimes. There they were landing interesting jobs, standing around smugly at exhibitions in expensive little galleries drinking the obligatory champagne. She suspected the only reason she ever received an invitation to these events was just so that they could show off their success to someone who had started from the same point but who had been left behind on the upward trek.

When she'd got the job with Danbrook Designs, she'd thought it would be interesting and creative, but in reality it had ended up boring and repetitive. It paid the bills though and had enabled her to find somewhere to live away from the increasingly bitter quarrels between her mother and father.

Lately though, there had been rumours flying around at work. A merger was about to happen, although any details were being kept quiet. Naturally, this meant that everyone came up with their own outlandish theories. Cat listened without adding anything to fuel the fire. She had always been a believer that if you just got on with your work, you would be all right.

When the whole department was summoned to a meeting on a Wednesday morning and it was announced that the merger was officially under way, she didn't worry too much. But then they received letters from Personnel Department informing them that their offices would be relocating to a new green field development in the New Year. She looked the place up on a map and realised it would mean a seventy mile round trip every day. Given the price of petrol and the unreliability of her old Austin Allegro, it wasn't an option. She toyed with the idea of moving, but she liked her flat and she'd lived in Fairham all of her life. Why move away from your familiar haunts and the friends you'd grown up with to keep working in a job that was boring at best? The offer of a decent redundancy package for those who decided not to relocate made her mind up.

The beginning of nineteen eighty-six saw her unemployed, but with money in the bank and an optimistic outlook. It was a chance to change her life. She spent her days revisiting old projects she'd put aside and starting new ones. Each week, she checked the situations vacant section of the local paper, but nothing really caught her eye. To be honest, she didn't really know what she wanted to do, just that she didn't want to end up in another office. However, as time went by and her bank balance began to dwindle, she started to think about applying for jobs that would simply pay the bills for the time being; bar work, waitressing and the like.

She went out for lunch with Amanda, an old school friend. Despite having vastly different outlooks on life, they'd kept in touch over the years and she knew she could rely on sensible advice from her.

'If you're going for jobs like that you'll need to re-write your CV,' Amanda said. 'You're over qualified. They'll take one look and realise you're not in it for the long term.'

'Oh come on. No one does those jobs for the long term. And I don't believe in lying.'

65

'It's not lying. Just editing. Everyone does it. You have to play the game. Or marry well.' She smiled smugly, having recently taken the second option herself. Expensive diamonds twinkled in her ears. The engagement ring had apparently cost as much as Cat earned in six months, back when she still had a job.

'How is Robert?' Amanda's new husband did something in the City. Cat had asked him once what it involved and regretted the question for the next forty minutes.

'Poor darling works far too hard. He's on the train at seven every morning and not home until eight or nine at night. But he should be getting a good bonus this year.'

If he doesn't drop dead first, she thought. 'That's nice,' she said.

'We're going to book a holiday in Thailand. Five star resorts, the works.'

'Thailand? James is there at the moment. Or he was three weeks ago when I got his last postcard.'

Amanda looked blank. 'James?'

'He was at college with me. We went out together for nearly a year. Remember?'

'Oh, that James.'

'Well, anyway, he's been off travelling for quite a while now. Works in bars, does portraits of the tourists, you know the kind of thing.' That was one of the reasons they'd split up. James had always longed for adventure, while she had been more of a stay-at-home type.

'He'll come back with some dreadful tropical disease.'

'Don't be so negative. I might do the same with my redundancy.' What was left of it, anyway. Maybe that was the reason she'd not found work easily; fate pushing her to get off her ass and do something daring for once in her life.

'Oh Cat, you can't. It's not safe. You could get raped, or murdered. Or both.'

'Or I might just live happily ever after somewhere warm and tropical. Tell you what, if I don't find anything in the next few weeks, I'm going.'

Having said it out loud made her vague ideas turn into a definite plan. She started thinking about what to take and where to start. She woke in the night, imagining herself getting off a plane carrying a huge rucksack, feeling lonely and vulnerable. Finding a room in a cheap hotel where cockroaches climbed the walls and you had to check for snakes under the bed. Having to be suspicious of people's motives because you couldn't be sure if they were trying to help you or rip you off. Could she really do it? Did she really want to?

Then salvation came in the shape of an advert in the local paper. 'Fairham Cinema requires full and part-time staff.' After the Gaumont closed, she'd taken the opportunity to transfer to Fairham, and had worked there for the remainder of her college course. It had been a much busier cinema and she'd enjoyed the experience, although it had never been quite as much fun as the wacky world of the Gaumont.

A little voice (sounding like her mother) nagged at her, saying that career-wise it was a retrograde step. Fair enough, she argued back, but at least it will pay the bills and it's the kind of job I can forget about when I'm not there, so I have the creative space to get on with my own projects. Plus, I've worked there before, so I have a good chance of getting back in. And if I don't then I promise I'll take off and travel the world.

She dialled the number, gave a few details and was asked to go along for an interview the next day.

As soon as she walked in, she recognised the cashier, Gina. They chatted for a short while.

'Mr Jessop has gone, you know. He works in the West End now.'

The former manager had always been a bit of a showman, so it didn't surprise her. 'So who's in charge these days?'

'His name's Garner.' She leaned closer and lowered her voice. 'Call me old-fashioned, but I think he's too young to be a manager. He needs a few more years in this game first.'

'What do you mean?'

'He came in here and started changing everything. A company man, they say. Ambitious.'

Mr Garner was tall, very thin and although not much older than she was, totally bald. Cat imagined him as a cartoon hot dog, singing and dancing on the big screen and had to suppress a giggle. In his office, a large ginger cat sprawled on the desk. During the interview, he stroked it occasionally. The cat kneaded the paperwork between its claws and butted its head against the in tray.

Unlike her first cinema interview, this one asked the kind of questions that made her mind go blank. Questions such as 'What do you see as your strengths and weaknesses?' and 'What skills can you bring to the role of customer service assistant at this cinema?' His pen scratched as he wrote down her answers, most of which she'd cribbed from a library book called *How to Impress at Interviews*. She became more and more convinced that she was going to end up backpacking to the Far East after all.

Eventually, he said, 'I see you've worked in the cinema business before. Why do you want to come back?'

She thought for a moment, decided to forget the textbook answers and just be honest. 'Well… I don't mind working evenings and weekends. I've been floor staff, ice-cream sales and on the kiosk.'

He nodded encouragingly.

She went on. 'There's something about the cinema that you don't find anywhere else. I love the atmosphere and the way films can make people forget their everyday lives for a few hours. It's great to be a part of that.'

The cat purred loudly. Mr Garner smiled. 'When can you start?'

So that was it. No need to uproot, to sleep in mud huts and eat insects as James had done somewhere or other on his travels. Back to safe regular employment. Back to the cinema business.

The uniform had changed. Out had gone the awful overalls. On her first day she was issued with two yellow and white striped shirts, a bright blue skirt and jacket and the standard torch, which gave out very little light and ate batteries. Apart from Gina, and Mrs Thomas, the assistant manager, all the other staff she met had only started working there after she had left the last time.

Jimmy, her appointed mentor, took his training duties very seriously. 'This here's the ticket needle,' he said, peering up at her from beneath his raggedly cut fringe as he showed her the implement. 'You have to thread the torn halves on, like this…'

'It's all right,' she said. 'I've done this job before. I know about having to keep the tickets so they can be checked. And I know not to shine a torch in people's faces when I'm showing them to their seats and that they can smoke on the left side of the auditorium.'

He continued regardless '…And then, at the end of the night, you hang it up in the office, I'll show you where, later.'

It was a quiet Monday afternoon. They stood in the upper foyer, leaning over the decorative railing. From below rose the smell of popcorn, hot dogs and some sort of lemony-fresh floor cleaner. Gina was knitting behind her Automaticket machine. Watery spring sunshine spilled through the windows.

A door to her right opened. From her past experience, Cat knew it led to the projection box for Screen One. She had never been up there. The Chief, a miserable old man, had kept it firmly locked and she had only rarely seen him when he came out to shout at someone. He had gone too; retired at last, Gina had told her.

A young man emerged, a large bunch of keys jingling from his belt. He walked quickly towards them. 'All right, Paul,' Jimmy said cheerily.

Paul nodded to acknowledge him and then was gone, bounding down the stairs.

'He's a projectionist,' Jimmy told her. 'He puts the films on, like.'

'How many projectionists are there here?'

'Just Paul and Alfie. There used to be another one, but he left a coupla months ago.' He cleaned under his grimy nails with the point of the ticket needle. 'Why did you leave your last job?'

'They moved the office and I didn't want to travel.'

'Bet you can't guess why I left my last job?'

She thought for a moment. 'Because you always wanted to work in a cinema and the chance came up?'

'Nah. I hit the boss. Knocked him down with one blow!' And he mimed the move, punching the air so forcefully it spun him round and he nearly fell over.

Cat helped to steady him. 'Why?' she asked.

'He was trying to chat up me girlfriend.'

'That's not good,' she sympathised. 'Does she still work there?'

'Nah. She went off to join the circus.'

'Wow. So I suppose you don't see her so often now, if she's on the road?'

He shook his head. 'I'm going to join her, soon as I've saved enough money.'

The jingle of keys signalled the approach of Paul the projectionist and sure enough, he came into view, running up two stairs at a time. 'You look busy,' Cat commented as he approached.

'These bloody timesheets,' he said. 'Up and down like a bloody yoyo. Start screen one, then five minutes later it's screen three and now I've got to go back upstairs to shut it down for the sales break.' He disappeared through the door.

Jimmy squinted at his watch. 'If it's nearly time for the sales break, I've got to get the tray out. Come on.'

He led the way downstairs to the ice room, slid open the lid of one of the chest freezers and lifted out a tray ready stocked up with tubs, Cornettos and plastic cartons of Kia-Ora. 'I'll do this one. You can watch me and have a go next time.'

She thought of mentioning that she'd sold ice creams before, but after the ticket needle incident, realised it would make no difference.

So, for the remainder of the day she dutifully followed him around the screens, listening to his instructions (and trying not to yawn). When he wasn't telling her how to perform a particular aspect of the job, he kept on talking about his colourful life. As most of his stories ended with how he'd knocked someone out 'with a single blow' she decided that given his diminutive size and stature they were probably all wishful thinking.

During her next few shifts, she discovered that Fairham had almost been closed down the previous year, but had been given a temporary reprieve along with a new manager. If Mr Garner could manage to increase admissions and cut costs, the cinema would continue to stay open. Because of the cuts, it was now impossible for staff to watch a whole film in one sitting. Once the last show was running, only one member of floor staff stayed on until the end and they were supposed to check inside each screen every fifteen minutes.

Being conscientious, Cat kept to this schedule. When she wasn't doing her rounds, she generally sat on one of the well-worn Lloyd Loom settees in the upper foyer, drawing or reading a book, glancing at her watch occasionally to see if it was time yet to make another check.

Paul often stopped for a chat during that last hour; once he had all the shows running he was able to relax.

'I don't like sitting up there.' He gestured up toward the projection box. 'Not now we're single manning. Once everything's on, there's nothing to do and no-one to talk to.'

It turned out that Paul had been a projectionist for four years and had worked for the previous chief.

'I only ever saw him when he came out to shout at the manager. Sometimes at the staff, too. I kept out of his way.' Cat said.

'He wasn't too bad. He just hated managers; well, pretty much everyone who worked outside the box, really. He was okay with projectionists. Once I got the hang of making his tea just the way he liked it, he was fine.'

'So how did you get into projection?'

'My aunt used to be an assistant manager. Not here; it was over in Plowbridge. While I was still at school I was down at the cinema every weekend, tearing tickets, selling popcorn and watching films. I soon got into the box and started learning that side of it too. Then just after I left school, there was a vacancy here for a trainee and that was it.'

It was very easy talking to Paul. It soon became part of her routine to make him a cup of tea when she had her own. Sometimes he stopped to drink it with her, other times he had to go and check the films were running as they should.

'If anything goes badly wrong, like a film break, an alarm goes off. But other things can happen too. A couple of months ago, the amplifier failed in screen two. No-one came out to say anything for about ten minutes, just sat there watching the film with no sound. But that's the sort of thing that can happen when you only have one projectionist looking after three screens.'

'Which is why you're always rushing round,' she said. 'Alfie takes it a lot slower.'

'He's nearly sixty. Pretty fit for his age, but all those stairs take it out of you. I wouldn't like to think how many stairs we go up and down in a day.'

After a couple of weeks, when she had proved reliable, she found that she was given more shifts on the kiosk than on the floor. She soon found out how rude customers had become since she last worked in the cinema.

'Hot dog,' they demanded.

'Give me a Coke.'

'I want one of those.' Pointing at the popcorn boxes.

It seemed that saying please and thank you had gone out of fashion.

'The trouble is, they think they're better than us,' Gina said. 'It's not the ordinary people, it's those snobby types who live in the big houses and have jobs in the City. They think that if we're working here, we've got no brains.' She glanced over at Jimmy, standing at the top of the steps in his oversized uniform. 'Well, they might be right in some cases, but being polite never did anyone any harm, did it?'

One afternoon she was in the kiosk on her own. Since opening at one-thirty, she had only sold twenty-three tickets. Many of these were to men who had gone in to watch *Flesh and Blood*. She'd thought it was just another historical drama and the 18 certificate due to explicit battle scenes until Jimmy said, 'Nah. It's got some really dirty bits.'

During the film's run, everyone had noticed that if he couldn't be found, he was usually in the back of Screen Three. 'Just checking to make sure they all behave themselves,' he protested.

As it was so quiet and there were only so many times you could re-arrange the After Eight mints and fluff up the bags of sweets, she was reading *Cathedrals of the Movies,* which she had borrowed from the library. It was a well written and beautifully illustrated history of British cinemas and their audiences, concentrating on both the architecture and social aspects of cinema going.

Her reading was disturbed by the sound of a heavy step ladder being carried through into the foyer. It was Alfie. 'While it's not busy, I thought I'd lamp up out here,' he said.

She got out of the way as he manoeuvred the unwieldy steps into the kiosk, putting her book face down on the Automaticket machine so she didn't lose her place.

He glanced at it. 'That looks interesting.'

'It is. I never knew some of these places existed. Well, quite a lot of them don't any more, which is a pity.'

He set up the ladder. A couple of the spotlights over the kiosk were out. 'Can you turn off that switch by the pillar?' he asked her. 'I've found out the hard way the wiring in this place isn't to be trusted.'

In a few minutes he'd replaced the bulbs. Cat switched the power back on. Two of them still didn't work.

'Either those are dead lamps or there's something else wrong. Best check, I suppose. Can you turn them off again?' He replaced them a second time, still with no joy. 'Ah well, another couple of jobs to add to the list.'

He folded the steps up. 'You must be the girl young Paul's been talking about. Not been here long, have you?'

'About five weeks now. I worked here before, though, a few years ago. And I was at the Gaumont down the road until it closed.'

'The Gaumont? Now that one deserves a place in your book. It used to be a real show place.'

'Not when I was there. Everything was falling apart. But behind the decay, there were glimpses of splendour.'

He nodded. 'It was a shame. That's what happened to my old show, as well. Too big for modern audiences and not worth tripling, so they shut it down.' He gathered up his box of lamps. 'Paul says you're an artist.'

'Well, yes.'

'So how did you end up here?'

She told him the story, in brief. 'When I saw there was a vacancy here I remembered how happy I'd been in the cinema. How it always makes me feel like I'm… home. That sounds stupid, I know.'

'No it doesn't. You've just got the bug.'

'The bug?'

'Not everyone gets it. Some people come and go. But the ones who stay, stay for good. And it's because whatever else you do, nothing gives you that same feeling.'

She nodded. 'No one's ever put it like that. I just thought I was weird. Well, a lot of people say that about me anyway.'

'Don't take any notice of them. And if you ever want to come up and have a look round the box, you're welcome.'

'Thanks. I will. I bet it's nothing like the Gaumont.'

Now if that had been Clive making an offer like that, it would have felt creepy and she would never have taken him up on it. But she didn't sense anything odd about Alfie's offer. He was just a nice old guy who felt the same way as she did about cinema.

Her opportunity to have a look round came quite soon. Some of the ice tray lights weren't working and she volunteered to take them up to the box. The projectionists seemed to fix everything in the cinema, not just the equipment in their own domain.

She detached the light mechanisms from the rest of the tray and carried them up the narrow, winding stairs. Alfie met her half way down and she wondered how he had known she was there. Later, she discovered he had rigged up a micro switch on the lower door connected to a buzzer in the staff room. 'So that we know if anyone's on the way up. It's good to have a bit of warning.' But such confidences were in the future.

'They asked me to bring these up. They're not working.' she said, offering the parts.

'The others usually bring the whole tray.'

'Well, this bit comes off easily and it's the only electrical part.' She wondered if she had done something wrong. 'I can get the rest if you want.'

He shook his head. 'You're right. This is all I need. Most of that lot downstairs don't have the sense of a louse.'

'And… if you've time now, could I have a quick look round?'

'Of course. This way.' He climbed up the rest of the stairs then turned left. As the door opened she heard the unmistakeable noise of film travelling through the machine; the sound that had first guided her to the Gaumont box. Inside, she saw two metallic grey projectors facing the auditorium. Beside the nearest stood a large piece of equipment with shiny horizontal discs. As the discs rotated, a ribbon of film travelled over rollers fixed to the wall, catching the light as it moved.

'What's that?' she asked. 'I've never seen one of those before.'

'It's called a cakestand. That's how we show film these days.'

Compared to the Gaumont, it seemed futuristic. 'The projectors look different than I remember.'

'These are Victoria 8's. The Gaumont had Kalee 21's running twenty minute changeovers.' He was clearly warming to the subject.

'I used to think it looked a bit like you'd imagine Doctor Frankenstein's laboratory.'

He chuckled. 'I suppose it did. I used to do relief work there sometimes. When the amplifiers misbehaved…'

'You had to hit them with the broom handle,' she finished. 'I once saw Steve, the senior, doing that.'

She walked toward the projector. For a little while she watched the film moving through the mechanism. Each tiny frame was illuminated then magnified; transformed into memorable images. The constant mechanical purr made a hypnotic background noise. It was fascinating, magical; a fundamental part of the cinema experience. She wondered what it would be like to stand up here and put on the show for an expectant audience.

'I remember coming here when I was small,' she said. 'I used to look back toward the porthole and if I saw anyone up there, I waved at them. That was when it was just one screen. There used to be this amazing light display that changed colours like a rainbow during the interval.'

'They took all that out when it was tripled.' He sighed. 'Back then, we took a real pride in the job. Nowadays they just want it on screen slap, bang, wallop. No finesse. Then at the end of the film, it's get 'em out as quickly as possible and shunt the next load of punters in. There's no sense of occasion anymore.'

'Some people still want a good show. I always enjoyed it and I was just a kid.'

'It's not what the patrons' want that counts. It's whatever costs the least money. They could have kept all the dimmers up here, but the system needed work doing to it. It wouldn't have been cheap. Plus it was manually operated, so you needed more men in the box to run it. It wouldn't have worked with single manning.'

'Paul's always on about single manning, too. But it's not new, surely? At the Gaumont, there was only ever one projectionist working at a time.'

'With a single screen, though. When twins and triples first came along, there were always two on duty. It's only recently they cut the manning levels. Now we're only allowed to have two people on together when we change the films on a Thursday.'

Conscious of having taken up his time and not wanting to outstay her welcome, she said quickly, 'Well, thanks for showing me around. I suppose I'd better get back downstairs in case I'm needed.'

He checked his watch. 'You're right. I've been rambling on a bit, haven't I?'

'Not at all. It's very interesting. Thanks.'

As she sat in the kiosk later on, she thought about the film steadily moving through the projector, showing its story to each audience in turn. Even those people who abruptly demanded popcorn down here were transported for a few hours as they sat in the darkened auditorium.

The trouble with working front of house - apart from the rude customers - was that the higher you progressed, the further you were separated from the essence of the business. You started off tearing tickets and seating people, but when you proved reliable and quick to learn, they put you on the kiosk. If you were good at that and decided a career in cinema was for you, the next step up was an assistant manager's job. And then you ended up stuck in the office, counting money, ordering confectionary and filling in anywhere else when members of staff didn't turn up. But to be up there, in the electric darkness, showing films… Up there, you were a part of the machine, the final link in the chain of film making, ensuring that the magic of cinema was kept alive.

She'd never really considered becoming a projectionist before. For one thing, she'd never seen the job advertised, although common sense told her that sometimes it must be. Another reason was that all the projectionists she'd known so far were men. Was there perhaps some kind of superstition that for a woman to handle film was unlucky? She'd have to find out. Paul would be the best person to ask; he had, after all been through the process fairly recently.

Her opportunity came the following afternoon. It was quiet again. A few senior citizens had just gone inside. They were clearly not regular cinemagoers.

'Please may I have one for the circle, my dear,' an immaculately dressed old lady had asked.

'I'm sorry, we don't have a circle any more. What do you want to see?' She didn't think it would be *Flesh and Blood* or *Jewel of the Nile*, but you could never be sure.

'The one with Robert Redford and Meryl Streep. *Out of Africa.*'

'It's showing in screen two. That's just through the doors over there.' She pointed out the sign.

'Thank you so much,' said the lady. 'We don't come to the cinema much, do we?' This last was addressed to her companions, another two ladies of similar vintage and appearance. 'When was the last time you went to the pictures, Agnes?'

'I think it was for *Lawrence of Arabia*.'

Having paid separately, the ladies had then taken some time before deciding that to share a box of Maltesers wouldn't be too extravagant, or spoil their appetite and had finally gone through to take their seats.

Cat settled down and continued sketching out the details for a mural a customer had requested for their daughter's bedroom wall. She was starting to get some freelance work now and it made a welcome addition to her regular cinema income. This one was a fantastical theme; brightly plumaged birds and delicately winged fairies flitting from behind exotic flowers in the foreground. The background showed an enchanted forest giving way to hills and a moated castle that she was just beginning to realise bore a distinct resemblance to the Disney logo seen at the opening to their films. Oh well, no harm in that. Disney had taken inspiration from Neuschwanstein Castle in Bavaria for their design.

'That's looking good,' said a voice from above. She looked up to see Paul leaning over the railing.

'Come down and have a closer look, if you've time.'

He checked his watch. 'I've got ten minutes until the scope change in Screen One.'

He jingled his way down the stairs. She laid out her sketches on top of the tiered rows of sweets

'Yeah, that's lovely. I like the Disney castle, too.'

'This is the easy part. Once it's complete I'll show it to the customer, then I'll have to set aside a day to paint it on the bedroom wall. It's a surprise present, so it has to be done before the little girl's birthday.'

He glanced at the foyer clock. Projectionists were always checking the time, she'd noticed.

'I just wanted to ask you something.' Here goes, she thought. 'How exactly do you become a projectionist? Do they advertise, or do you have to be recommended by someone? I suppose you got to know about it because of your aunt.'

'Well, kind of. I think they advertised it internally too. You know, in the company bulletin. A lot of the time, someone knows somebody who wants to move sites, or is after a promotion and that's how it gets sorted.'

'Right. So, er, how often do vacancies come up?'

'Why? Are you interested?'

She felt herself blushing. 'Well, I sort of wondered…'

'It's a great idea, but you really need to talk to Alfie. There's been some talk about us getting a third man – ah, person – here.'

'Okay, I will. Thanks.'

'Right, I'd better go.' He started to leave.

'Paul!' she called after him. 'Don't mention it to Alfie, will you. I'd like to tell him myself.'

'Yeah, sure.' He was off through the inner doors and up the stairs.

She didn't get to see Alfie for nearly a week, due to days off and the different shift patterns.

Jimmy had called in sick at the last minute, so until Darren, one of the evening staff, came in at six she was the sole member of staff responsible for selling tickets and sweets and also directing the odd few customers to their respective screens. It wasn't ideal – people could inadvertently wander into the wrong screens – but as it was just her and Mrs Thomas on duty there was no other way around it. Mrs Thomas never liked to be out of the office much. Today she had the perfect excuse as she had to figure out all the times for next week's films and send them through to the local papers.

Cat had finished the design for the mural, so today she was keeping herself occupied sketching the foyer's original features. It was a good job the architect had designed it with an open portion in the centre, as it had prevented them putting in one of those horrible suspended ceilings she'd seen at other cinemas. From her visits as a child, she remembered a large hanging light fitting that had taken up much of the empty space, but the details eluded her memory.

Voices from the inner foyer made her look up. Alfie was just coming out of the office with the timesheets in one hand. She knew that he always liked to check them personally. It was impossible for one person to be in two places at the same time, but that didn't stop the managers from scheduling in unworkable clashes. He crossed the foyer briskly. This was her chance.

'Er, Alfie,' she called, as he passed by. 'Could I just have a quick word?'

He looked over. 'Hello, Cat. What is it?'

'Well, I was talking to Paul the other day about something and he said I should speak to you.'

Alfie looked puzzled. 'About what?'

'I was thinking… I mean, I was wondering…' Deep breath now and straight out with it. 'If there are ever any vacancies for projectionists and if there are, how I'd go about applying for one.'

'Hmm, I see.' He paused for a moment. 'So why do you want to become a projectionist?'

'Well, like you said, I've got the cinema bug. I like the business and projection seems to me to be the closest you come to the heart of it. I've been thinking about it for a while, but I didn't know what I needed to do. So, I'm just finding out if there's a chance, really.'

'As it happens, we've been trying to get someone else here. We're supposed to have an establishment of three, but since Graham left, we've been one short. Mr Garner's desperate to cut back on overtime. Mind you, he'd prefer to take on someone experienced, so they could go on shift straight away.'

'Oh, right.' So that was it, then.

Alfie continued. 'Only trouble is, we've not had any suitable applicants so far. These days, it can be hard to get the right person.

There's just one problem I can see, apart from you needing to be trained up.'

'And what's that?'

'You're a girl.'

'Woman,' Cat corrected quickly.

'Well, female anyway. When you get to my age, anyone under forty is a lad or a girl. Though it can be hard to tell the difference these days. I'm not prejudiced myself. Plenty of women did the job through the War. I worked with a lady projectionist for years and she was one of the most conscientious operators I've known. But you'd have to get through an interview with the zone engineer and he's a bit old fashioned. You'd have to prove you were capable.'

'But how would I do that if I've not been a projectionist before?'

'That's the catch,' he said. 'But there might be a way. Let me go and have a think about it.'

Cat carried on sketching, but her nerves were on edge. Having made the move and asked the question, it was all she could think about. Which must mean she really did want the job, she supposed. Something she'd started off thinking about in an abstract sort of way had solidified into reality.

It was just before five o'clock when Alfie came back down to the foyer. Under one arm he carried a dusty black folder.

'Here you go. I knew it was about somewhere,' he said, handing it over. 'If you're really serious, then study this. Get all the facts and figures in your head. You might be in with a chance then.'

It was heavy with the weight of knowledge contained inside. The pages were yellowed and smelled old. *Motion Picture Presentation Manual* was stamped on the cover.

'I've been having a think,' he said. 'There's a lot to be said for taking on someone who's already working in the cinema. At least you're comfortable with shifts. You can get someone from outside as a trainee and then find out they don't want to do every other weekend, late nights and the like. You spend months training them up, then they leave.' He shook his head sadly. 'It's happened a few times.'

81

He sounded, thought Cat, as if he was definitely warming to the idea.

'Now, assuming we don't get anyone experienced applying – which might still happen, you know – then if I drop a hint there's someone already here who's interested in projection, you could get an interview in – ah – about a month. That should give you time to get enough theory in your head so you stand a chance of impressing old Abbott. How's that sound?'

'Brilliant. Thanks, Alfie.'

As soon as he had gone she opened the manual and read the first line to herself.

Good presentation means better business and better business means a better future for you.

Well, that sounded promising.

For the next few weeks she spent her free time at home and the quiet hours at work delving into its pages. Sometimes the manual raised more questions than it answered. Even though it had only been published in nineteen sixty-one it seemed written for a bygone age. There was no mention at all of cakestands but lots about carbon arcs. Alfie told her they had stopped being used once cinemas were tripled and single manning came in. 'But learn it anyway. Like I said, Abbott's from that era himself. Last time he was a chief they still had five men running one show. And it was always men in those days.'

She enjoyed reading about the art of presentation and film make-up, yet longed for the day when she could actually acquire the practical skills instead of just filling her head with theory. But she also had to keep reminding herself that the job wasn't hers yet. There was no point in getting her hopes up only to see them dashed. She hadn't been so focussed on anything since she took her final exams at college.

When the day came she was nervous, but prepared. The interview would be taking place during her normal working hours so she didn't have the additional worry of choosing what to wear. Her office clothes weren't formal enough (they had been fairly laid back regarding dress code) and her only suit, bought for a wedding, was cream and had a skirt.

'Don't look too girly, if you know what I mean,' Alfie had said.

Unfortunately, her cinema uniform also came with a skirt, but at least that was just down to company policy so she couldn't be blamed for choosing it.

The interview took place in the projection room. Mr Garner, Mr Abbott and Alfie sat on one side of a table that had been carried up from the bar. She faced them across its expanse. Mr Abbott had obviously spent some time enquiring about her punctuality and reliability as she could see from the notes on his clipboard. Being able to read upside down was a useful skill sometimes.

'So what makes you want to become a projectionist?' he asked. 'Enjoy films, do you?'

Alfie had warned her about this one also. 'Whatever you do, don't say you like films. Abbott's got this theory that if you do, you'll spend all your time staring out of the porthole and not doing any work.'

'Well, I watch them occasionally,' she said slowly. 'Working front of house you have to, in case customers want some advice about what's showing.' She cast a glance at her manager, who nodded reassuringly. 'But I don't consider myself a film buff by any means.'

Abbott scribbled some notes.

She remembered the aspects of the job stressed by the manual. 'It costs a lot of money to make a film and a projectionist can make a huge difference to someone's enjoyment by making sure what they see and hear is as close as possible to what the director intended. I studied art and photography at college, so I've a good eye for detail.'

He made a noise that sounded vaguely approving. 'And what about the technical aspects of the job? Maintenance, electrics and so on.' He cast a glance at her hands, making her glad for once of her unglamorous short nails.

She had decided it was best to be honest. 'I'll admit I don't know much about electricity, except for what we learned at school, but I'm practical and I learn fast. I don't mind getting my hands dirty.'

The questions continued. How did she feel about being alone for hours at a time? Could she lift a film? Did she intend to start a family in the near future?

Then it came to the technical part. What did she know about projectors? How did the intermittent movement work? How many frames of film went through the gate in a second? And what about feet per minute?

Afterwards, she felt drained, but certain she couldn't have done any more. If Mr Abbott wanted to find fault and give the job to someone else, he would.

They had said they would let her know the same day whether she had been successful, but as time continued to pass with no word, her anxiety grew. At around four o'clock Mr Abbott came downstairs and left the cinema without as much as a goodbye. This convinced her that she hadn't made the grade. Surely, if she had done enough, he would have offered some kind of congratulation as he passed by?

The house phone rang. She stared at it for a couple of seconds, unwilling to break the spell. In the next few moments, either her hopes would be dashed, or not.

She picked it up. 'Hello.'

'Ah, Cat.' It was Mr Garner. 'I expect you want to know what we've decided, don't you?'

'Er, yes.' This was it.

'Well, I'm pleased to tell you we'd like to offer you the position of trainee projectionist.'

He kept on talking, but she wasn't really listening. She'd done it!

'… can't start you straight away as we need to recruit someone to cover your current role. You should be able to move across to projection in a fairly short time; hopefully by the end of the month.' Mr Garner continued.

Cat felt like whooping in celebration, but restrained herself to a small, triumphant, 'Yes!' and a silly little dance she hoped no one saw.

'Well done,' Alfie told her later. 'Abbott was impressed, and that's not easy to do. They didn't want to lose you from downstairs either and I think that persuaded him you're a good worker.'

If the time until the interview had dragged, it was nothing to that last few weeks in the kiosk. She felt as though she was going through the motions as she didn't really want to be there anymore. The customers seemed surlier than usual, the hours of boredom longer. She kept the manual under the shelf, reading it through to remind herself that better times were coming, that this wasn't forever.

Her first day as a projectionist was a Monday. She'd handed in her front of house uniform and it felt strange and liberating to come to work in jeans and a T shirt, not to mention starting so many hours before the cinema opened. Alfie showed her where to hang her coat and put her things safely out of the way then began her training with the words, 'Let's have a cup of tea before we start, eh?'

Tea, she learned, was an important part of the projection box routine. It was imperative to start the day with a cuppa, also to offer drinks to any visiting contractors or engineers to keep them sweet. The projectionists all put a pound a month into the kitty to pay for tea bags, instant coffee, milk and sugar.

Tea over and mugs duly washed and put away, it was time for a tour of the building. It wasn't as vast as the Gaumont, but there were still numerous interconnecting corridors and stairs; rooms with yellowed paintwork and peeling varnish on their doors which housed the spare lamps, projection parts and all sorts of stuff that might come in useful one day. Next came the film dump, where the delivery drivers dropped off features in battered metal cases, trailers in cardboard boxes held together by parcel tape and advertising reels for each screen.

'Now we go further down, into the bowels of the cinema,' Alfie said. 'Careful on those steps, they're a bit rickety.'

The steps led under the stage, into a huge, empty basement illuminated only by three dim light bulbs. It was a horror film director's dream, with pipes overhead and a bank of industrial grey switch boxes against one wall. Two deep holes were covered by metal grating. Peering through, Cat saw dark water.

'This end of the building's below ground level so it gets flooded when it rains. The pumps are supposed to switch on automatically, but sometimes they clog up and stop working. Once I came down after a storm to find the water lapping around the mains intake.' Alfie pointed at a thick, black cable which snaked up the wall into one of the large, grey boxes. 'If water ever gets in there, we'll go out with a bang. So you need to keep an eye on those pumps.'

They climbed back up and onto the stage. The boards creaked in protest as they walked across. Voices were lost in the high darkness above their heads. Cat expected to hear the sound of pigeon wings; that panicked flurry of sound, but there the resemblance to the Gaumont ended. The blacked out windows at the rear of the stage had been covered in chicken wire to prevent birds getting inside. Alfie pointed out the massive old speaker cabinet at the centre of the screen and the new, smaller speakers that had been recently installed for Dolby Stereo in screen one.

He led the way to the mini screens, served by a single projection room behind the auditoria. 'This is what's called rear projection. There's not many of these about, but we didn't have enough space to have the projection room at the back, like it is upstairs. That's one of the reasons why the picture's so small.'

The projectors faced outward at an angle through large windows. On the other side an equally large mirror reflected the picture onto the back of the screen.

She learned that the cakestand was properly called a Philips non-rewind. Alfie explained briefly how it worked. 'We take out the ring the film's wound on to and thread the beginning through the feed module. It goes over all these rollers…' he pointed them out, fastened to the wall by brackets. 'Then through the projector. It comes back along these bottom rollers and winds on to the same ring which we've placed on an empty plate. So at the end of a show, the whole print has moved to a different plate and we start all over again. No rewinding needed; you always run from the middle.'

The film lying on the top plate was covered by a sheet to stop it getting dusty overnight. Cat's first job was to remove this and fold it neatly. Then she learned how to clean down the projector. It required a thorough clean each morning, then a brush of the sprockets and wipe down of the film path between each show.

For the rest of the day, she followed Alfie around, lacing the film from the cakestand to the projector and learning which buttons to press on the programmer to select the take up and feed plates. By late afternoon her feet ached from the number of times she'd climbed and descended the stairs, following the workings of the time sheet and the noisy demands of the end sequence alarm that indicated when a programme had finished and was ready to be laced for the next show.

The work came in sudden bursts. You started the adverts and trailers in one screen. Then, fifteen to twenty minutes later, there would be a return trip for the feature change. If the feature was widescreen – the same as the programme – then it was just a matter of closing the curtains, raising the lights briefly, then reopening them on the certificate and setting the sound to the correct level for the feature. For Cinemascope films, the lens and masking also needed to be changed. Alfie did this so automatically he could carry on talking to her at the same time.

'It looks easy, because I've done it so often. You'll be like a learner driver when you try. You'll be thinking too much about what button to press next. Don't expect to get it right first time. No-one does.'

By the time they stopped for yet another cup of tea and something to eat, her head was hurting as much as her feet. 'How long do you think it will take for me to learn all this,' she asked.

'I reckon by the end of this week you'll be able to start shows. And once you've laced up a few times, it'll be second nature. When you've mastered that, we'll go on to film make-up.'

'The manual says it takes four years to learn the trade.'

'Back in the days when it was written there was a proper scheme, with a college course and all, but these days that's all gone. Garner will want you to be able to go on shift as soon as possible so he can stop the overtime payments. Most trainees nowadays are ready in about six months.'

Six months didn't seem like very long; not when you knew that at the end of it you would be in sole charge of the cinema. At this stage, even the routine stuff seemed overwhelming, let alone knowing what to do when something went wrong. She kept telling herself that if someone like Clive could manage, then she'd be fine. It was just a matter of practice.

As it turned out, Alfie was right. By the end of her first week she felt like an old hand at starting shows, and could lace up through the projectors as well as the cakestands.

'You're doing really well,' he said. 'You've got nimble fingers and a good memory, which is half the battle.'

She had already fallen into the habit of checking her watch every five minutes and glancing at the timesheet frequently to make sure she would be in the right screen at the right time. 'Why do they write the times so we're up and down the stairs all day?' she asked, exasperatedly. 'Couldn't they do it so that screen one is on before we need to go and start one of the minis?'

'Sometimes they can. It depends on the length of the films and how many performances a day booking department want us to fit in. They also like to stagger the times so that if it's busy, you don't get lots of people waiting outside the screens and filling up the foyer.' He took a deep draught from his eleventh – or was it twelfth – cup of tea that day. 'Some other cinemas have it easier than us, with automation to start the shows and even to do lens and masking changes, but this company likes to keep it as manual as possible. We're lucky to have the end sequence to shut the projector down at the end of the show.'

'No need for gym membership when you're a projectionist,' Cat commented.

It was during her second week of training that something unexpected happened. It was early evening; a short break between houses. She had just sat down for a cup of tea and something to eat when the house phone rang. 'Can you come downstairs, Cat. There's someone here to see you.'

She wondered who it could be and wished they could have left it for another ten minutes so that she'd had a chance to rest her feet.

'I won't be long,' she said to Alfie, and went down to the foyer.

She recognised him even before she walked through the inner doors. He was thinner than the last time she'd seen him and tanned, of course. 'James!' she called out. 'When did you get back?'

He turned to meet her and grabbed her in a bear hug, whirling her round the foyer. It was a good job there weren't any customers about; it was bad enough in front of Gina and Jimmy. 'Put me down,' she hissed in his ear. He took the hint.

'Sorry. Just glad to see you again. My flight only landed at lunchtime. Your dad said you were working here now.'

'So, how long are you back for?' She led him back through the doors to the foot of the circle stairs. At least they weren't in full view there.

'Well, that's it…' he paused. 'I'm back to stay. I've had enough of travelling. I've decided to settle down and get a "proper job" as my parents would say.'

'This isn't the greatest time for that. The country's in the middle of a recession. I got made redundant last year.'

'Yeah. I was surprised to hear you were back in the cinema again.'

'It's a long story. I'll tell you all about it some time, but I need to get back to work now. Give me a call tomorrow. I'm off then.' She was all too aware of her congealing dinner and the need to lace up Screen Three fairly soon.

'Um, well. I needed to ask you a favour.'

Typical James. 'Oh yes, and what's that?'

'I need somewhere to stay. Just until I sort things out. A few days, maybe?'

'What about your parents' house?'

He shook his head. 'They're having an extension built. It's a mess. There's no room.'

'Your brother's?'

'He's just got a new girlfriend. He doesn't want me there, getting in the way.'

'So you want to stay at mine?'

He gave her a roguish smile. 'You don't mind, do you?'

'There's not much room. You'll have to sleep on the sofa.'

He looked as if he was about to protest at that. Cat wondered if she was being a bit cruel. But she didn't want to sleep with him again and she hadn't asked him to come back, so that was his problem, not hers.

After a few seconds he finally said. 'Well, as long as I've got somewhere to put my head down I'll be happy. You won't even know I'm there.'

'I will,' she said. 'You snore loud enough to wake the dead.' She checked her watch again. 'Just wait here and I'll get the keys.'

Her mind was whirling as she raced back upstairs. What was she doing? Letting James back into her life would make things complicated. But she couldn't leave him to sleep on the street, could she?

'Everything all right?' Alfie asked when she got back to the staff room.

'Sort of. It's an old friend. I just need to give him these.' She waved the keys she'd dug out of her bag.

Alfie looked a bit puzzled.

'He's got nowhere to stay – just got back from travelling.'

'Don't forget screen three.' The end sequence was already shrilling its insistent tone, audible even through the closed door. It would carry on until she got there and silenced it.

'I won't. I'm on the way now.'

Having given James the keys and pointed him in the right direction, she carried on with her work. On her way back upstairs, Jimmy stopped her.

'Is that your boyfriend?'

'He was once,' she said. 'We split up a few years ago.'

'You looked happy enough to see him again.' He grinned.

'Well, I've worried about him. He's been all over the place; Malaysia, Thailand, Vietnam.'

'Vietnam? In the war, like *The Deerhunter*?'

'I think that finished about ten years ago. Anyway, got to go now.' Being a projectionist meant you always had a good excuse to get away from Jimmy.

It wasn't easy, having James staying at her flat. By the time she got home that night, he'd already taken over a large part of the living room. Her day off was wasted by having to clean out the filter on her washing machine when a load of his filthy clothing blocked it up. She also felt obliged to make him a meal after he mentioned how he'd longed for English home cooked food while he'd been sweating in the Tropics. As expected, he snored badly, keeping her awake. Going back to work seemed like a rest.

The next morning, Alfie set her in front of a spool of old trailers at the bench. 'Now it's time to learn the art of rewinding. You'll need to be able to check adverts and trailers on the bench, as well as the individual reels of film before they get put together and run on the cakestand. Hold the handle with your right hand, and put the fingers of your left hand on the edges of the film.'

She did as instructed. It felt strange.

'Now, you need to start turning the handle, nice and slowly.'

As she did, the film jumped out from between her fingers and ended up in a messy pile on the bench before she managed to stop the winder. 'What did I do wrong?'

'You might have been holding it a bit too gently.'

She tried again. As she started to wind, the friction caused by the edges of the film burned her fingers. 'Ow!'

Alfie laughed. 'That's better. The faster you go, the more it hurts until your fingers harden up, so keep it slow. And watch the spool you're winding it on to. There shouldn't be any proud edges if it's done right.'

She carried on, concentrating hard.

'So how's your young man?'

That took her by surprise. She stopped again and ended up with another mess of film. 'He's not my "young man". I'm just helping him out.'

'Ah.' Alfie helped her to sort out the film. 'Jimmy's been telling everyone you're an item.'

'Oh, great. I told him the other night that James wasn't my boyfriend.'

'You'd best have a word with him, then.'

'Don't worry, I will.'

'Now, have another go.'

That morning, she wound and rewound until her right arm ached and her fingers felt as if they were about to spontaneously combust. She wondered if she'd end up with a muscly right arm and a puny left one from all the winding.

One of the more pleasant aspects of the job was viewing films. Before showing them to the public, Alfie liked to rehearse the prints.

'When you make it up, you might notice a light scratch on, say, reel two. But until you see it on screen, you can't be sure if that will show up or not,' he explained. 'Plus you have to decide on the sound level. Different films need to play at different levels, you'll find.'

So finally, she got to watch films, undisturbed, with a nice cup of tea. Even better, she was alone in the auditorium, with no smokers to spoil her enjoyment. Even when you sat on the non-smoking side, the air soon became polluted.

Two weeks passed and James still inhabited her living room. The flat no longer felt like home. Prior to his arrival, she'd been able to relax on her days off and even do a bit of painting, but there was no chance of that now. Because he didn't have a car meant that she had to keep ferrying him around. Well, she didn't have to, but he had a way of persuading her.

'I need to go over to Mike's today. Any chance of scrounging a lift?'

She hadn't intended going out. 'Where does he live?'

'Just the other side of town.'

She sighed. 'We do have buses in this country, James.'

'Yeah, but they're expensive. And I'm not earning anything yet. He's going to see if he can get me a job with his dad's firm.'

'Oh well, I suppose so.' The sooner he got a job, the sooner he might be able to rent a place of his own.

'Cheers, Cat. I don't know what I'd do without you.'

Over the next few weeks, Cat learned about not just film handling and presentation, but how to clean the pump filters, change drive belts on the air handling units and top up the secondary lighting batteries with distilled water. Alfie mended everything from ice cream trays and poster frames to the office kettle. Cat helped him to put up new shelves in the stockroom and climbed through ceiling voids unrolling cable for the soon to be installed computerised ticketing system. After one busy weekend, they spent most of Monday morning unblocking the drains. It wasn't quite what she had expected, but it was varied and most of it (apart from the drain rodding) was enjoyable.

The job offer didn't materialise, so James was still moping around the flat. Cat had managed to persuade him to go and sign on. At least he was getting the dole now and going to the Jobcentre a couple of times a week to look for work. The rest of the time, he seemed to spend entertaining friends.

It was after one hectic Thursday when they had a lot of film changes that she got home to find the flat stinking of dope. There was nothing left in the fridge for her to eat and greasy pizza boxes were scattered around the floor. She dumped her bag down and glared at the little group sprawled over her sofa.

'That's it,' she said. 'I've had enough.'

James and his friends exchanged glances. One of them started to giggle.

'And you can shut up!' she said. 'This is my home. It looks like a pigsty. And it stinks in here. My neighbours will probably get high just climbing the stairs.'

'Sorry, Cat,' James said, giving her that 'dejected little boy' look that had worked for him in the past.

'Are you? Are you really?' She turned and slammed the kitchen door behind her, then cracked open a bottle of Shiraz. At least they hadn't started on her wine. She took a drink and wondered if she was being unreasonable. Her tone of voice had reminded her horribly of her mother just then.

She heard voices and the sound of the front door closing. A few moments later, James opened the kitchen door.

'They've gone,' he said.

She sighed. 'I didn't mean to go on like that. I've had a hard day at work.'

'I wish I could do something to help.' He moved closer and put an arm around her.

She wanted to throw it off, but restrained herself. 'You can, by finding somewhere else to live. This place is too small for two people.'

'Maybe we could get somewhere bigger. Together.' He pulled her closer.

This time, she did move away. 'Look James, we aren't in a relationship any more. I don't want to live with you. I'm quite content on my own at the moment.' She took a breath and steadied her voice, aware she was becoming angry again. 'I was happy to help you out when you got back, but it's been almost a month now.'

'I can give you some money towards the bills, if that's what this is about.'

'No, it's not. I just want my home back.' Perhaps his friends could put him up, she wanted to add, but didn't.

'Okay, okay. I'll see what I can do.'

As her experience increased, Alfie left her to run the mini screens alone. Paul had booked a week's holiday, so there would be a couple of days when she'd have to work with a relief projectionist. 'Just carry on the way you've been going and you'll have no problems.'

On the following Tuesday, she arrived early to meet the relief. He was a fat little man with a comb over hairstyle covering his bald patch. 'I'll look after screen one if you can manage the minis,' he said, before making his way into the staff room. She put her bag in its usual place and tried to start a conversation. 'It must be interesting going around to all the different cinemas.'

He sat down heavily in the only comfy chair. 'It pays well.' He took a magazine out of his bag. 'You'd best get downstairs and open up, hadn't you?'

She checked her watch. 'There's plenty of time.' She had been going to have a brew before she started. That was the usual routine, but it was clear she wasn't wanted up here so she left him to it.

She got the projectors cleaned and laced up, replaced a few lamps in the foyer and toilets and still had twenty minutes to go before the doors were due to open. By then she was gasping for a cup of tea and something to eat. There was nothing for it but to go back upstairs.

He was still sitting in the same chair, filling in a crossword puzzle. The floor was speckled with biscuit crumbs. A film transit case propped the door open. She saw from the label it contained *Mona Lisa* which needed to be made up.

He looked up briefly. 'Capital of Chile. Do you know it?'

'Sorry?'

'Four across. Eight letters. Capital of Chile.'

'Er... Santiago I think.'

'That'll fit.' He filled it in, his pencil scratching the page.

She made her tea, and got the Tupperware box out of her rucksack. Normally, she'd eat up here, where there was some daylight and fresh air. Downstairs in the mini box, it was stuffy and there was only a plastic chair to sit on. The silence deepened. She was obviously not welcome, unless he got stuck again. She ate her sandwiches on one of the Lloyd loom sofas in the upper foyer, feeling as if she had been banished from her natural environment.

When she came back five hours later for dinner, he was in the same place. So was the film. 'Shall I make that up?' she asked.

'If you want,' he muttered. 'No hurry, is there? It's not playing until Friday.'

'We usually make up films as soon as they come in, so we can run them through and check them.'

He sighed heavily and folded his paper. 'No one cares any more. Not the manager, not the company, no one. You'll realise that in a few years' time, but by then it'll be too late.'

'Too late?'

'Once you've been in this trade a while, you're stuck. Cinema is all you know.'

'I like it,' she protested.

'That's not much help if they shut the place, is it? I give it ten years, tops. It might see me out, and Alfie too, but I don't reckon you'll have a job for life.'

She took the film downstairs and made it up anyway.

Having survived two days with the relief (to whom she had given the name Mr Doom and Gloom), it was good when things went back to normal again. Alfie started to let her run all three screens alone, as this was the best way of getting her ready for the day she went on shift.

She still had the safety net of knowing he was on site, but had to deal with any problems that arose. The most common and easy to fix were film breaks. The tape joins between adverts occasionally failed, even though they were checked on the bench when the new week's adverts came in. Despite the pressure to get the show back on, you had to be careful to cut and splice the film correctly so it was the right way round when it went back on screen.

Things were slightly better at home now. James had made an effort to keep the place tidy and if he invited friends around, they were always gone by the time she got back from work. He was also taking his job search more seriously and had some interviews lined up. Hopefully, he'd charm his way into one of them and would soon be in a position to move out.

One weekday afternoon Alfie was busy making up trailer sets and Cat was lacing up Screen One projector when the phone trilled insistently. She answered.

'There's no sound in two,' Jimmy said. 'A bloke just came out and said it's been off for about ten minutes.'

'Right. Okay, I'll go and have a look.' She felt her heart rate quicken. This was her first real problem.

'What's up?' Alfie said, coming over.

She told him.

'Right, then. We'd better get down there. Save a bit of time and think about what you're going to check. Best finish lacing up first, though. One screen's got a problem, but you still need to keep the rest running normally.'

While she ran the leader back to the cakestand, she thought out loud. 'First of all I'll check that the sound's in the right format and the right level. Mind you, it was okay when I put the feature on an hour ago, so I don't think that's going to be the problem.'

Alfie nodded sagely. 'Then what?'

They made their way down the stairs. 'Make sure the amplifier's on? It might have failed, or the power's gone off.'

'Good.'

As they crossed the foyer, Jimmy raced over. 'What's wrong? When's it going to be fixed?'

'I've no idea,' she snapped. 'I'll let you know when I've got there.'

Jimmy backed off, muttering something about the customers wanting something done about it right away.

'Well done,' Alfie said. 'Last thing you need is interruptions when you're thinking. Can you remember where you were?'

'Check the amp's got power. If it's dead, check the breaker. Swap it for the spare.' They were almost there. She fumbled for the key to the mini box door. Once inside a quick glance verified that the amplifier's lights were on, and all seemed fine with the settings.

She glanced at the projector and saw at once where the problem lay. The exciter lamp, which illuminated the optical sound track, was dead. 'Shall I stop the projector?' she asked.

'You might as well, for now. If the film's off and the lights are on in the auditorium, it'll let them know we're doing something. You know where the spare exciters are kept?'

She nodded, went over to the cupboard and got one. When she flicked open the cover, the old lamp looked fine; it wasn't at all blackened and the filament was intact.

'Change it anyway,' Alfie said.

She did. The old lamp was cold, proving it had been unlit for some time. The replacement remained dark when she fitted it. 'It's not the lamp. Not unless the new one's no good as well.'

Alfie remained calm. 'Possible, but unlikely. What's next?'

She thought a moment. 'You've always said that if something's not working, we need to see if it's got power going to it.' She looked at the projector base. 'The switch is still on. Maybe a fuse has blown?'

The fuses were at the back of the projector. They were labelled in Italian, but someone had written a translation on a bit of card taped next to them. She found the right one and unscrewed the housing. The fuse inside looked fine, and when Alfie tested it with a meter, proved to be intact.

The house phone went off. Alfie picked it up. 'No, haven't found it yet. This one might take a while. Yes, probably best to give them a refund then.'

'Does this mean we've lost a show?' All through her training it had been stressed to Cat, not just by Alfie, but by everyone else in the cinema trade that to lose a show was the worst possible calamity.

'It happens sometimes. As long as it's not your fault – which this isn't – then we just have to accept it. Look at it this way; they'd already missed ten minutes of the film and at least another ten's gone by while we got down here and did these checks. We might be able to get it back on soon, but we can't rewind to the point where they lost sound and those people are already fed up of waiting.'

'I suppose so.'

'Carry on running the film through to the end so it's ready for the next house. I'm going to check if there's power going up to that switch.'

Cat had to run back upstairs to start Screen One and when she returned Alfie had found the problem.

'The power supply for the exciter lamp's failed.'

'Can we replace it?'

'We could if we had one. But they're too expensive to keep sitting around on a shelf just in case, so we don't. I'll have to call the service engineer and get him to bring one along tomorrow morning.'

'Does that mean we'll be off screen for the rest of the day?' Losing one show was bad enough.

'No. Luckily I have just what we need in the car.'

He returned with a battery charger and after a bit of fiddling and cursing to find the supply wires among the rat's nest of cabling in the base the lamp lit up again. 'That'll do the job. You might be able to hear a bit of a hum if you're up close to the screen, but at least we've got sound again in time for the next show.'

Cat wondered how many years it took before you knew all that kind of stuff. Would she ever have that same easy confidence and ability to improvise?

Once everything was back on screen again they had a break for something to eat and a refreshing cup of tea.

'I'd better warn you now about the engineer,' Alfie said. 'He's a bit of a character, but his bark's worse than his bite. You're going to have to meet him sooner or later, so you might as well come in early tomorrow and introduce yourself.'

She realised this must be the same engineer who had put the fear of God into Clive at the Gaumont. His name was Bertie. A cigarette remained clenched between his crooked yellow teeth as he fitted the new power supply, swearing and coughing and cursing the machines in their native Italian. As he worked, something stuffed inside one of the bulging pockets of his jacket began bleeping. He scrabbled around until he found a paging device, squinting at the number displayed.

'It's that fucking idiot at Plowbridge again. What's he broken this time?'

He called the offending cinema from the box phone. 'Come on, come on,' he muttered, blowing out clouds of smoke like an angry dragon. 'First he pages me in the middle of a job, then the bugger can't be arsed to pick up the phone!'

Eventually the phone was answered. Cat couldn't hear what was being said at the other end, only that Bertie became more and more annoyed. 'You've checked the fuses? You sure about that? Good. Because if I drive all the way out to you and find there's nothing wrong, there'll be hell to pay.'

Cat made a mental note to always double and triple check the simple things. Both Alfie and the manual had stressed that already, but Bertie's ranting hammered it home.

He finished the call, banging down the phone. 'Trouble is there's too many idiots in this game these days. I'm going to have to finish up here and get out to him.' He fixed Cat with a scary gaze. 'Let's hope this one turns out better than the rest.'

'She's fine,' Alfie said quickly.

'A bit quiet.'

'Can you blame her?'

Bertie laughed, which set him off coughing again. 'Come on, let's get this thing sorted.' He checked his watch. 'I should have time for a quick coffee before I hit the road.'

While they had a coffee, Cat laced up ready for opening, mostly to keep out of Bertie's way. It was easy to see why Clive had been scared of him. By the time she returned to the staff room to get her sandwiches, there was no sign of him. 'Has he gone?' she asked before settling down.

'Yes. Off to frighten the bloke who called him earlier.' Alfie must have noticed her look of relief. 'Bertie's not so bad once you get to know him. He's a bloody good engineer. I've never come across anything mechanical he can't fix. One time, he stripped down a crossbox to replace a worn striking pin. Saved us having to pay out for a new one and it's still running fine today. He likes you,' he added.

'Does he? I thought I was just another idiot in his opinion.'

'Not at all. He was asking when you'd be going on shift. I told him another month or so.'

'But I've only been training for four months now. Do you think I'm ready?' Being left in sole charge of the place seemed like a huge responsibility. She wasn't sure how she would manage if a major problem arose.

'Don't look so worried. You'll be fine. You know enough to cope with all the day to day routines and basic fault finding. Everything else is down to experience and you only get that by doing the job.'

Her first week on shift was planned for the beginning of December. It was a quiet time of the year, and as Alfie said, it gave her a chance to get used to single manning before the Christmas holidays arrived with early openings and packed houses. 'Plus, with three of us on the rota, we can all get some time off over Christmas and New Year.'

On her next day off she went to pick up some shopping at Sainsbury's. As she loaded bags into the boot of her car a Jaguar pulled in to the space next to her. When the doors opened, she recognised James's parents at once. His mother was perfectly turned out as usual. Not a hair dared to move out of its assigned place.

His dad noticed her first. 'It's Cat, isn't it?' She had always got along better with him than his wife, who seemed to be of the opinion that Cat wasn't good enough for her little boy.

'That's right.'

'So what are you doing with yourself these days?' he asked cheerfully.

'I'm training to be a projectionist. In the cinema.'

'The cinema?' James's mother said, 'Gracious.' She sounded faintly disapproving.

Cat ignored the perceived slight. 'So how's your new extension coming along?'

'Extension?'

'Yes, on your house.'

James's dad looked perplexed. 'We aren't having any work done.'

'Oh. I thought…'

'Wherever did you get that idea?' James's mother said.

'Actually, James told me.'

'Oh well, with him being abroad, he probably misunderstood something I said,' his dad put in.

'But he's here. In England. In Fairham.' Now it was her turn to be puzzled.

'No he isn't. He's doing voluntary work in Cambodia,' his mother insisted.

'He's been back since, oh, September. He told me he couldn't stay at home because you were having an extension built.'

There was an uncomfortable silence. For a moment, Cat felt guilty at having told them anything. But then, she'd fallen for his story. Presumably, they had also believed whatever he chose to tell them. 'He's been staying at my flat ever since,' she continued. 'I thought you knew.'

James's parents looked at each other, then back to her. 'Perhaps we'd better ask James himself what's going on,' his dad said.

They followed her back to the flat. She knew there was going to be a scene. Part of her relished the idea. But she also hated confrontations and usually did her best to avoid them. Why hadn't James told the truth?

When she'd left, he'd been asleep on the sofa. As she opened the door, he was sitting up and scoffing a Pot Noodle. The look on his face as he saw who was behind her was priceless.

He glared at her. 'What's all this about?'

'Why not ask mummy and daddy that? If you hadn't told us all a pack of lies to begin with...' She could feel her temper starting to bubble.

'Yes, why didn't you just come straight home, darling?' his mother said.

James put on his 'dejected little boy' look. 'I didn't want you to know how badly things went wrong out there. I felt as if I was a failure...'

'Oh, come on.' Cat said, exasperated. 'You've been back nearly two months. Surely you could have told them by now.'

James stared at the floor, his Pot Noodle forgotten. 'I'm really sorry,' he said, his voice quavering slightly. 'I just couldn't face telling you,' he said to his dad.

His mother went over to hug him. 'Well, it's all right now. You can come home with us.' She looked around the room. Cat expected her to add 'out of this squalor', but she refrained from saying it.

'Yes, get your things together, son,' his dad said. 'We'll sort things out.'

'And you'll be home for Christmas,' his mother said happily, blinking back tears.

In just a matter of minutes, he'd stuffed his things into the giant holdall he'd brought with him and was walking out of the door like a prodigal son. Cat watched in amazement. All the stress of the past two months was melting away.

'Have a lovely Christmas,' she said as he left.

James's dad turned to her. 'Thanks for taking care of him,' he said. 'Maybe you'd like to join us for Christmas dinner?'

Cat saw the horrified look on his wife's face. 'It's very kind of you to offer,' she said. 'But I've already made plans. Bye.'

She shut the door behind them. Her home was her own once more.

She returned to work in a more relaxed frame of mind than she had felt for a long time. Even the thought of going on shift was less worrying now.

Although single manning meant that theoretically there was only one projectionist on duty at a time, having three people available meant that in practice there was an overlap during the middle part of the day. One person would start early – usually at eleven o'clock during term time – and work until five. It was their responsibility to do any maintenance jobs prior to the doors opening and to get the projectors laced up and ready to run. Another projectionist came in at two o' clock and stayed until the last film finished at night. Fairham didn't run late night shows, so they were always out of the building before eleven. This meant that customers and staff were able to catch the last bus home, or get in a drink at the pub before last orders.

Cat's first day alone was on a Tuesday. It was a late shift, so by the time she arrived, the cinema was already open, the first performance having started at one-forty.

Gina was sitting behind the pay desk. 'Good luck,' she said.

'Thanks.' She made her way up to the staff room and dumped her bag in its usual place. Paul must still be downstairs, she thought, so she went through into the main box and peered out of the porthole. He'd already raised the lights and the non-sync music was playing softly; something by James Last and his Orchestra. A few people had taken their seats. She patted the projector softly. 'Be nice to me,' she said. 'Don't go wrong today.'

Back in the staff room, she put the kettle on for her first cuppa as a fully-fledged projectionist. She heard Paul bounding up the stairs. 'Tea or coffee today?' she asked as he joined her.

'Coffee, please. How are you feeling?'

'Slightly nervous, to be honest.'

'So was I, the first time I was left on my own. Mind you, I'd been a projectionist for nearly two years before single manning started, so I had a bit of experience behind me. It's a lot tougher for you.'

He sat in the battered Lloyd loom chair, which was too tatty for the foyer, leaving her the comfy chair. 'Everything's ready to go. I've lamped up the mini screens, the boilers are on and we've got next

104

week's timesheets from the office. There's nothing in the film dump yet, so you should have a nice easy day.'

'Good.'

'And I'll take care of the minis until it's time for me to go home.'

Cat smiled. 'Thanks Paul. I really appreciate it.'

All too soon it was five o'clock. He packed his things away and said goodbye. Outside, it was getting dark. The neon sign at the front of the cinema sent a pink wash through the staff room window. Although she knew the timesheet by heart, having checked it multiple times during the afternoon, she glanced at it again. Next to start was Screen Three. There was time to eat dinner before she went downstairs, but she wasn't very hungry.

Putting the next lot of shows on made the time fly by until seven o'clock. By then, she was starting to feel peckish, so heated up some soup on the Belling. After eating it, she went through into the main box again. The cakestand plates turned slowly, reflecting light onto the ceiling and the projector purred like a contented cat.

As she crossed the upper foyer on her way to lace up the minis for the final time that day, a gentle buzz of voices rose up along with the smell of hot popcorn. When she started the last show upstairs, it was a wonderful feeling to look out and see quite a few heads above the backs of the seats. She timed the feature change perfectly, with the curtains swishing apart just as the censor went on screen. She remembered the feeling of passing her driving test; how good it had been to take off the 'L' plates and drive off alone. This was a comparable moment.

How worried she had been at the start of her training; how impossible it had seemed that she would learn everything she needed to know and yet, here she was, on shift. A full member of the projection crew. This time last year she had been facing redundancy and an uncertain future; now she was starting out on a career that would, hopefully, last a lot longer than Mr Doom and Gloom had forecast.

At the end of the evening, when she turned off the box lights and shut the door behind her, she began a habit that would continue through all her years at Fairham. 'Goodnight,' she said softly to the cinema. 'See you tomorrow.'

Reel 3

The Multiplex Boom

Graham: 1992 - 1993

Uncle Peter often told stories about the Palace cinema where he worked. He'd come round to the house a couple of times a month, usually close to meal time.

'Scrounging again,' mum used to say, but not unkindly. He was her older brother by several years and was a projectionist at the scruffy cinema close to the town centre. Graham had never been there. On the rare occasions his parents took him and his brother to see a film they went to the Cannon at the top end of the High Street. 'Don't mention to Peter we've been,' mum always said. 'He'll want to know why we didn't go to his place.'

'Someone from work took his girlfriend there once,' dad put in. 'She was bitten by fleas. And the film broke down. I don't care how cheap it is, I'd rather go somewhere decent.'

Truth was he'd rather not go to the cinema at all. Dad had recently bought a large screen TV and an expensive home cinema system. His collection of video films filled three of Ikea's tall Ivar shelving units. 'It's much better to watch films at home,' he said. 'You don't get any yobs disturbing your enjoyment. I can have a beer or two. You guys can eat as much pizza as you like. We can stop it whenever we want.'

'And we can have it as loud as we like,' said Graham's older brother, Matt.

'As long as it doesn't disturb the neighbours,' said mum. 'These houses have such thin walls.'

On his journey home from the senior school he'd recently started, Graham passed by the Palace cinema. It was just across the road from

Woolworths, which was always worth a visit for the pick and mix sweets. A lot of the kids from his school did the same. The trouble was some of them stole things, which made the staff suspicious of everyone. Graham knew they sometimes pounced on any random school kid, even if they hadn't done anything. Johnny Fowler was accused of taking a liquorice bootlace and ended up being brought home in a Police car. He'd got into loads of trouble. The ones who should have been caught got away scot free.

He always avoided that lot if he spotted them. They were troublemakers in school as well as out and they'd pick on you for no good reason, especially when you were slight for your age and preferred to learn stuff rather than muck around. That was how he ended up going into the Palace for the first time one October afternoon.

He'd just turned the corner when he saw a big group of them go in to Woolworths ahead of him. For a couple of minutes, he hovered uncertainly outside, peering in through the glass doors. Maybe he could hang around somewhere in the vicinity and get his sweets later after they'd gone? That was when he glanced over the road and spotted his uncle up a ladder outside the cinema. Chatting to him would kill some time, and there was the added bonus that if the gang came out they wouldn't dare bother him if he was with an adult.

'Hi, Uncle Peter,' he said when he was close enough to be heard.

'Where are you off to, son?'

'Just home,' he shrugged.

'What's for tea tonight? Did your mum say?'

'Dunno. Think it's fish fingers and chips.'

'Fish fingers, eh. I might give that a miss. It reminds me of something that happened here a few weeks back. Pass us those pliers out of me tool box, will you?'

Graham did as he was asked and watched as his uncle expertly stripped a cable. 'So what happened,' he asked after a while, when it seemed Peter might have forgotten what he'd been going to say. Adults did that a lot, he'd noticed.

'Oh, right. Yes. This young couple came in a few weeks ago. They'd stopped at the chippy on the way - not that they're supposed to bring in takeaway stuff, 'cos it stinks the place out. And it means they don't buy anything from us either, so the manager gets annoyed.' As he spoke, he twisted strands of wire together, joining two cables which he then fitted into a plastic block. 'So there they were, sitting near the back of screen three, tucking in. All of a sudden, the usherette hears this unearthly scream. Thought maybe a rat had run across someone's feet. That's happened a few times.'

'There's rats in the cinema?'

Peter nodded. 'Didn't I ever tell you about them? And cockroaches, too. Mind you, we haven't got them any more since the pest control bloke came in and dusted the place overnight. I was crunching dead roaches underfoot all the next day.'

'Yuck.'

Peter connected up another pair of wires. 'Maybe this bugger will work now. Held together with string and gaffer tape, this place is.'

Graham nodded. The plastic cover from the poster frame was criss-crossed with cracks and scratches. Graffiti too. THIS IS A DUMP! was scrawled in red marker pen across the front.

'Anyway, where was I?'

'There was a scream. Was it rats?'

Peter shook his head. 'No. It was worse than that. Joanne – that's the usherette - went down there to see what was up. And what she saw, she'll never forget. See, this girl had been helping herself to chips in the dark and she'd got one that she thought was a bit too crispy. It was so hard that when she tried to bite it, one of her teeth broke – that was why she screamed. But it was when Joanne put her torch on that it really kicked off. You see…' he leaned down from the ladder conspiratorially and lowered his voice, even though there wasn't anyone around to hear. 'It wasn't a chip at all. It was a man's finger!'

'Whoa. Gruesome!'

'See, the bloke who chips the potatoes had an accident with the machine that morning. They were supposed to chuck them all out, but the boss couldn't bear the thought of losing money – just like the skinflint who runs this place – so he got them to rinse off the blood and fry them up as usual. Last time I ever get my supper from there, I'm telling you!' He slid dramatically down the ladder, landing lightly. 'Right-ho. Keep an eye on all this lot while I nip back inside and turn on the juice.'

He disappeared inside the cinema. Graham had enough time to wonder if there might be a bang and some sparks, like when dad drilled through a cable in the kitchen wall. He stood back slightly, just in case, but all that happened was that the long tubes flickered a few times, then burst into life just as Peter returned.

'Blimey! It works,' he said, sounding slightly surprised. He started to put the frame back together.

Graham's attention wandered. He glanced over to Woolworths, where the group of boys were just being evicted by a member of staff. He might be in luck, once they'd cleared off, of course.

'Fancy coming inside to have a look round? Bet you've never seen a projection box before, have you?'

'No.'

'Come on then.'

The foyer was dark and smelled stale, as if the air trapped inside had lain undisturbed for far longer than a day. There were big wire cages over the sweets on display.

Peter turned on some lights which made the foyer both brighter and shabbier at the same time. The carpet was stained and threadbare in places. Graham wondered if you'd spot the fleas jumping up before they bit you.

'Not bad, is it?' Peter commented. 'Me and the boss gave the walls a lick of paint last April and I put up those new spotlights over the kiosk. Got 'em out of a skip.'

The doors creaked as they were pushed open. Deeper inside the cinema, the prevailing smell was of air freshener overlaying something nasty. It became stronger as they passed the door leading to the Gents. Graham held his breath for as long as he could, all the way down some stairs and into a dimly lit corridor with walls and ceiling the colour of old meat.

Peter stopped and searched through a huge bunch of keys hanging from his belt loop, using one of them to unlock a door labelled PRIVATE. He led the way up some worn wooden steps into a tiny room.

'See that.' Peter pointed behind the projector at a giant reel. 'That's the film. It runs from this spool here at the top then back to this one at the bottom. When it's finished, you have to rewind it. Whole thing takes about five minutes at full speed.'

The film was black and shiny, like an old-fashioned record. Graham had a thought. 'Does every cinema still use film? Someone at school said it was all on video these days.'

Peter made a noise somewhere between a grunt and a snort. 'That's what they'd like, believe me. Then the manager could just put the cassette in and press play. But no, everywhere - from here right up to the big London cinemas - shows film. And that's the way it'll be for a long time yet. Making a video picture look good on your television is a lot easier than blowing it up to the size of a cinema screen.' He looked thoughtful, then continued. 'Plus it'd cost a lot of money. All of this equipment was second hand when it was put in and it'll last another thirty or forty years. It was built to last, not like modern technology that's out of date as soon as it's out of the shop door.'

Graham knew this was one of his uncle's favourite gripes. When he came round to the house he was always going on about how everything made these days didn't last five minutes. But then, dad said that there was no point in making things that would last forever, because people wouldn't want to keep them that long anyway. 'When I bought us a new television it wasn't because the old one was broken, but because this model is bigger and better.'

'No, film will see me out all right,' Peter continued. 'Here. You can have a piece to take home, if you like.' He dodged round the back of the projector and over to a tiny bench. Unrolling some film, he snipped it with a pair of scissors. 'There you go.'

'Thanks.' Graham stuffed it into his school bag. 'I'd better go now or I'll be late.'

'Go on then,' Peter said, 'Enjoy those fish fingers. Let me know next time your mum's doing steak pie.'

Peter called in a few more times before Christmas. When he mentioned that Graham had popped in to the cinema one afternoon, mum picked up on it instantly. 'You're not to go bothering your uncle when he's at work,' she said.

'It was no bother,' Peter said. 'It's nice to see someone his age taking an interest.'

After his uncle had left, mum rounded on Graham. 'That cinema isn't a playground. I don't want to hear about you going there again.'

'It won't be around for much longer anyway.' Dad looked up from the paper. 'It says in here there's a new eight screen multiplex going up on that retail park they're building.'

The bus Graham caught to school went past the site. Over the next few months he watched as tall steel frames rose up from the mud. By Easter, the buildings were taking shape. The supermarket was the first to open, followed shortly by a DIY store and several furniture and carpet shops. The cinema opened its doors in early May with a preview day inviting people to go along and watch films and trailers free of charge and even enjoy a complimentary soft drink and popcorn.

Graham went with some friends. The first impression he had as they went inside was of light and space. Everything was new, shiny and bright. There were film posters and cardboard standees everywhere. The kiosk was huge and there was a pick and mix selection to rival Woolworths, although much more expensive. On one side of the foyer was a licensed bar, while opposite stood an arcade with loads of gaming machines. They spent an hour or so playing on these before venturing further inside.

As everything was free, they went in and out of all the screens. Some of them were showing trailers, while in others whole films were playing. The seats were really comfortable; the picture was wall to wall and the sound awesome. Graham was so impressed, he stayed to watch the whole of *Wayne's World*, even though he'd already seen it on video. It was totally amazing. With a cinema like this to come to, even his dad might agree that it brought another dimension to the experience of watching a film; one that you just couldn't match at home.

Bill: 1993

The industry was getting back to its feet, that was certain. If the early part of the nineteen-eighties would be memorable for all the closures; nineteen eight-five onwards heralded the start of a new cinema boom. That was the year the first multiplex opened in Milton Keynes; a modern cinema complex in a city that had only existed for twenty years. It also marked the first year that admissions began to rise again, following the post-war decline in cinema going.

Since then, Bill had visited a couple of multiplex cinemas; he liked to keep up with modern developments. As he grew older, his main fear was of becoming one of those people who moaned about the way the world was going and who refused to learn anything new. Apart from the obvious fact of them having a lot more screens under one roof than any previous site, what set them apart was the way they ran.

The first wave of multiplex cinemas had been built by American companies. The two main British exhibitors, Cannon and Odeon, were slow to jump on the bandwagon. It was their usual attitude toward anything new; wait and see what will happen before committing yourself to action. Look how long it had taken for them to start retro-fitting Dolby Stereo.

The new cinemas had no choice at first but to take on existing projectionists. They offered a competitive salary and the attractive proposition that projection meant just that; no more mending seats and coaxing recalcitrant boilers into action. Less appealing were the long hours; open at around eleven o'clock every morning with the last film finishing around midnight. Most of them ran late night shows on a Friday and Saturday as well, so on those nights, you'd get out at around three in the morning.

Bill had quite a few old friends who now worked in multiplexes. 'Look at it this way,' Geoff had said. 'With an eight screener opening just a mile away, I knew my old show wouldn't last, so I thought I might as well jump ship while the offer was there.'

He'd gone to visit Geoff at the new cinema on one of his days off. Like many of the multiplexes, it had been built on an out of town site. From the outside, only the signage and poster frames marked it out as a cinema. Its construction was very similar to the other retail units on the development; Bill supposed that if it didn't perform as expected, it could easily be converted back into a DIY store or supermarket.

There was certainly no shortage of parking, especially at this time of the morning when the shops were just beginning to open. He walked over to the front doors and peered through. The foyer was a vast, carpeted space with a rectangular retail counter in the centre of it. Wide corridors led off to the auditoria; four on each side with giant plastic numbers fixed to the walls to guide people to the right screen. The whole place was unlit and seemingly deserted.

Bill looked around for a doorbell. Most cinemas deliberately placed them high up, out of reach of kids who would otherwise ring them incessantly and drive all the staff mad. He spotted it in the top corner of the right hand door frame and pushed it. The bell was so distant, he didn't know if it had worked or not. Finally he saw a figure coming across the foyer and Geoff opened the door.

'You found it all right then?'

'You couldn't really miss a place this big. And there's signs up all over town to the new multiplex.'

'Come on in, then. I'll give you the full tour.'

The building smelled of new carpets and fresh paint. He noticed that sensibly, they had put lino down around the retail area so that spilled fizzy pop didn't soak into the carpets. The foyer had a high suspended ceiling with recessed spotlights.

'How do you get up there to change those?' he asked.

'We've got a fancy hydraulic tower. The auditorium ceilings are the same. You don't have voids in these new buildings, so all the lights have to be changed from below.'

He led the way into Screen One. 'This is the biggest. Four hundred and twenty seats.'

Bill sat in one. It was far wider than the old seats he was used to; made for modern size bums and very comfortable. 'You wouldn't mind watching a three hour epic sitting in this,' he said. The sightlines to the screen were excellent. It was just the right height to avoid neck strain and as the auditorium was gently raked, unless someone very tall sat in front of you they wouldn't interfere with your view.

Another feature common to the multiplexes he'd visited was their plain interiors. Here, the walls had been painted in dark red, with fabric covered panels providing acoustic treatment. The surround speakers for Dolby Stereo were dotted around the side and rear walls. It was nothing like the architecturally splendid creations of the first cinema boom in the nineteen-thirties. He doubted that people would ever campaign to preserve a building like this.

'They're all the same, decoration wise. The only thing that varies is the number of seats and the size of the picture,' Geoff said. 'That's why they put up those big numbers. Mind you, people still go into the wrong screen. We had a couple in who sat through forty minutes of *Strictly Ballroom* before they finally realised it wasn't *Last of the Mohicans*.'

They walked down the remainder of the corridor and through a door that led upstairs. 'This way to the projection suite.'

'That sounds posh.'

'Well, you can hardly call something the size of this…' Geoff threw open the door to reveal an area that seemingly ran the full length of the cinema, 'a box. We tried room and gallery before settling on suite. Let's leave "booth" for the Americans. It always makes me think of a fairground tent where you go and see the bearded woman or the baby with two heads.'

The walls were painted mid grey. Each screen had its own projector and cake stand. A tall rack held the multiple amplifiers and

Dolby processor. Large numbers were prominent on the back of each lamp house and on the walls too.

'It's really easy to get them confused when you're in a hurry,' Geoff said. 'Like downstairs, it all looks the same. We put highlighter on the time sheets too, so you know where you are at a glance.'

The time sheets took up a full A4 page and looked complicated. It was bad enough these days in a triple with two films generally showing in each screen every day. 'What's the maximum number of films you've shown in a week?' Bill asked.

'So far, seventeen's the record. It'll be beaten soon. We have kids' shows on Saturday and Sunday mornings, old folk's screenings on a Tuesday and late nights Friday and Saturday. It soon builds up. You know, if someone had said to me ten years ago I'd be making up that amount of film, it wouldn't have seemed possible.'

Back at home, Maureen heated his meal in the microwave. 'Did you have a good day out, love?'

'Yes, I did. Geoff seems to have settled in there.'

'Mum, where's my blue shirt gone?' Philip called from upstairs.

'In your wardrobe,' Maureen called back. 'Where I hung it up,' she said to Bill. 'He leaves his clothes all over the place. It's a wonder he can find anything.'

Bill smiled. 'He makes more mess than the other two put together.' It was far quieter now that Neil had moved out and Robert was at university.

The microwave pinged and Maureen brought the plate over. 'There you are.' She'd already eaten earlier, so she sat with a cup of tea while he tucked in.

'Do you think they'll build one here? There's been another story in the paper about the old gasworks site being developed.'

'I just hope it'll be our company that gets a bid in there. I wouldn't like to have to start all over again with a different one. Mind you, Geoff's done all right. His old site's hanging on, but they've reduced prices and that's always a bad sign. He thinks it'll close by the end of the year.'

'Pity he didn't stay on for the redundancy.'

'Yes, but at least this way he's got another job and it's still local.'

Maureen sighed. 'I always think it's sad to see a cinema close, even if there's another one opening in the same town. There's all those memories wrapped up in it. Remember the first time we took Robert and he thought what was on the screen was real?'

Bill chuckled. '"Don't let those hippos eat me, dad." That's what he said.'

'And we've a few memories of our own in there too,' she smiled. 'Remember when we were courting? Do the staff still get up to things like that these days?'

'They certainly do. Geoff was telling me two of the girls on the kiosk had a fight the other night. One of them caught the other girl snogging her boyfriend in the stock room.'

'Passion among the popcorn,' Maureen laughed. 'That would make a good film title.'

Cat: 1993

Bertie settled back in the staff room's only comfy chair and lit another cigarette. 'So, Alfie, when is it you're going?'

'September the ninth,' he said. 'Just three months left.' He still didn't sound wholly enthusiastic about it. Cat already knew he had mixed feelings.

'Retirement's all very well,' he'd said to her. 'At first, it'll just be like taking some holiday. The wife's got a whole list of jobs for me to do. But when the novelty wears off, what then? What do you do with all that time?'

'So they'll be after a new chief for this place. Hmm.' Bertie looked over at Cat. 'I hope you're going to apply.'

'I'd not really thought about it,' she said. 'I don't think I've got enough experience.'

'Everyone has to start somewhere,' he pointed out. 'Alfie thinks you're up to it. So do I. And if you don't you could end up with some idiot getting the job. There's plenty of them to go around these days.'

'I suppose so.'

'I had an emergency call the other day. They've got a ghost a mile high in screen six, this so-called chief tells me. Says he can't sort it out himself so I need to get there a.s.a.p.'

Cat had a sudden vision of Bertie dressed like he was one of the main characters in *Ghostbusters*, before she realised he was talking about a misaligned shutter blade rather than things that go bump in the night.

'Anyway, when I got there I told him to put a light on the screen. "That's not a ghost," I said to him. "Take the fucking porthole out." So he did and bingo - no ghost! Some bloody fool had cleaned the porthole the day before and left smears on it. And this is a chief who's been doing the job nearly fifteen years!' Bertie stabbed the air with his cigarette. 'So don't do yourself down, girl. You're capable of doing a better job than most of those buggers.'

'They're advertising it next week,' Alfie said.

'Right. You get your letter in pronto. Make it look like you're keen.'

Cat nodded. You didn't have a lot of choice when Bertie got an idea into his head. And he had a point. She'd been lucky working with someone as good as Alfie, who had taught her so much over the years. She never dreaded going in to work and didn't want that to change.

It was apparently quite commonplace for potential applicants to come and have a look around the cinema before the interviews, to get a feel for the current condition of the cinema and its equipment. This would enable them to plan their answers to interview questions such as 'What would you do to improve presentation at this site.'

The week after the advert came out, one of the candidates arranged to come in on a Tuesday afternoon. Alfie was due to be off that day and gave her some advice. 'Show him around and answer any questions honestly. But don't make the place seem too appealing, if you know what I mean.'

This candidate, on paper anyway, seemed the best of the lot. At least his application had been word processed and was literate. One of the other letters had come in scrawled on the back of a paper bag and had more or less said that the person was applying because it was better pay than his current job and was nearer to where he lived.

Cat was getting Screen Two ready for opening when the phone chirruped with the internal call tone and she was told the prospective chief was waiting in the foyer. She finished lacing up, conscious of feeling slightly nervous. Get a grip, she chided herself. He's probably feeling the same way.

Even with several customers waiting to be served, it was easy to tell which one had come about the job. He was wearing a suit and carrying a briefcase. Cat thought he looked like a nervous sales rep on his first day alone. She went up and introduced herself.

'Hi, I'm Cat Taylor. Senior projectionist here. You've come for a look round?'

'That's right.' His handshake was firm, but slightly clammy.

'Where would you like to start?' She smiled.

'Well, the main box, I suppose.'

She led the way up the stairs, deliberately going slightly faster than normal, so that by the time he reached the top he was slightly out of breath and probably a bit too hot in his suit.

'This is screen one.' It was already running. She hoped he would notice how clean everything was. Alfie had always kept the box pristine and she'd been happy to maintain the same standards. It had shocked her when Bertie said what a filthy state some places were in.

'You've no automation at all here?' he asked, looking around.

'No, none. We keep very fit,' she said cheerfully.

'I expect they'll put some in when it goes up to five screens.'

Cat sighed. 'Yes, if that ever happens.'

He looked a little concerned. 'What do you mean?'

'Well, they first came up with the idea oh, two or three years ago. But then we got listed by English Heritage so all the plans had to be redone. Since then it's been on and off more times than I've had hot dinners.'

That had definitely hit home. She decided to play with him a bit more. 'I'm sorry if I'm sounding pessimistic. But that's how it is.'

'No. I appreciate your honesty. I heard a different story, that's all.'

Cat shrugged. 'Well, I guess they wouldn't want to put you off applying, would they? I mean, we all know what happens to little cinemas like this when multiplexes open nearby.' She checked her watch. 'I need to start screen two in five minutes. Would you like to come down there with me?'

On the way down, he asked a few more questions. 'This place is counted as two boxes on two levels?'

'That's right. Even though we have much further to walk between boxes than some cinemas, it's still the same money.'

'Do you get much overtime?'

She laughed drolly. 'I wish. The manager's really tight. He doesn't like paying out, so Alfie keeps it to a bare minimum. The only time we get any extra is if someone's on holiday.'

He had a quick look round the mini box while she started the adverts. 'I've never seen rear projection before,' he said.

'It's fine, once you get used to it,' she said. 'The main thing you have to watch for is this light on the switch panel.' She pointed it out. 'It tells you the curtains have opened up there in the auditorium. As we're behind the screen, it's the only way we know the customers can see the picture.'

He nodded, and pointed at the side wall of the box, where the reflected image from the porthole glass could be seen. 'What are those lines painted there for?'

'So we can check the racking this end. Otherwise you can walk all the way back up there only to find you're showing a racking line at the top or bottom of the picture when it's playing in scope.' She checked the film was on all the rollers before flicking the alarm and end sequence switches on. 'So what's it like at the cinema where you work now?'

'Four screens since just over a year ago. It's similar to this one, apart from the rear projection. But I've been there for ten years and the chief's only forty-eight. He doesn't want to move on, so I'm going to have to if I want promotion.'

She nodded understandingly. He was quite a likeable chap, she decided. Be ruthless, her inner voice said. Just because he's inoffensive doesn't mean he'd be any better than you at running this cinema.

'Your engineer's Bertie Arkwright?' he asked.

'Yes.'

'I've never met him, but I've heard some stories. Didn't he throw someone down the stairs once?'

'He's not that bad, really. Alfie gets on well with him, because he's old school and can pretty much fix anything that goes wrong. But I've seen Bertie shouting and swearing at people down the phone. I was terrified of him when I started in case I made a mistake and called him out for something stupid.' That was definitely the truth and no exaggeration. She'd learned since that Bertie fostered his reputation to deliberately make people think twice before crying 'emergency'. Once he decided you could be trusted, he toned down the act considerably.

'Would you like to see anywhere else?' she asked. 'The boiler house, backstage and suchlike?'

'No, that's fine. Thanks for your help.'

'Not at all.' She showed him back to the foyer and went back down to the mini box to wait for the feature change. She felt slightly mean, but everything she'd said was the truth, more or less. It made her realise how much she wanted the job.

As it happened, her best efforts didn't put him off; his application stayed in place. Cat was quite glad when she heard this. At least, if she got through, it would be fairly and honestly. The contest was just between the two of them; paper bag man didn't get onto the shortlist.

She swotted up on all the things that she thought they might ask and two days before the interview Bertie came in to grill her.

'Right,' he said, sitting back in the comfy chair while the broken Lloyd loom poked her in the back. 'Tell me about the crossbox.'

She took a deep breath. 'It's also known as the intermittent movement. There's a shaft with the intermittent sprocket on one end and a Maltese cross on the other. A cam with a striking pin rotates via the projector mechanism and as it engages with one of the four slots on the cross, the intermittent sprocket moves a quarter of a turn. That pulls down a frame of film.'

Bertie was nodding encouragingly, so she continued.

'The cam rotates against the curved face of the cross, holding the frame steady while it's being projected.'

Bertie took a swig of coffee. 'Good. So tell me what the shutter's doing.'

'While the film's being pulled down, the shutter blade cuts off the light. It's rotating forty eight times a second, so it also cuts off the light a second time while the frame's held steady in the gate. That's so we don't see a flicker.'

'And what if the shutter and the intermittent movement go out of sync?'

'If any light gets through while the film's moving, you see a ghost. That's basically streaks of light either above, or below the image depending on which way the shutter has gone out of alignment.'

'So how can you tell the difference between a ghost and a dirty porthole?'

'If it's the shutter, the streaks flicker as the shutter turns. If it's on the glass, the streak stays still.'

Bertie snorted. 'At least you know more than that fucker down the road. Right. Let's say your sound fails in the middle of a show. What are you going to check?'

The questions went on for nearly an hour. At the end of it, Cat felt totally drained.

'You'll do fine,' Bertie said. 'You know your stuff. And the boss of technical services is nowhere near as tough as me.'

The interview proved him right. Cat felt as if she sailed through the technical section. Even the standard questions weren't as tricky as she feared and with her knowledge of the cinema and its operations, she didn't find them hard to answer. The combined recommendation of Alfie and Bertie Arkwright must have clinched it, as the following day she was offered the position. She wasn't quite as jubilant as on the day she became a trainee projectionist, because that really had felt like a victory against overwhelming odds. It was still a slightly daunting prospect to think that she would soon be responsible for the smooth running of all technical aspects of the cinema.

'I'm always on the end of the phone, if you need advice,' Alfie said. 'And I'm happy to be leaving the place in the hands of someone like you who really cares about it.'

'Drop in whenever you like. There'll always be a cup of tea and the comfy chair waiting.'

'As long as Bertie hasn't got there first.'

Graham: 1994

The multiplex cinema was certainly a success. Most weekends, Graham caught a bus out there with some friends, watched a film and then had something to eat at the recently opened McDonalds.

The town centre started to die slowly. Now that there was a big DIY store out of town, the funny little shop that had sold everything from washing line to letterboxes and paint to garden tools saw the business dwindle until the owner finally decided to call it a day. The town centre supermarkets went the same way and the toy shop couldn't compete with the prices and variety at the massive superstore on the retail park. The High Street became pocked with boarded up windows.

'It's ridiculous,' said Graham's mum. 'All that's left in this town are charity shops and estate agents.'

The Palace struggled on for nearly a year after the opening of the new cinema, lowering its prices and becoming even shabbier than before as the owner gave up maintenance almost entirely.

'We're hanging on by the skin of our teeth,' Uncle Peter said gloomily. 'Someone ripped one of the screens last week and all we could do was stick it together at the back. More bloody gaffer tape.'

'Never mind, love,' Graham's mum said sympathetically. 'Have a bit more pie.'

Graham wasn't surprised. He'd seen enough films now at the multiplex to realise that no-one would choose to go and watch a blockbuster on the Palace's tiny screens with old fashioned mono sound. He liked to sit as close as he could to the screen so he felt as if he was right in the middle of the action. He'd watched *Jurassic Park* there and remembered the awesome bass roar of the T Rex and the way the surround sound made it seem as if the velociraptors really were creeping up behind you. He didn't like to see his uncle so depressed, but there wasn't much he could do about it.

Just over a month later, things got worse. The Palace shut its doors for the last time without any protest and only a short paragraph in the local paper. Peter was made redundant and without work to keep him busy, dropped in at meal times even more often.

'It's hard finding another job,' he complained. 'That's the trouble with being a projectionist. It's too specialised. I went into it straight from school, learned everything I needed to know by doing the job. I haven't got any paper qualifications and that's all they want these days.'

'It's a shame,' Mum served up a plateful of stew with dumplings. 'But I'm sure you'll find something.'

Peter turned to Matt and Graham. 'You two make sure you do well at school. Don't end up like your poor old uncle.'

After a few months of unsuccessful applications and interviews, Peter had a lucky break. One of the projectionists at the multiplex decided to take early retirement for health reasons, meaning that a vacancy came up. The chief had known him for years and had tried to entice him away from the Palace a few times when the Cannon was still in the town centre. When he asked if Peter would be interested, he went to have a look round. He came over to the house that evening brimming with enthusiasm.

'It's good money. Different though. Like going from the Millennium Falcon to the USS Enterprise. The box has even got air conditioning. And you wouldn't believe the amount of film they make up in a week!'

'Are you going to go for it?' Graham's mum asked.

'Course I am. You can't pass up on something like that. It's nothing like the old Palace, but it's still cinema. I'd rather work there than have to take a job out of the business.'

Peter started more or less straight away. It was inevitable that during one of Graham's summer visits to the cinema, he met his uncle by the kiosk, putting a plug on a hot dog warmer.

'This is my nephew,' he told the kiosk girls. 'What have you come in to see today?'

'*The Flintstones.*'

'Have you got your ticket yet?' one of the girls asked. 'It's been packed every show.'

Graham nodded, and showed her. 'I came in earlier to get one.' He'd gone to McDonalds while waiting. It was a lot cheaper than buying snacks at the cinema.

'There you go,' said Peter, holding up the plug. 'All sorted. Enjoy the film, son. If you want, you can have a look round upstairs afterwards. Just ask one of these girls and they'll let me know.'

Graham remembered visiting the tiny, dark box at the Palace and thought it would be interesting to see the difference here. 'Okay,' he said.

Two hours later, Peter opened a shiny grey door. 'So this is it. Ta daa!'

The box was bright and clean and seemed to go on forever. The part he could see had four projectors in a line, pointing out of their separate portholes, then disappeared round a corner. 'Which is the one I was in? Screen two.'

'I'll show you.' They started to walk down and had to flatten themselves against the wall as a girl with a long blonde ponytail sped round the corner on a skateboard.

'Sorry,' she called as she disappeared down the box.

'That's Fran. She's another one of the projectionists. I keep saying we should have speed limit signs up here.'

Around the corner was a vast area with cupboards and shelves for storage and two large work benches against a wall covered in film posters. 'This is where we make up all the film.' Peter pointed out. 'It's a full-time job in itself. On days when lots of prints come in, there's one person on the bench all day, while the other one runs the shows.'

They turned the next corner to find another four projectors. 'There's screen two.' It had a large number two stuck on the back of the machine.

Graham went up and looked out of the viewing port. Members of staff were busily sweeping up all the spilled popcorn before the next show.

'Fran's already laced up so it's ready to start again,' Peter said. 'It takes them longer to clean up down there than it does for us to re-lace the projector.'

Graham looked to his right. 'This is for the sound?' he asked. The rack of amplifiers was almost as tall as he was, with lots of red and green lights and the gently whirring sound of fans running.

'Yup. Dolby SR. You've probably seen the signs downstairs. That's what gives the bass such a kick, compared to plain Dolby Stereo. Not that I'd heard either before I came here. Next year we're supposed to be getting this new digital sound system. Chiefy went up to London for a demo and said it was incredible.'

'Wow.' Graham wondered how it could possibly be better than what he'd already heard. Just below the viewing port was a beige coloured square box. On the front were little green plugs stuck into holes. 'What's this?'

'That's the automation. We have all mod cons here. When it's time to start, you just push that button.' He pointed it out and checked his watch. 'It's nearly time for screen four to go, so you can do the honours if you want. Come on.'

Screen Four's projector looked exactly the same, but with a large number four on the back. Peter counted down. 'It starts at four thirty-five. About... now.'

Graham pressed the button. For a moment nothing happened. He heard a click and then a loud beep before the projector next to him sprung into life. About five seconds later, the light came on and the curtains rose slowly in the auditorium below as the picture hit the screen.

Peter turned a knob on one of the amplifiers so they could hear the sound was working. 'Now I just have to make sure it's all running smoothly and that's it. We always come back to make sure the feature's gone on okay, especially if there's a lens change, but basically it'll just run itself until it stops at the end.'

'So when it's all on, what do you do?'

'Little jobs, like you saw me doing earlier. Plus with eight screens there's always something finishing and ready to lace up again. And even though the place is almost brand new, things still go wrong occasionally so we're here to deal with any problems.'

They passed the bench again. 'Remember I gave you a bit of film once?'

'I've still got it somewhere.'

'Well, here's another piece. Try and break it.'

Graham pulled at the ends then tried to rip it in half across the middle. The film stretched a bit, but didn't break at all.

'That's this new stuff. Polyester. You can tow a car with it. It's good in some ways, because it doesn't break, but that causes other problems. At one place a projector got pulled over when something jammed because it's so strong.'

'Can I have this?'

'Go ahead. We've got plenty.' He pointed at the shelves.

'Don't they want it back?'

'The films, yes. Trailers too, most of the time. But there's lots of other little bits and pieces like the day titles, leaders and film spacing that get changed regularly, so we're always chucking out film.'

Graham heard the sound of an approaching skateboard and moved out of the way as Fran appeared again.

'We've already started number four.' Peter called.

She skidded to a halt. 'Great. I can get back to my tea.' She flipped the board around and headed back in the direction she'd come from.

'Anyway, where was I?'

'Does she do that all the time?' Graham asked.

'Most of it. To be honest, if I could ride one of those things I'd do it too. You walk a fair few miles during a day at this place.'

'You could learn.'

'No. I'm too old for that. And I was never very good on skates, so I'd probably break something. My leg, or one of the projectors.'

They strolled back to the end of the box. 'Call in any time you're around,' Peter said. 'We never see anyone up here, so it brightens up the day having a visitor.'

Graham had always visited the cinema a couple of times a month, but once Peter got his staff pass, entitling friends or family to two complementary tickets a week, he started to go even more often. Because the tickets were free, he didn't mind taking a chance and watching films he might have thought twice about paying for. He was still too young to get in to see a 15 certificate legitimately, but some of them he saw from the viewing port, listening to the sound through the monitor speaker. He watched *Speed* and *True Lies* in this way. Peter drew the line at letting him watch 18 certificates though, so he didn't get to see *Pulp Fiction* until it came out on video.

If he had nothing else planned, he often stayed around after the film had finished. During the summer months, most of the staff spent their breaks out in the delivery area behind the cinema, where it was sunny and sheltered. Fran had a business going on the side fitting sound systems to the various staff cars parked out there. Her boyfriend, Keith was often around too, tinkering with his motorbike and impressing the staff by doing doughnuts and wheelies until the site security staff came over to see what was going on.

'Miserable gits,' Fran said. 'Mind you, I got one over on them the other week. After I changed one of the xenon lamps I blew up the old one outside their hut. You should have seen them come rushing out! They thought someone had taken a pot shot at them. I nearly died laughing.'

'How come they didn't see you?' Graham asked.

'I lobbed it from the railway embankment and hid in the bushes until they went back inside again.'

Another popular pastime for the staff was looking through the skips outside the back of the retail units. The carpet shop regularly threw away offcuts and samples. One time there was a rug with slightly frayed edges which ended up on the projection staff room floor, making it seem a bit more homely.

'The only trouble with this place is you can't see out.' Peter said. 'All the old cinemas had staff rooms at the top of the building, near the original projection box. And they always had a window. Not that you spent all day looking out of it, but at least you could tell what the weather was doing. Once you're in here, you lose track of whether it's day or night.' To compensate for the lack of a view, they put up pictures on the walls; a seaside scene and a sunset over mountains.

As autumn brought cooler weather, less time was spent outside. Graham kept up his weekly trips to the cinema, usually on Sunday afternoons, sometimes helping out in the box. If Peter was busy elsewhere, he could start a show. He also helped with film make up by getting the individual reels tail out using the make-up table, while Peter or Fran joined the parts together and wound them onto spools at the bench. It gave him an insight into everything that went on in the background to keep a cinema running.

In the town centre, the old Cannon had already been demolished. The Palace's boarded up façade blossomed with graffiti and posters advertising local gigs. One of the outside walls had turned green where rainwater flowed down the brickwork from a broken gutter.

'I hate to think what it's like in there now,' Peter said sadly. 'There must be mushrooms growing out of the walls with all the damp.'

Graham looked around the clean, bright surroundings of the multiplex. 'It must be loads better working here.'

'It's got its advantages. But I looked after that old place for years. It had a soul. This... this is just a film factory. Still, I'm lucky to have been able to stay in the business, so I can't complain. A cinema's still a cinema, after all.'

Bill: 1995

It had taken a few years to happen, but finally a multiplex was being built in the town. There had been lots of false alarms over the years. Every time a site came up for development, it was reported in the local paper that a multi-screen cinema might be included, but all of these rumours had come to nothing.

Bill's old cinema had remained the sole venue in which to see films and they'd done well enough considering they only had four screens in which to show the ever-increasing number of cinema releases. It had also been fortunate that the nearest multiplex was twenty miles away along a winding single lane 'A' road much frequented by tractors. That generally put people off driving the distance.

Now, at last, the people of Saxfield could look forward to the opening of an eight screen cinema. Bill would be keeping his job as luckily it was being built by the same company he had worked for since the start of his career. The old site would close the day before the new one opened.

On his days off, he'd sometimes go into town and watch the steelwork rising up behind the hoardings. A department store had originally stood there, demolished in the nineteen-eighties and used as a temporary car park ever since. As such, it was a comparatively small footprint, meaning that they had to build upwards to fit in the eight screens. Although it would have new projection equipment and modern sound systems, in many ways it would be more like running a traditional site due to the multiple levels and separate projection boxes. Bill didn't mind that. He'd seen the plans and liked the way the cinema had been designed to blend in with the surrounding buildings in that part of town. Unlike some of these multiplexes, it looked as if it might stand there for at least as long as the old cinema had done.

'You don't realise how much stuff you bring in over the years until you have to think about moving it.' Andy, the senior, had started to clear out the cupboards in the projection staff room. 'Blimey, I'd forgotten about this toasted sandwich maker. Fancy a ham and cheese toastie, chief?'

'I'll pass on that, thanks.' Bill leafed through the old *Cinema Technology* magazines that had recently been unearthed, brushing away dust and spiders as he turned each page. 'These are worth keeping.'

'Let's hope there's plenty of storage at the new site, then. A bigger film dump would be good, too. This week the driver had piled it so high the advert box fell on my head when I opened the door.'

'I had a word with him last month,' Bill said. 'He'd put three transit cases on top of the new xenon lamp I'd ordered. Ignored the "fragile" stickers all over it. Thankfully it was still intact or they'd have been paying for a replacement.'

Bill reached into the cardboard box Andy had dug out from the depths. 'Look at this. An original drawing for the Projectomatic we used to have in Screen One.' The paper was brown with age, the folds so sharply creased they had begun to come apart. It looked as if it might be hundreds of years old, rather than dating from the mid-sixties. He pored over it, recognising Harold's writing among the various alterations and notes written by long retired – and mostly dead – chiefs and engineers. Underneath was one of the old logbooks they'd had to fill in daily, to be checked and signed off by the Regional Engineer on one of his regular visits. Bill's own writing covered many of the pages. 'Hot dog machine repaired,' he read from one page opened at random. 'Some things don't change.' He dropped it onto the growing pile of stuff he'd decided should be kept because throwing it away just wouldn't feel right.

Andy picked it up and flicked through. 'What's Thawpit? You had two gallons of it delivered on August the second.'

'Carbon tetrachloride. We used it for de-greasing and cleaning. Long since banned, of course.' He picked up some Dolby information sheets for the CP50 sound processor. 'I doubt we'll need these at the new place. We should be getting CP65 processors all round and a DA20 in Screen One for the digital sound.'

'I can't wait to hear what it's like.'

'That demo I went to was so loud I nearly lost my eardrums. Mind you, they were trying to impress us all, so I'm not surprised. If it helps add to the realism of seeing a film, I'm all for it.' He threw some projector manuals onto the same pile. 'Pity we can't take the Vic Eights with us. They're a lot sturdier than those Fives they're putting in nowadays.'

'I wouldn't fancy carrying one down all those stairs though.'

'True. I remember helping carry the rectifiers up here when we were tripled. If I had to do it these days, it'd probably give me a hernia.'

Andy checked the clock. 'Better go and start four. Do you think we'll get automation in the new place?'

'I hope so. Five boxes on three levels won't be easy to run without it. But then, I've been to quite a few multi-screen sites where they cope with just an end sequence, so don't be surprised if we get the same.'

He heard Andy's footsteps getting fainter as he went downstairs and sifted through what remained in the box. There were some old timesheets from the early days of tripling, back when they only ever showed one film per screen. He remembered wondering back then how they would ever cope with all the extra film-make up. Now, it seemed so easy, even with the fourth screen added back in nineteen eighty-nine. Adapting to eight screens would take some getting used to, but they'd manage. He'd ask around for some tips to improve efficiency and save time.

The phone trilled and he picked it up. 'Your wife's on the line.'

'Go ahead and put her through.' It was unusual for Maureen to call him at work. Maybe she wanted him to pick something up from the shops on the way home.

'Hello, love,' he said.

For a second or two she didn't speak. Then, very quietly she said. 'Your dad's been taken to hospital. They think he's had a heart attack.'

'Oh.' It took a few moments for the information to sink in. Bill's dad was seventy-five, but fit for his age. They'd been over to his parents' house the previous Sunday and he'd been the same as always. 'What happened?'

'Your mum said when he got up this morning he didn't feel too good. She went to get him a cup of tea, and when she got back he'd collapsed. So she called the ambulance and they took him straight in. I thought I'd better let you know.'

'Yes, of course.' His thoughts raced. He could get off early. Andy would be fine on his own. 'Look, I'll come home and we can go down to the hospital. Mum must be worried sick.'

'She's taking it really well. Your sister's with her, so she's not been left on her own.'

'Good. Right. I'll just let them know I'm going and I'll be with you in about twenty minutes.'

'Don't drive too fast.'

'No. Course not.' He rang off. It still didn't seem entirely real; not when he explained to Andy, or the duty manager. Not while he was driving home, cursing the traffic jam at the roadworks on Priory Street. It was only when they arrived at the hospital and he saw his mother's face that it began to feel as if this was really happening. Then, seeing his dad looking small and pale in a hospital bed, wired to all the medical paraphernalia you normally only saw on TV programmes, it finally hit home.

He was rostered off the next day anyway. Most of it was spent at the hospital, waiting around for news and reassuring mum that dad was in the best place.

'It makes you feel so useless,' he said to Maureen as they had a coffee together. 'If only there was something I could be doing, I'd feel a lot better.'

She squeezed his hand. 'I know exactly what you mean. But there isn't so this is all we can do.'

By the following day, nothing very much had changed. Bill was due back at work for the evening shift. 'You go on in,' Maureen said. 'It'll take your mind off things.'

She was right. All that waiting was exhausting. At least while he was working, it distracted him and stopped him worrying too much, although he couldn't help wondering if there had been any changes and if the phone would ring at any moment to give him good – or bad – news.

He got home just before midnight. Maureen was waiting up, as she always did, and brought him a fresh cup of tea. 'How's it been?' he asked.

'Similar to yesterday. They said his condition was "stable", so I suppose that's good.'

Bill took a sip of tea. 'Something like this makes you realise that you can't take anything for granted. Dad's never smoked and he doesn't drink much. I'd have said he was in good shape for his age. So would he, for that matter. Yet, out of the blue, just like that, he has a heart attack.'

'He'll be fine,' she reassured. 'He's a strong man.'

She was right, as always. Over the next few days, his condition did improve and by the end of the following week, he was allowed to go home.

'I'm lucky to still be here,' he told Bill. 'If that had happened back in the old days, I'd have been a goner for sure. Now all I've got to do is be well enough for the opening of your new cinema. Have they set a date yet?'

'Sometime near the end of October is what they're aiming for. Just over eight weeks. We can't even go in yet; it's still a building site.'

'Well, don't forget to reserve tickets for me and your mum.'

'I've got an order in already.'

Every week they had meetings inside a tiny Portakabin to review the progress. Bill went along with Felicity, the general manager, picking their way across the site wearing borrowed hard hats. Towards the beginning of September, they were allowed into the cinema building for the first time. It still looked as if it had a long way to go, even though they had been assured everything was going to plan. The foyer area was full of pipes and cables. The projection boxes were dusty shells, with markings on the walls showing where the isolators and distribution boards would go. Holes had been cut for the projector and viewing ports and Bill looked through into similar chaos on the auditorium side.

'Hard to believe we'll be running film in here by Christmas,' he said.

'Well before Christmas,' Felicity put in. 'I've just heard the gala opening is set for the first Thursday in November.'

Weeks rushed by. A horde of new front-of-house staff had been taken on and two new managers as well. Bill would be entitled to another projectionist to run the increased number of screens and levels, giving them a total of four, including himself. The last time he'd been part of a team that size was back in the sixties, when they were running just one screen.

After a few rainy weeks in September, one of the builders had to give Felicity a piggy back across the sea of mud to the next site meeting. Bill brought his Wellington boots. Inside the foyer, all the fixtures and fittings were shrouded in dusty plastic. The projection boxes were ready for the equipment to come in at last, although the floors were in a dreadful state, with ingrained dirt and scuffs marking the blue lino. New rewind benches were already in place and the staff area (inside the largest box) had been fitted with a stainless steel sink that was full of filthy mugs. Getting this place clean enough to run film was going to be a real challenge.

On his days off, he usually visited his dad, who was becoming frustrated by his slow progress back to health. 'I wish the weather was better. If only I could get out more.'

'Don't worry, dad. These things take time. I bet you'll be out on your allotment again next spring.'

'It'll take me months to get on top of the weeds,' he grumbled. 'You turn your back for a moment and the twitch starts creeping in. Anyway, how's it going at your cinema.'

'We're getting there. The gala film's going to be *Crimson Tide*. I think you'll enjoy it.'

He'd been spending more time at the new site than the old one, trying to get everything ship shape. As the engineers finished the installation in each screen, his job was to run old films to check the equipment was working properly. The cleaning was endless. Dust was settling all the time. When they weren't being run, the projectors and platters were covered for protection.

Just a week before opening, the flat roof above screen seven developed a leak, so they had to rig up a piece of plastic above the platter and avoid using the top plate while the builders tried to sort out the problem. The automation in three of the screens was suffering from issues which meant that it kept shutting down for no reason. Despite being told numerous times not to, workmen kept taking short cuts through the boxes, trailing in more dirt. Bill was amazed that there hadn't been any film scratched considering the environment was still so dusty.

He'd wanted to spend some time at the old site on its last day, but it wasn't to be. He was over at the new cinema from nine in the morning until ten at night. Although he felt shattered at the end of it, he didn't seem to have achieved very much due to constant interruptions, meetings and phone calls.

The Gala Opening day dawned. Two prints hadn't yet come in. One of those that had already arrived proved to be damaged when checked on the bench, so they were waiting for a replacement. There were eight sets of adverts to check and twelve programmes to be made up for the new films starting on Friday. Andy was bringing some of the films across from the old cinema in the back of his Sierra estate car. Bill left them to it as he ran through the newly revised schedule for the Gala Opening and cleaned down the projectors yet again. The boxes were nowhere near the condition he would like them to be in, but they would have to do.

One of the installation engineers was re-cutting an aperture plate for screen eight, while another was still trying to fix the automation problem. Bill had already decided that he would run the Gala show in Screen One manually to avoid any chance of the film stopping mid performance. As he crossed the foyer for the umpteenth time, he mused on the fact that there were at least fifteen staff busy cleaning and stocking up the retail area and extra managers had been drafted in from other sites to help out with the opening. Up in projection, it was just the usual team and although they were all working flat out with no breaks, they would be hard pressed to get everything done. He'd thought that by the time it got to this stage, everything would have been ready in good time, with a chance to rehearse the opening ceremony amid an air of calm confidence.

His walkie talkie crackled. 'Bill, can you set up the PA system. We need to rehearse the speeches.'

'Right. I'm coming.' He tried not to sound as stressed as he felt. They'd already been through the speeches the previous day, but he guessed they had changed the order again.

He couldn't put the PA system in its final position as there were workmen up a scaffold tower over that precise spot. Experience had also taught him it wasn't wise to leave easily portable equipment lying around an insecure area if you wanted it to still be there when you came back to it later, so after they'd finished messing around he locked it back in the office. He was just about to go back upstairs when he saw Bertie Arkwright pushing his way through the new front doors. That was all he needed right now. Bertie's visits were always welcome when you had a broken down projector or a slow afternoon to listen to his stories and the latest circuit gossip, but neither of those applied today. Officially, he would only start looking after the site once it had properly opened and the installation team had completed all the snagging work.

Bertie spotted him and came over. 'How's it going?'

'Hectic.'

'You look like you need something to drink. Let's try out this new espresso machine they've got.'

Bertie guided him over to the café area and ordered one of the managers to make them both coffees. 'Sit down, Bill. Have a break for five minutes. You look knackered.'

'I feel it. There's so much needing to be done and just not enough of us.'

Bertie looked around at the swarming foyer. 'Plenty of bodies around here.'

'Well, that's always the way, isn't it? This is the bit everyone sees. We're up there out of sight.'

Bertie laughed. 'You're starting to sound cynical in your old age.' He took a long drink from his coffee. 'Not bad. Not bad at all.'

Bill sipped his own coffee. Funnily enough, just sitting down for a while helped clear his thoughts. By the time he'd finished (and Bertie had knocked back his second Espresso) he felt ten times better. Maybe Bertie coming in wasn't such a bad thing after all.

They went up to the main box. Bertie spotted one of the engineers at the far end. 'I'm off for a chat. You carry on with whatever it is you need to be doing.'

'Thanks, Bertie.'

The rest of the afternoon flew past. Some builders tried to go through one of the boxes and met Bertie who told them in no uncertain terms to fuck off. They seemed to get the message. In the foyer, scaffolding was being cleared away and carpets hoovered. Bill inspected all the auditoria to make sure they were looking presentable should any of the distinguished guests wander inside.

In the manager's office at the old site there had been a black and white picture of the auditorium taken on opening day, with palm trees stationed either side of the proscenium. It had all looked wonderfully tidy and calm, but now he couldn't help but wonder if, just out of range of the photographer's lens, there were builders sweeping up rubble and tools being stashed in cupboards, just like today.

Just after five o'clock, he ate the sandwich Maureen had packed for him that morning, had a strong mug of tea and wondered if he should change into his suit yet. The show was due to start at seven-thirty, but people would start arriving for the champagne reception and buffet any time after six, especially those from head office.

'Those buggers love to fill their glasses and stuff their faces before the other punters can get a look in,' Bertie said. 'If you lot want any of it, get in there quick.'

'I don't know if we're invited,' Bill said. 'No-one's said we are.'

'No-one's said you aren't either,' he retorted. 'Without you, they wouldn't have a show to watch.' As it happened, he went down there himself and came back with a tray loaded with food, an unopened bottle of champagne and several glasses. 'Enjoy it,' he said. 'You've all worked bloody hard.'

'I'll leave mine until I've got the show running, if you don't mind,' Bill said. He didn't want to breathe alcohol fumes all over the Mayor if he came up to the box.

'You make sure you get a drink, mind. One of those spare managers down there had the cheek to ask me where I was taking all this. "Up to the workers," I said. "Up to the ones who really matter." He didn't know what to say.'

Bill got changed and went downstairs to mingle for a short while. He spotted Maureen with his mum and dad after a few minutes and went over to see them.

'How's it all going, love?' Maureen asked.

'Fine,' he replied, 'It was a bit hectic earlier, but we're sorted now.'

His dad looked around. 'This is a grand place,' he said. 'Did you know, I went to the old cinema the first week after it opened. I thought it was the bee's knees, but it didn't hold a candle to this.'

'Glad you like it, dad.'

'I had my doubts when you said you were going to get a job in the cinema. So did your mum. But you've certainly made a success out of it. I'd be proud to say to anyone that my son's the chief projectionist at a place like this.'

'Thanks, dad. Now, I'd best get back to my post. Enjoy the film.'

They began ushering the guests into the auditorium at around seven-fifteen. A few had already made their way inside, eager to get the best seats. From the viewing port, Bill saw Felicity showing the Mayor and his wife to their reserved places. He also spotted his parents and Maureen just to the left of the centre aisle. He re-checked the film was correctly laced up and that the automation was safely isolated so as not to cause problems.

'Let me know when everyone's inside and it's time to start,' he said into the walkie-talkie.

'Will do,' came the reply. 'We're just waiting for the last few to take their seats.'

He struck the lamp and waited for the word. It was good to look out and see heads above nearly every seat. He hoped that when they opened to the public tomorrow, attendance would be as good.

'Right, Bill. Start the show.'

'Okay.' He pressed the button to dim the houselights (which he'd set to a nice, slow fade), then the pageants. He started the projector, waited until the lights had fully dimmed then opened the tabs on the certificate of the feature. The first show at the new multiplex was well and truly underway.

Cat: 1996

'So what's wrong with <u>this</u> one,' Amanda sighed. 'If you don't settle down soon, it might be too late.'

'Too late for what?'

'You're thirty-six. Your biological clock is ticking.'

'Oh, that.' Cat dismissed it with a shrug. 'If I'd wanted kids I'd have done it years ago. Probably without saddling myself with a man as well.'

Amanda laughed. 'It's not easy to get pregnant without one.'

'I mean living together, marriage, settling down. The whole thing.' She could see from Amanda's face that she just didn't get it. Well, how could she? She'd gone down the conventional route a long time ago. 'The trouble with men is that as soon as they move in, you end up looking after them. And that's where I am with Guy.'

Amanda looked puzzled. 'When I met him, he seemed lovely.'

'Snap. That's why I fell for him. And we've had some really good times together. But I don't want the same things that he wants. And sometimes, he gets in the way of what I do want.'

'Like what?'

'Well, take last Saturday. I was off work and I wanted to spend some time on those cityscapes I've been painting. I'd been thinking about what I needed to do the previous evening and I was itching to try it out. But he wanted to go out for the day. And he made me feel bad for not wanting to do the same. So I ended up going along with it and wishing I hadn't. Then when we got back, he just plonked himself down in front of the TV and expected food to be provided.'

'You have to make compromises in a relationship.'

'Do I? He doesn't. If I'd insisted on staying in, he'd have been hovering round and getting in the way until I gave in. Why is my life less important than his?'

Amanda shook her head. 'I don't understand you, Cat. You've met someone nice at last and you've moved out of that poky flat. Isn't that enough?'

'No. It's not.'

'Well, have you spoken to Guy about all this?'

She stirred the dregs of her coffee. 'I've tried. Several times. But he doesn't seem to listen to what I'm saying.'

'That's men all over.'

'Exactly,' she said. 'And I've had enough of it.'

They settled the bill then Amanda dropped her back at the house. 'See you again soon.' She waved as she drove off, back to her uncomplicated life.

Cat let herself in. It was a lovely house, in a pleasant part of town. She knew she'd miss the garden and the views. When it was clear, you could see the top of Canary Wharf's tall tower shining in the sun, far off in the heart of London.

She went upstairs to the back bedroom; the one she'd set up as her studio. In the ten months she'd been living with Guy, she'd hardly done any work. Other stuff always got in the way. She sat on the padded bench and stared out of the bay window. The garden lay still beneath low, grey cloud. Horse chestnut leaves were just beginning to turn as autumn approached. Next door's tabby cat prowled along the top of the fence. The rooftops along the curve of Magnolia Drive led the eye down the hill, toward the red brick bulk of the cinema's stage end.

In her mind she dissected the structure and opened it up like a page in a child's pop-up book. There was Screen Five, across the width of the old stage, Screen Four at the front of what had once been the stalls, the original minis behind them. And her favourite, Screen One, the former circle. She thought of all the romances that she'd shown there; all the happy-ever-after Hollywood endings. 'Life isn't like the movies,' she said softly. 'Life is much harder.' It was a quote from one of her favourite films; *Cinema Paradiso*. It seemed to strike a chord with nearly all projectionists. Even Alfie had enjoyed it, despite the subtitles.

Alfie was still a regular visitor at the cinema. When they weren't touring in the caravan, he and his wife came to the Wednesday morning screenings. For a reduced price, customers could enjoy a cup of tea or coffee and free biscuits before going in to watch a film that was only a few months old. Sometimes he stayed around afterwards to sit in the staff room for an hour or so and have a chat.

'I had it lucky, when I think about it. Never dreaded going in to work, not like some that I know. I reckon I saw the best times in this business. Still, I'm glad I retired when I did. There's too many who put it off then by the time they take the plunge, they're not well enough to do all the things they dreamed of. It's been good to be able to do a bit of travelling.'

'Where is it you're off to this winter?'

'Spain again. Down near Marbella. We'll be meeting up with some friends for Christmas and New Year then coming back near the end of February.'

'Sounds wonderful.'

He nodded. 'So how are things here?'

'Same as ever. They seem to be trying to pack in more and more films each week. Although we've only got the five screens, there's always at least ten different features showing. I never thought I'd be making up so much film.'

'Still, good to be busy, eh?'

'Yes. Better than being bored any day.'

She remembered that last conversation, just the previous week. She wasn't ever bored at work, but home was another story. Here she was, staring aimlessly out of the window, unable to summon the enthusiasm to do anything. So how was she going to get out of this mess?

She grabbed a notepad and a pen. Writing a list always helped to get things straight in her head, whether it was planning out the week's duties at the cinema or contemplating changes in her life.

1) *Talk to Guy. Explain that I feel stifled and unable to do the things I want to do.*

Well, she'd already tried that, as she'd told Amanda earlier. He either couldn't (or didn't want to) understand what she was getting at.

'You have plenty of time to do the things you want when I'm at work and you're off,' he'd said. 'When we're both free, it's good to do things together, don't you think?'

He made it sound so reasonable. How could she explain that when she lived alone it was just so much easier? Guy wouldn't take it well if she stayed up late when he had to get up early for work the next day. He was a light sleeper and the noises she made moving around the house or in her studio would disturb him. And when she was off for a day, she had to do stuff like food shopping, washing clothes and keeping the place tidy rather than being able to concentrate on being creative. Back in her 'poky little flat', she only had to consider herself; if she couldn't be bothered to change the duvet cover every week there was no one to complain about it. If she decided to spend all day painting and eat yesterday's leftover curry reheated in the microwave that was fine too.

'But I help around the house as well,' he would protest. 'I iron my own shirts. I can cook if I need to. It's just you have more spare time during the week.'

Then there were all her books, piled in boxes in the garage. Guy didn't like books in the house, saying that they harboured dust which aggravated his allergies. Bringing them indoors made her feel inconsiderate and made him reach for the anti-histamines.

2) *Find out if there are any properties I can afford to rent locally. Then tell him that I am moving out.*

She paused half way through that one, making an elaborate doodle that looked like a swirling black hole in the middle of the page. There, she'd written it down. Leaving was the only way out. It wasn't a question of if, just the practicalities of when. Maybe if she had her own space again, they could go back to the way it had been when they first met? Except, deep down, she knew it wouldn't. That would suit her, but Guy didn't like living alone. If she moved out, he'd move on.

She looked up. Sunlight had burst through the clouds and somewhere among the trees, a blackbird was singing. She knew what she had to do. It would make things harder in the short term, but better in the long run. There was no choice but to take the plunge before this stifling routine dug so far into her life she was unable to break free of it.

Graham: 1997

It wasn't the first time Graham had gone to see a staff preview of a blockbuster new film, but this one was special.

The projectionists always ran through new releases to check for quality and sound levels before the first public showing; the only exception to this being when a film came in late on a crossover from another cinema and there was no time to check it on screen before opening. Run-throughs were normally on a Thursday or Friday morning, meaning he was only able to attend in school holidays. Thankfully, this one was taking place on a Thursday evening, after the cinema closed to the public.

It was strange, arriving as all the customers were leaving. The lights from the foyer blazed out across the shiny wet tarmac, with the neon signs making pools of bright blue which scattered and re-formed as the cars drove by. He knew it would be late when he'd get home and he'd be yawning all day tomorrow at school, but what the hell – it was nearly the Easter holidays and they wouldn't be doing much in the way of work. Anyway, there was no way he was going to miss this one. Tonight's show was the long-awaited re-release of *Star Wars: Episode IV – A New Hope*.

Graham had never seen the film at a cinema. Born in 1981, two years before the release of *Return of the Jedi*, his experience of the Star Wars trilogy had always been at home, on video. Even though they had a large screen TV and surround sound, it wasn't the same as seeing it on a really big screen, in the darkness of a cinema auditorium. Ever since he'd read about the plan to re-release the entire trilogy to commemorate the twentieth anniversary of Star Wars cinema debut, he'd been eagerly waiting for this moment. Most of the front of house staff, who were just a few years older than him, had the same sense of anticipation. They too had owned the action figures and played the video games.

'Back in those days, we'd get films months after their first release in the States.' Peter had told him. 'They showed *Star Wars* in nineteen seventy-seven; we didn't get it until early seventy-eight. We'd all heard about what a hit it had been over there and there was this big expectation about the business it was going to do. And boy, did it do the business! Queues round the block for weeks. It was like turning back the clock, as far as admissions went. Best of all, it was a family film. Everyone could see it. And pretty much everyone did.'

He went inside, waving to some of the staff, who were waiting by the kiosk. They knew him as Peter's nephew and a regular at the cinema. He made his way past the darkened screen entrances and up the stairs to the projection room. It would be in Screen One, of course; the only auditorium so far to have been equipped with Dolby Digital sound.

Fran was leaning against the wall watching Peter lace up the print. 'Hi there,' she said to Graham. 'So this is it. The big moment, at last.'

Peter peered out from behind the projector. 'I'll let you kids get downstairs before I start it, so you don't miss anything.'

'Full Fox opening,' Fran said. 'I bet you'll blast our ears off.'

Peter grinned. 'I might.'

'Mind you don't blow the sub bass, or Chiefy won't be happy.' She pushed off from the wall. 'I'll let you know when to start.' She patted the walkie-talkie clipped to her belt. 'Come on, Graham.'

They made their way to the auditorium. A folding table had been placed in the back aisle, and the delicious smell of pizza rose from the opened boxes.

Fran selected a piece. 'Tuck in, before these ravening hordes devour the lot. Now, let's get to the best seats in the house.' These were a bit further back than Graham usually chose to sit, dead centre to the screen. 'This is the sweet spot for the sound,' she explained.

Graham knew that the original had been one of the first films in Dolby Stereo, although back then, not many cinemas had been equipped for it. The latest format, Dolby Digital was not just capable of being played louder without any distortion, but gave two separate surround channels to increase the sense of realism. All the films he'd seen so far hadn't disappointed. *Star Wars* was going to sound amazing.

Fran looked around. 'Is everyone here?' she yelled.

'Susie's in the loo,' someone called back.

'Okay, we'll wait for her.'

The atmosphere was more like a party than a cinema screening. People were chatting loudly and calling out to each other. A couple of the doormen started singing, 'Why are we waiting?' and there were cheers when Susie finally turned up.

Fran unclipped the walkie-talkie. 'Right, Peter. Everyone's here now.'

Graham glanced back at the porthole. Peter gave him the thumbs up sign. As the houselights slowly faded, the voices subsided. The footlights began to go down and the festoon curtain opened just as full darkness bathed the auditorium. As the censor hit the screen, there was a brief cheer, followed swiftly by someone hissing, 'Ssshhh.'

The Fox logo was much louder than Graham had heard it before, louder than you would ever play it to a normal cinema audience for fear of complaints from delicate ears. As the famous opening title appeared, Graham took a bite of pepperoni pizza. Life didn't get much better than this.

Bill: 1997

Bill cut off the leader from reel one of *Dante's Peak*, attached the usual nine feet of black spacing and removed the spool from the rewinder, stacking it under the bench. Once the kids film was plated off, it would be ready to run on to the platter. Another job ticked off the list. He strolled over to the staff area and put the kettle on. There was just time for a cuppa before screens four and six finished.

As it boiled he completed the film report. *Used print. Treated. Slightly buckled. Light base side scratch reels one and two opposite soundtrack.* It was close to the edge and probably wouldn't show up on screen. In any case, as they appeared to be sending out used American prints for this film, even if he asked for a replacement there was no guarantee it would be any better.

His walkie-talkie crackled. 'Can you come down to the foyer right now, Bill?' The voice sounded panicky. 'It's urgent! There's water coming through the ceiling by the pick and mix.'

'On my way.' His tea would have to wait.

As he made his way down, the walkie-talkie crackled again. 'Need any help, chief?' It was Greta, the trainee technician. She must also have heard the message.

'I'll let you know. Can you look after my screens? Four and six will be off soon.'

'No problem.'

In the foyer several members of staff stood around staring as water dribbled into a bucket. A suspended ceiling tile had fallen, having turned into a grey, porridge-like mess which was now splattered all

153

over the carpet. Someone had been sensible enough to move the pick and mix hoppers closest to the deluge.

'When did that happen?' Bill asked.

'The ceiling fell down about five minutes ago. Then the water started coming in.'

He glanced out through the front doors. It wasn't raining. In any case, there was another level above the foyer, so it was unlikely to be caused by a leaky roof.

'I'm going to see if I can find where this is coming from.' He made his way up the stairs, trying to work out what exactly was above that part of the foyer. He had a bad feeling that it was the first floor toilets.

He didn't even have to go inside the Gents to find the answer. Water had already seeped from beneath the door and was soaking into the carpet. He pushed it open and found the whole place awash. The water may have only just found its way through to the foyer below, but this had been going on for quite a while, he guessed. Thankfully, it wasn't a burst pipe or a smashed toilet. Someone had used most of a toilet roll to bung up the drain on two of the urinals. Every time the cistern flushed, a cascade of water poured over the rim. It made for quite an attractive indoor water feature.

He rolled up his sleeves and fished out the soggy papier-maché, dumping it in the bin. The water began to drain straight away. As he cleared the second urinal, the door opened.

Felicity, the general manager, stood there, trying to avoid getting her feet wet. She took in the situation quickly. 'I'll send someone up with a mop.'

'Good idea. It's just a pity we can't get the moron who did it to clear up his own mess.'

He washed his hands thoroughly then went back down to the foyer. 'Panic over,' he told the staff, who were still gathered around watching drips fall into the bucket. 'It was an overflowing urinal – well, two of them actually.'

One of the girls gave a little shriek and stepped back.

'Don't worry. It's just water. Well, mostly.'

Felicity came over. 'Can someone go up and help Craig mop the floor.' One of the lads dashed off. 'Bill, do you want a coffee now you've saved the day?'

'Why not? I was about to have a drink when all this happened.' He made his way to the office and settled down.

'Here we go,' she said, pushing the door open and putting down the cups.

He left his to cool for a while. 'Thanks.'

Felicity gave a sigh. 'You give folk a nice new cinema and they do their best to wreck it. I can never understand why some people behave like that.'

'Neither can I. Still, at least we caught it before it did too much damage. We can get the tower out tomorrow morning and put up a new tile.'

'I'll have to write off all that pick and mix.' She took a sip of her coffee. 'Oh well, at least we're having plenty of admissions this week.'

'Good old *Star Wars*. I never thought I'd be showing that again, twenty years on. Mind you, there's a whole generation out there who've only seen it on video.'

'And who come in to block up our toilets! Little wretches.'

Bill blew on his coffee. It was still scalding. 'I'd best check on Greta.' He unclipped the walkie-talkie from his belt. 'Are you okay to carry on running everything for another ten minutes or so?'

'Fine. I've just laced up four and set the timer, so if you don't get back in time it'll start on its own.'

'Thanks for that.' They only used the timers when there were unavoidable clashes. Bill was old-fashioned enough to feel uneasy about letting a show start totally unattended. Nine times out of ten everything worked as it should, but there was always the possibility of something unexpected causing a problem.

'She seems to be getting along well,' Felicity said.

'Yes. She's a quick learner. Very conscientious, too. I think she'll be ready to go on shift in another month or so.' It wasn't such a big jump these days. Generally, it was only first thing in the morning, or once the last shows were all running that only one technician was on duty.

'Excellent. Oh, and while we're on the subject, I've just remembered there was something I needed to talk to you about. At the regional meeting last Monday one of the things we discussed was the possibility of setting up a scheme to improve training for you guys. After all, we've had structured management training for several years now.'

'It's been talked about before,' Bill said. 'I've always thought it's a good idea. The main problem with the way things are done at the moment is that – well - we all know that at a few sites it just doesn't happen. I feel sorry for some of those trainees.' There were a variety of reasons. In some cases, the chiefs didn't want to pass on their knowledge; a few Bill had met were afraid that if their staff knew too much, they might be after their jobs. There were others who didn't have the knack when it came to teaching. And at some sites they were just too busy to have the time to train someone properly.

'Well, in the next few months HR will be setting up a working group to try and figure out a way forward. I hope you don't mind, but I suggested they should contact you.'

He felt absurdly flattered. 'I'd be happy to be a part of it.'

'I thought you would.' She paused and took another drink. 'How's your dad getting along?'

'Not so good. He's not doing as well on this new medication as the doctor had hoped.' For the past few years, since his first heart attack, Bill's dad had seen his health steadily declining.

'Well, if you need any time off, just let me know.'

He nodded. It was good to have an understanding boss. 'Anyway, I'd best get back upstairs now.'

'What about your coffee?'

'I'll take it with me and let it cool a bit.'

He got up there with a minute to spare before Screen Four started, then made his way to the main box. A training scheme would help to improve standards all around the circuit, he thought. It was another example of how the company was changing that they had even considered such a move. He'd always remember the attitude that used to radiate from head office down – that projectionists were some kind of sub-human species. A few years back, he'd had to ring one of the head office departments with a query about his pension. After a few minutes the woman he'd been speaking to had found his details and had said, in a somewhat surprised manner. 'But you're a projectionist! How come you're so intelligent?' The comment had left him so stunned, he'd not thought of an appropriate retort until after he'd finished the call.

He heard the projection room door open and looked around the corner to see who it was. 'You must have smelled the coffee,' he said as Bertie Arkwright strolled into view.

'I was passing so I thought I'd drop in and see how things were going.' He sat down heavily.

'Not too bad, apart from a flood in the Gents.'

'Is that lens turret still playing up?'

'No, it's been fine since your last visit.'

'Glad to hear it.' Bertie took out his cigarette packet.

Bill looked pointedly at the No Smoking sign. 'Don't forget there are smoke detectors in here. You'll have to go out on the stairwell by the window.'

Bertie huffed then put the packet away. 'Bloody killjoys. I'll have one later.'

Bill handed him a mug of black coffee and sat down to finish his own drink. 'So what have you been up to today?'

'You're not going to believe this one. I get a call yesterday evening to say the sound's gone in screen three at Wishbrook Road. "Have you checked the amplifier?" I say to him. He tells me yes. "And is the exciter working?" I ask. He says, "It's the speaker that's the problem." So I ask him what's up with it. "It's gone," he says. "What, you mean blown?" I ask. "No, gone," he says. Turns out some fucking thief has walked off with it down the fire exit. And this was during a show!'

'That's a bit of a rough place, isn't it?'

'You're telling me. I keep expecting to find my car up on bricks when I get back to it. So this morning I had to drag another one in and connect it up for them. Chief's no help because he's got a bad back.' He sighed heavily. 'I'm getting too old for this lark. Still, only another three years to go before I retire.'

Bill wondered how Bertie would survive without his regular supplies of black coffee and gossip. No one had ever seen him eat. If Gordon Gekko hadn't said it first, 'Lunch is for wimps,' could have been Bertie's catchphrase. 'What are you going to do with yourself?' he asked.

'I've got it all planned. Next year I'm going to buy a bigger boat; a seventy-footer. Narrow beam, so it can get through all the locks. I'll fit it out myself then once I've finished we'll rent out the house and set off round the country.'

'Sounds good.' Bill imagined the colourful language wafting over the canal if another boat got too close and scraped Bertie's paintwork.

'It can't come soon enough. The business is full of fucking idiots and lazy bastards these days – present company excepted.'

'Come on, Bertie. Not that much has changed. Back in the sixties, we had a co-chief who did nothing but sit around all day. And he wasn't unique by any means.'

'At least most of them know their arse from their elbow back then,' Bertie protested. 'They didn't call engineers out for stupid faults like they do now. I blame these.' He waved his mobile phone. 'It's too easy to get hold of us, so instead of using what little brains they have, they just pick up the phone.'

He had a point there. 'True. Maybe if this new training scheme gets under way things will improve.'

Bertie snorted. 'I've been telling them for years it's what's needed.'

'Well, someone's heard. They're setting up a working party I'm told.'

'They've not roped you in to help, have they?'

Bill felt defensive. 'I've said I'm interested. I think it's a good idea.'

'There's nothing wrong with the idea. It's what's made of it. Might end up being all waffle and no action. Like most other things this company dreams up.' He slurped his coffee loudly. 'Now, have I told you about the twat who threw a bucket of water over a smoking rectifier last week?'

Cat: 1997

Showing *The Empire Strikes Back* in Screen One gave Cat a strange sense of foreboding. She kept telling herself that this was stupid and irrational. All because they had been given the news of impending closure during the film's first run at the Gaumont didn't mean anything bad was going to happen this time around.

Her life was settled these days. She had finished with romantic complications and now lived in a small garden flat just ten minutes away from the cinema. It was attached to a tall Victorian house with peeling paint on the doors and window frames and dark green ivy holding the brickwork together. When Cat had first called after replying to the advert, she had thought it looked like the stereotypical haunted house in a film. Standing on the cracked black and white tiled step, she'd had an absurd urge to run away before the door creaked open. Fortunately she hadn't.

When the door finally opened (with no creak), the smell that greeted her wasn't cobwebs and corpses, but freshly baked bread. 'You must be Cat,' said the cheerful old lady. Her name was Miss Cooper. The house had belonged to her parents then passed down to her. While they'd still been alive, they'd had the basement converted into a flat so that she could live independently, but be close enough if they needed help. Now she lived in the main house and the flat had stood empty for several years. 'I've often thought of renting it out, but never got round to it until now.'

Cat guessed she needed the money, but was reluctant to share the property with a stranger. She'd probably feel the same way herself. She reassured Miss Cooper that she didn't play loud music until the early hours and that painting was a relatively quiet hobby.

'An artist! How lovely. Ronald used to paint.'

She got the full life story; how Miss Cooper – Phoebe – had been engaged once, but her fiancé had gone missing during the Second World War. 'And he never came back. So that was it. I'd never felt that way for anyone else and I knew I never would again.'

Several cups of tea and slices of cake later, they had agreed on a very reasonable rent and two weeks afterwards she'd moved in. It was the ideal situation. Neither of them bothered the other, but both had company when they felt like it. Phoebe enjoyed having someone practical around the place.

Earlier this spring, Cat had begun to clear the overgrown garden; glad someone was there who could tell her what was a weed and what should be kept. Plants that had been deprived of light for years were starting to sprout. She found herself checking each day to see what they were up to. The colours and textures of the new growth were inspiring. It helped to take her mind off the way the business was going. It was nothing to do with the technical side of the job; she knew the building and the equipment well enough by now. It was the management, or rather the lack of continuity caused by the comings and goings of various general managers. A small, town centre site such as Fairham was seen as an ideal first step for young, ambitious people. Their need to be noticed by the higher echelons meant that each time one moved on, another came along full of new ideas and enthusiasm.

'We need to extend the opening hours,' one of them had stated. 'We should finish later so that we can fit in two evening shows instead of just the one. At my last cinema it made a huge difference to admissions.'

It was pointless to argue that this was primarily a commuter suburb, not a city centre site. Late closing was what all the multiplexes did these days, so late closing it would be. It meant that the first evening shows – starting somewhere between six and seven o'clock – were just that bit too early for people getting in from work and wanting something to eat before going out to the cinema. The last shows went on between nine and ten, meaning they finished close to midnight; too late for the majority of the audience who liked to be in bed at ten-thirty so they could be on their trains to the City bright and early the following morning. But the company seemed happy with the arrangement, and that manager was soon promoted.

The following manager came up with the idea of late night shows on a Friday and Saturday night. Apparently that was what they did in the multiplex where he had done his fast-track training. Fairham had last run late night shows back in the eighties; films such as *Pink Floyd's The Wall*, *The Blues Brothers* and *Withnail and I* had done particularly well. But special shows weren't part of the plan this time around, just another performance of the regular films. Cat didn't mind the extra hours; projectionists were paid double time after midnight, but it was depressing to put shows on for just a handful of drunks and insomniacs. Most weeks, at least three of the films ran with no-one watching. The non-rewind equipment meant that you had to run the film all the way through, so to save a bit of electricity if no-one had come in fifteen minutes after the advertised start time, they turned off the xenon lamp.

The newest manager, Joanne, had only been in place for a month. She hadn't yet come up with any changes that affected Cat and the projection team, but the front of house staff weren't happy at the latest alterations to their breaks and rotas.

'They're just so set in their ways,' she moaned to Cat. 'At my last cinema, most of the staff were students. Much more flexible.'

Easier to push around, Cat thought, remembering how shy she had been as a teenager.

Joanne seemed to see her as a kindred spirit, despite their age difference. 'I'm amazed you aren't bored with this place,' she said. 'Don't you ever want to move on to somewhere bigger?'

'Not really. I've done some relief work at other sites, but I like Fairham. And I live locally too, so it's convenient.'

162

'Well, you may not have much choice about it soon. Old cinemas like this won't be around forever. The company prefers to invest in multiplexes.'

'We'll see,' she said. The thought of working in a multiplex horrified her. She'd visited one or two and thought them soulless and sterile. Most of them operated from one huge projection room. Once inside, you didn't see another soul all day. Although it was inconvenient to have to go up and down the stairs between boxes at Fairham, at least you heard the hum of voices when the foyer was packed and felt as if you were a part of the cinema.

Joanne spent most of the time in the office, poring over spreadsheets and business plans. Cat only ever saw her when she went past on her way to the switch room. That was another characteristic of these new career managers. Most of them were rarely seen by the customers, except when someone demanded to see them to sort out a problem. She often wondered why they had chosen to be in the cinema business. They seemed more interested in pick and mix sales than in films. But that was the way the company was going. The foyer had been refitted at least three times over the past decade, but no-one wanted to spend money on upgrading the projection equipment. It was almost as if they were slightly embarrassed about what went on in the screens behind the glossy retail area.

Of course, there was one reason Cat was aware of that might have made Joanne decide on a cinema career rather than managing a supermarket; she was rubbish at mornings. Most cinema people were at their best late in the evening rather than rising with the lark. Joanne often turned up with just minutes to spare before the doors opened. This wasn't too much of a problem; Cat and her team all had keys for the building and the staff could get themselves ready for opening with one exception. The duty manager was the only person who had keys for the safe, and the safe contained the cash floats necessary for the ticket sales and retail areas.

It was on the Sunday after the clocks went forward that this became an issue. Cat was on early shift; her Senior Technician having

163

worked the late night show on Saturday. As she got the screens ready to open, she heard the staff chatting over the walkie-talkies. 'Anyone seen Miss Morgan yet?'

'No, she's not in the office.'

'Late again,' someone said. 'Good job she's not hourly paid like us, or she'd get her wages cut.'

Cat glanced at the clock. It was just ten minutes before the cinema was due to open. Joanne was cutting it fine. On her way through the foyer she saw that there was already a queue of people waiting outside. Well, it was Easter Sunday and *Star Wars* was showing, so it was bound to be busy.

'What are we going to do if she doesn't get here in time?' asked Nadia, one of the more practical Customer Service Assistants. 'That lot will go mad.'

'I can hold up the film for a while. There's plenty of time between shows. I could even pull out the ads and trailers if it gets too late.'

'They won't be happy though.'

Cat considered the options. It was entirely possible that Joanne had forgotten the clocks had gone forward and was still sleeping soundly. She thought quickly.

'Does anyone have any change? I bet that most of those people will have pre-booked their tickets, so as long as we have enough for them to buy sweets and stuff, we should get by.' She could raid the projection tea fund. 'Just make sure you write down who put in what, so you can get it back again.'

'I've got a better idea,' Nadia said. 'I'll call my father. He can lend us some change from the restaurant to get going.'

'Will he do that?'

'If I ask nicely.'

'Well, give it a go, then.' Cat ran off to rustle up all she could muster.

A few other people contributed too, and just after they opened the doors to let in the hordes, Nadia's dad arrived with fifty pounds worth of coins. 'I'll expect some free tickets for this,' he joked.

'Brilliant, thanks.' Cat said. 'You've saved us from being lynched by this lot.' She escaped upstairs as soon as she could, and was able to start the first show on time, forestalling any complaints.

Joanne turned up half an hour later, looking red and flustered. 'Thank goodness you managed to open up,' she said. 'I forgot to set the alarm this morning. Then my car wouldn't start and I had to get a neighbour to help.'

'Oh well, it wasn't too much of a problem. At least we kept the customers happy.'

Later that week, Alfie had called in and she recounted the episode to him.

'It's not the first time that's happened and I'm sure it won't be the last,' he commented. 'Just goes to prove the old saying.'

'What old saying?'

'You can open a cinema without a manager, but you can't open without a projectionist.'

Graham: 1998

'Five weeks now we've been showing *Titanic* and they're still coming in their droves.' Peter paused only to cram his mouth with another forkful of mashed potato. 'It's a sell out every night. Some people have been to see it three or four times already.'

'Do you think I'd like it?' Graham's mum asked.

'Why don't you come and see for yourself. You can use some of my complementary tickets.'

Graham's dad shook his head. 'We'll probably wait until it's out on video.'

'Dad!' Graham said. 'It's made for the big screen.' He had watched it once as a preview and a second time during a public showing. The love story was a bit boring (although Kate Winslet posing in the nude was a bonus) but there was no denying it was a spectacular film.

'Everyone knows how it ends anyway. The ship sinks.'

'You can say the same about a lot of films, even if they aren't based on true stories.' Graham protested. 'I mean, we all know the bad guy isn't going to actually get to kill James Bond, but we still want to see how he'll escape this time.'

'Yes, come on, Colin. Let's go out for a change.' Mum obviously warmed to the idea. 'I've not been to the pictures for years. More veg, Peter?'

'Please.' He held out his plate.

'You and dad could go for a meal as well – have a real night out.' Graham saw the look of annoyance on his dad's face. Dad could be so set in his ways sometimes it was fun to wind him up.

'Ooh, yes. That would be lovely, not having to cook for a change.'

'Well, as long as it doesn't finish too late. I have to be up for work the next day,' he grumbled.

'You could go on a Friday,' Graham suggested. 'Or even a Saturday.'

'It'll be packed. We'll end up having to sit too close to the screen.'

Peter waved his fork. 'I'll make sure to reserve the house seats near the back, so don't worry about that.'

Graham's mum had a glint in her eye. 'The back row, too! It'll be like when we were courting.'

On Saturday afternoon, Graham went to the cinema and watched *The Postman*. It was a lot better than he had expected from the reviews he'd read, but that was often the way. He probably wouldn't add it to his list of favourites, but it hadn't been a wasted afternoon. After it finished, he made his way up to the box staff room to say hello to Peter. He noticed the title they'd written on the tail of the film as identification; *Post-Apocalyptic Pat*. That summed it up nicely.

'Fran thought of that one. She's good at that game,' Peter commented.

'Well, tonight's the night,' Graham said. 'Mum and dad's big night out. I can't remember the last time they went anywhere together. And it's not even as if they need to stay in these days, what with Matt at uni and me in the sixth form.'

'It's just a habit,' Peter said. 'Your dad was never really one for going out much.'

'He's so boring,' Graham said. 'He's done the same job for twenty years. If I was stuck in an office my whole life, I think I'd die of boredom.'

'Well, I can't argue with that, being as I feel the same way. But he's a good bloke. He earns a decent wage and your mum's never wanted for anything. Neither have you two boys, for that matter.'

Graham shrugged. 'I bet he'll complain about the food at the restaurant. He always does when we eat out. It's dead embarrassing.'

'I wonder what he'll think of the digital sound?'

'Probably say it's not set up as well as his system at home.'

Peter chuckled. 'We get a lot of customers like that. They all think they're experts these days. Then you get the ones with the old-fashioned ears.'

'Old-fashioned ears?'

Peter explained. 'When you get a film like *Titanic* it brings in people who haven't been to a cinema for years. The last time some of them went it was back in the days of mono sound. We had a posse of elderly ladies in last Wednesday. They came out during the trailers and demanded to see the manager. Said it was far too loud and that it was coming out of the wrong place. "The sound's meant to come from the screen," one of 'em said. "Not from all around you. It's unnatural," she said.'

Graham thought that was funny, but that was the cinema business for you. It wasn't like any other. That reminded him of something that had been on his mind. 'You know, I've been thinking a bit lately.'

'Did it hurt?'

He smiled at his uncle's all too predictable comment. 'We've been having all these people in at school talking about different careers. All it's done for me is make me realise that what I really want to do is... well, this. Cinema projection.'

'Your mum would kill me.' Peter said. He had a drink of tea and continued. 'I know you've been helping us out here for a few years now, but I wouldn't want to see you end up like me. Remember when the Palace closed? It was hard for me to get another job because this was all I'd ever done. You need to get some decent qualifications. Go to university, like your brother.'

'It just seems like a waste of time when I already know what I want to do.' Besides, Matt was the brains of the family. Everyone always said so.

'I know. Believe it or not, I remember being young, even though it was back in the dark ages. You don't want to wait for anything. But the most important thing you can do is to get yourself an education.

You're interested in studying computers and all that sort of stuff, right?'

'Yeah, but...'

'No buts. Do your exams next summer. Then go to university. The cinema will still be around when you've done and if you feel the same way, then follow your heart. But at least you'll have a plan B if things go tits up.'

It sounded far too sensible. 'That's not going to happen, is it? Nowadays they're opening new cinemas every year instead of closing them. Business is booming.'

Peter had another drink of tea. 'Yes, but all because it's doing well now doesn't mean it'll last forever. The way technology's moving these days, who knows what people will be doing for entertainment in thirty years. And you'll only be in your forties then. You'll still need a job.'

It wasn't what he wanted to hear, but he could see that Peter had a point. 'I suppose so,' he agreed reluctantly.

'Good lad. Anyway, wherever you end up going to university, there's bound to be a cinema or two around. You could get a part time job there while you're studying. That'd be a good start to your career, if you decide it's still what you want to do.'

Bill: 1999

As Bill gazed out of the train's dirty windows, lambs gambolled in the spring sunshine. He reflected that while it was gratifying that the company had chosen to locate their new projection training centre in the midlands rather than the London area, Danton on Leen wasn't the easiest place to reach by rail. Wherever you came from, you had to change trains at least once. Rumour had it that one of the reasons Danton had been chosen was that it was the brewing capital of England. With such an enticement, even the most sceptical and reluctant projectionists might be tempted to attend the training courses on offer.

The yeasty smell of beer filled the air as he caught a taxi from the station, passing a massive brewery and a run-down looking independent three screen cinema on the way. The training centre was housed on the top floor of a huge Victorian granary building, only taking up a small portion of the available floor space.

This was the chance for the training committee to see the fruits of their work. Bertie Arkwright showed them all around. There was a perfect little cinema with a hundred seats; similar to many conversions inside old buildings. A door at the back led into the projection and training room, equipped with three different types of projector and platters and multiple sound systems. Engineers were busily putting the finishing touches to the installation. In less than a month, it would be open for business.

'Of course, all this was paid for by *Titanic*,' someone told him. 'After such a good year at the box office, it was the least they could do.'

'Hopefully it won't sink on its maiden voyage,' Bill quipped.

Bertie must have heard his comment. 'Luckily, there haven't been any icebergs sighted on the River Leen this year.'

Everyone laughed. Bill was sure they must all feel as he did; here was concrete proof of the company's changing attitude when it came to both projectionists and training. Soon, trainees would not have to rely solely on their home site to provide them with the skills for a successful career. Together with the training manual the committee had devised, the courses run here at Danton would ensure the next generation of technicians had a thorough foundation of knowledge.

They had a buffet lunch, followed by a few drinks at the town centre Wetherspoon's before going their separate ways. The next time they would be visiting would be for the Chief's Conference. For years, managers and their assistants had been invited to a regular conference; now the heads of each cinema's technical department were getting their own day out.

'Things are really changing for the better,' he said to Maureen that evening.

'Let's just hope your first grandchild doesn't decide to make an appearance the same day as this conference. You know that's the week Susan's due.'

'Since when do children ever arrive on time? I don't think any of ours did.'

'I know. But just be prepared to drop everything. They're going to have these things every year from now on anyway, aren't they?'

'So they say.' It would be a pity to miss the first conference, but he'd need to be at home to welcome Susan and Neil's baby into the world. 'Still, family's more important than work.'

Maureen smiled. 'I'd never thought I'd hear you say that.'

'I never thought I'd hear myself say it.' Losing his dad the previous year had put a lot of things into perspective. During his illness, the old man had spoken often about how he regretted missing out on family events due to work commitments. 'All that overtime I put in brought us extra cash, but you can never make up for lost time. There's no point having plenty of money if you don't have a chance to enjoy what it brings.' As a young man, Bill wouldn't have seen the sense in this advice; now he was older he could appreciate his dad's words. Back then, people never talked about having a balance between life and work. The best you could hope for was that you enjoyed your job.

The training centre opened on schedule. Bill's latest trainee, Grant, went along for some of the courses and came back full of motivation and handouts. During the course, as well as taking apart a projector and learning about film sound, he'd been able to get to know other technicians from all around the country. Bill realised this was one of the other advantages of going to a place like Danton. Unless you were based in one of the big cities, where there were several sites close together, you rarely got to meet with colleagues. Apart from the occasional phone call when you wanted to pick someone's brain for technical information, there wasn't much contact between cinemas at all. Each was like a separate island, with its own customs and ways of working, despite all being part of the same company. Having the training centre meant there would be a far freer exchange of ideas and information in the future.

'One of the others said it had been a hard job getting his manager to send him,' Grant told Bill. 'He was moaning about the travel costs apparently.'

'Funny how they never mind paying out when it's for a screening in London,' Bill mused. 'We expected that some of them would try to find excuses, even though they've been told they've got to send people for training.'

The box phone rang distantly. Bill never had any problem hearing it over the whir of projector motors and the ever-present tick-tick of film passing through the mechanism. 'Better get that.'

It was one of his fellow training committee members. 'Afternoon, Bill. Thought I'd best let you know about Bertie Arkwright.'

Bertie was on holiday this week, that much Bill knew from the engineers' rota pinned to the notice board. 'What about him?'

'He's died. On his boat. Heart attack, they say. Collapsed at the tiller, out like a light.'

'No?' It was difficult to take in. Bertie was one of those characters you thought would go on forever. It had been hard enough to imagine him retired and out of the business, let alone this. 'Are you sure?' Sometimes the grapevine passed on rumours that later proved to have been blown up out of proportion.

'Yes. I got it direct from Barbara in technical department. She'll be sending out an email later today.'

'I'll watch out for it.'

'Still, at least he got to see the training centre up and running.'

'There is that.' When Bill put the phone down he sat at the desk for a few moments. Bertie had been one of the constants of his cinema career. He always told an interesting story, even if some of them may have been a bit exaggerated. Plus, he was a good engineer. Bill had always been impressed by his uncanny ability to sniff out what was wrong with a projector seemingly by magic, although it was probably due to Bertie's years of experience. The realisation that he'd never walk in through the box door again was almost more of a shock that when Bill's own father had died. But that hadn't come out of the blue like this news.

Felicity came up later bearing a printout of the email. 'Sad news,' she said. 'Another larger than life character gone. I had a lot of time for Bertie.'

'He'll be missed,' Bill agreed.

'Wasn't he due to retire in a year or two?'

'Something like that. I remember him telling me him and his wife were going to cruise the waterways, full time. Now he'll never have the opportunity.'

Cat: 1999

Cat was making up a print - reel three of *Parting Shots* - when the phone at the other end of the box rang. She stopped the spool and went to answer it. It was her old friend Paul, now a chief at his own site.

'You'll never guess what's happened,' he said. 'Bertie Arkwright's died.'

'What?'

'There's an email come through about it. Get yourself down to the office to see it. The funeral's in a few days. All his cinema colleagues have been invited.'

She was stunned. Bertie had dropped in just the previous week, full of enthusiasm for his imminent holiday. 'See you when I get back,' had been his parting words.

She should let Alfie know. Even though he was retired, he'd want to go along to the funeral and pay his respects. She imagined phones ringing all over London and beyond, sending the bad news spiralling out.

Just to be sure it wasn't some dreadful mistake, she went down to the office. The latest manager was using the only PC, and reluctantly left off his marketing proposal to let her see the emails. There it was, in black and white. She printed and brought it back upstairs, then called Alfie.

As she checked the rest of the film, she found herself remembering how kind Bertie had been behind all the bluster. How he'd baled her out of trouble in more than a few occasions, talked her through fault finding over the phone and simply offered good advice when it came to non-technical problems. One of the many career managers who'd

174

passed through Fairham had been particularly hard to work with, but Bertie had kept her going. 'He's just an ambitious little shit,' he'd said. 'He'll have moved on in six months. Just keep your head down and do your job and you'll still be here when he's long gone.'

On the day of the funeral, she picked up Alfie and they made their way through unfamiliar suburbs to the crematorium. She knew some of the projectionists by sight and a lot more that she'd talked to on the phone. It was good to be able to match names to faces. Everyone looked slightly uncomfortable in rarely-worn formal attire.

'The last time I wore this suit was at my wedding,' one chief said.

'Lucky you can still get into it, mate,' someone riposted.

'His missus isn't feeding him enough,' added another.

Cat had attended a few funerals in her life and they all followed a similar pattern. It was hard to recognise the man she'd known from the eulogy, read by his next door neighbour. Cat wondered if everyone felt the same as she did; that the service had totally excluded them. Bertie had always kept his home and cinema life separate, but surely the point of a memorial service was to reflect on all aspects of a person's life and achievements.

After it was over, they all hung around in the car park, unwilling to go their separate ways as yet.

'It just doesn't feel finished,' Cat said. 'I don't feel like we've said goodbye to our Bertie.'

'Let's go to the pub,' came a suggestion, eagerly picked up.

'Yeah. Give him a proper cinema send-off.'

'There's a Wetherspoon's just down the road from here.'

And there it began. Everyone had some story to tell, some memory that made others nod in agreement. Bertie's many catchphrases and mannerisms were remembered. 'We should be toasting his memory in black coffee, not beer,' someone said.

There was much talk of it being the end of an era. 'All that experience, all that knowledge, just gone,' another chief lamented. 'Not many left from that generation now.'

Alfie introduced her to a tall middle-aged man called Bill. 'We used to see each other regularly at union do's,' he explained.

'So you're Cat,' Bill said. 'Bertie used to sing your praises.'

'Really?'

'Oh yes. "That girl in London's a bloody good chief," he used to say, only he didn't say "bloody".'

They laughed, then moved on to the forthcoming Chiefs' Conference at the new training centre.

'Chiefs' conference,' Alfie mused. 'Now there's a thing I never thought would happen. Bet the managers are none too happy about it. They like to have all the freebies and jollies for themselves.'

'Some of them,' Bill said. 'I suppose I'm lucky to have a decent manager, from what I've been hearing from some of them here.'

'Our latest one's not too bad,' Cat said. 'But they come and go so fast. All of them want to manage a multiplex, not stay at a traditional town centre site. I do worry sometimes if little cinemas like mine have a future.'

'I used to fret about the same thing,' Bill reassured her. 'The threat from the multiplexes isn't over yet. But you're in London and it takes a lot longer to travel anywhere, so even if they build one five or ten miles from you, people won't necessarily drive the extra distance.'

'I like the old cinemas,' Cat said. 'The atmosphere of them. That whole nineteen-thirties super cinema ambience. I like to think I'm just one in a long line of chiefs who've looked after the place and kept up the standards.'

Bill glanced at Alfie. 'Looks like your old site's in safe hands.'

Alfie smiled. 'Like Bertie said, she's a good chief. Now come on, let me get you another drink.'

Bertie's wake went on well into the evening. Cat wondered how some of the projectionists would manage to get home. She'd only had one alcoholic drink herself, as she had the responsibility of getting Alfie back in one piece. Eventually, they said their goodbyes and got away.

'That was some do,' she said, driving back up towards Fairham at last.

'Just like in the old days,' Alfie said. 'We always had a get together when someone well known in the business died. There'll never be another one like Bertie, will there?'

'There certainly won't,' she agreed.

Alfie carried on with his theme. 'Not many big characters like that left any more. Well, it's the end of the century soon, so things are bound to change.'

She supposed he was right. 'Let's hope the new century brings some positive changes.'

'Let's hope so.'

Reel 4

The Film Factories

Bill: 2001

It was a grey morning in late January when Andy and Bill pulled up in their borrowed van. They'd been on the road since six, and had spent a fair while finding their way round the one-way system before finally locating the entrance to the old cinema's car park. The vast red brick tower of the stage end loomed above them. Exit doors had been propped open and workmen were already busy with the strip out. Considering it had only closed the night before, the vultures had descended rapidly.

'We'd best get in while there's still some kit to be had,' Andy said. He was now chief at a three screen and was looking to acquire anything he could. His manager had been particularly keen to get some decent bits of carpet, whereas he was after projection spares and theatre lamps.

'There'll be plenty,' Bill reassured him. 'This is a big place. Bet our new owners have made a mint from the sale.' Ever since they'd fallen into the hands of venture capitalists, several sites that had always been viewed as secure had shut down. It no longer mattered whether they were profitable or not; what counted was maximising the returns on the investment. Many of these older sites had been built on their own land; land now eagerly sought after for redevelopment in town and city centres.

'This was a real showplace. Two and a half thousand seats. It was one of the first to be twinned in the sixties,' Bill said as they made their way toward the nearest door. Just inside, stacks of seats were lined up as if waiting for their marching orders. The sound of hammer drills filled the air.

181

Once inside the auditorium, they made their way carefully across the exposed floor. Bill spotted one of the service engineers up a ladder, removing a surround speaker from its bracket.

'Ay up, Keith,' he called. 'They keeping you busy?'

Keith turned and waved. 'Always busy these days. What have you come for?'

'Anything we can get. No chance of a couple of those surrounds, I suppose?'

'Get off. They're spoken for. Nothing's going to waste here. Best find your way to the main box – just off the foyer. Ian's the chief. He'll let you know what's available.'

'Cheers.'

Inside the main box, more engineers were working to remove the sound racks. Ian introduced himself and offered them a cup of tea. They stood out of the way, next to the original Cinemation console fitted against the rear wall. Bill admired its polished wooden casing and the styling reminiscent of jukeboxes from the same era. He also noticed that it was still powered up and working.

'That'll be the last thing to go off,' Ian said. 'It runs everything – lighting, boilers, heating and ventilation as well as the shows. State of the art, that was, when it was installed in sixty-four and it's served the place well. Do you want to look around, while there's still stuff left to see?'

'Might as well,' Bill said. Ian seemed to be taking the loss of his cinema fairly well, although that might just be that it hadn't quite hit home yet.

He led them back through the foyer. The kiosk was already partially dismantled, with all of the hotdog and popcorn warmers piled up ready to be moved to another site. Behind the glass of the paybox, pictures from a children's colouring competition hung askew, including a graphic rendition of the sinking of the Titanic.

'The manager's really cut up about this,' Ian told them. 'We were packed last night. He made a brilliant speech about how we've managed to hold our own, even though we had a multiplex open just down the street last summer. We weren't going to give up without a fight, but the company never gave us the chance.'

He opened the door to Screen One in the old circle. It was still vast enough to impress, and breathed that evocative smell comprising old carpets, wood panelling and years of cigarette smoke that had pervaded the fabric of the building. As yet, the auditorium was untouched.

'Although they're having the seats and speaker systems out of here too. Nothing's going to waste, which is some consolation.' Ian trudged up the central stairway. 'Now, if we go up to the top box, there's a few bits and pieces you might be interested in.'

Andy rummaged enthusiastically through the spares cupboard while Bill glanced out of the porthole, thinking of all the projectionists who had done the same over so many years. There was so much history here; recorded by the film posters, stills and promotional standees dotted around the box. It reminded him a lot of the old site he'd left behind when they moved across to the new one.

Coming from a multiplex, with newer equipment, he wasn't going to find much in the way of useful projection spares, although Ian presented him with several rolls of splicing and edge marking tape, chinagraph pencils and a spare footage counter.

'Andy's after carpet,' Bill mentioned. 'The lollipop design, if there's any to be had.'

'Tons of it. I'll show you where you can take it from. You need any exciter lamps?'

'No, we've got red light readers for the sound now.'

'Lucky you. Bet you'll have some?' he asked Andy.

'Please.'

'Did you hear the story about that stingy manager who wouldn't let the chief order any spare exciters? They had one fail on a Saturday night and couldn't get a delivery until Monday. He must have lost thousands for the sake of a six quid lamp.'

Bill sighed. 'It doesn't surprise me. They're told to cut costs and won't listen to common sense. I've heard of places running out of heating oil, xenon lamps and the like. Reminds me of the eighties again.'

'So where's all the money coming from for all this new digital stuff we keep hearing about?'

These days the trade magazines were filled with articles about the advent of digital projection – the next big state-of-the art game changer that was waiting around the corner. So far, there had only been a few releases in digital formats, trialled at West End cinemas for premieres and special screenings.

'Search me. They're so reluctant to spend anything, it's going to take years. Let's face it, they haven't even installed digital sound in every screen yet.'

Andy turned round. 'I'm sick of all this digital hype. Everything I read talks about having better quality pictures – no more scratched prints. If you have good projectionists, prints shouldn't get scratched anyway.'

'Agreed,' Ian said. 'But I've had prints come in on crossover from other cinemas that looked like they had been dragged across the floor. You know some of the multiplex companies employ sausage turners as projjies?'

'Sausage turners?'

'Front of house staff. They give them a bit extra money to do shifts in the box, but they don't really know – or care – much about projection. But it saves paying real projectionists a decent wage.'

'Let's hope our lot don't try it,' Andy said.

'Not while we've got the union agreement in place. The American companies never signed up to it, so they can do what they like.'

'It's a slippery slope,' Bill agreed. 'We're safe for now, but with all these mergers and acquisitions going on, who's to say what might happen over the next few years.'

'Stop being so bloody gloomy,' Andy said. 'It might see you out, but what about me? What about the ones who are younger than me?'

'Survival of the fittest,' Ian joked. 'Only kidding, mate. Nothing moves that fast in this industry. You'll be fine. The way I see it, there's bound to be a few changes, but they'll still need experienced projectionists.'

Bill nodded. 'That's my view as well. They're talking about showing other types of content, not just films. Concerts, live shows, hiring out the cinemas for conferences. All that sort of stuff needs proper setting up and someone technical on hand for when things need tweaking. Our jobs will change a bit, but that's the way it's been right through my career.'

Andy stuffed his hoard into a cardboard box. 'This should keep me going for a while. Can we go for the carpet next? My manager wants the bar tarting up and he'll never forgive me if I come back without a decent bit of carpet.'

'If you've room, we could let you have a couple of round tables too. And what about some spare quad frames?'

'Anything I can get in the van, I'll have.'

By the time they'd finished, the short winter afternoon was drawing to a close. They had a last mug of coffee with the engineers and said goodbye to Ian.

As they pulled away, Bill reflected on all the closures he'd seen over the years. It was never a happy occasion, but at least they'd salvaged something from this wreckage. And that was all you could hope for, really.

Graham: 2002 –2004

Graham wondered if he had made the right choice. He had begun his bright new cinema career, but as he sat in the gloomy staff room of this suburban hellhole cinema, he felt as if he had been dumped and forgotten.

He'd gone through university still keeping an interest in the business, working part-time in a local multiplex. It had been a very different set-up from Uncle Peter's cinema – one of the American chains – but he'd enjoyed the variety and working with other people who were as enthusiastic about films as he was himself. But once he finished his three year course he realised he wanted to get back to the less formal atmosphere found in the British run cinemas.

His parents had still not been entirely keen in his choice of career. 'Why go to all that effort of getting a degree to end up working in a cinema?' his dad had said. But mum had been supportive. 'He's got plenty of time, love. Just let him make his own choices. He's got other options now, if things don't work out.'

He'd been excited to see an advertisement in one of the trade papers. Potential trainee projectionists were invited to a workshop and selection centre in London's West End, with a view to fast-track careers in projection. There would be plenty of training and support and the opportunity to gain experience quickly working in a variety of different cinemas around the London and South East Area. The day itself had been exciting and inspirational and he'd been one of the eight successful candidates who were offered a position.

Bearing in mind the cost of living in London, he'd opted for one of the suburban sites; a recently refurbished and upgraded nineteen-thirties Art Deco cinema set in a leafy suburb. From the outside, it had looked promising, with fresh new paint and signage. The foyer was airy and inviting, the interior was finished to a high standard and new projectors and sound systems had been installed in each of the five screens. Two of them had Dolby Digital sound; the three smaller screens were Dolby SR only due to the inevitable sound breakthrough problems of a sub-divided cinema.

Annalisa, the general manager, was only a few years older than Graham. She had all sorts of ideas to increase revenue at the cinema. 'This is quite an affluent area, but before the refurb, audiences had dropped off considerably. This place was a bit grim. I want to encourage people to come back and see all the changes we've made.'

'Sounds good.'

'There's just one thing. Both the projectionists have been here for a very long time. They've got stuck in a rut. I'm hoping that introducing someone new might give them a bit more enthusiasm going forward.'

It had been the first inkling that the picture might not be as rosy as it had been painted. He'd met John, the chief, soon afterwards, up in the staff room. As soon as Annalisa had left them 'to have a chat', John made it quite clear that he wasn't keen on having a third member of staff around.

'Don't know why they've insisted on us having you. I kept saying I didn't want no trainee. How am I going to find the time to train you up what with all the other stuff she keeps wanting us to do these days?'

'It's okay,' Graham tried to reassure him. 'I've had some projection experience already. And I learn fast. They told us we'd be going up to the training centre regularly, and have site visits from the training advisor too.'

John sniffed loudly, dismissing this. 'Wait and see. This company's full of hot air and promises that don't come to nothing.' He hauled his considerable bulk up from the armchair and flicked on the kettle. 'I've been in this business a long time and I can tell you, they're all the same. Last lot just wanted to cut costs and run the place down. We didn't have no money spent here for years. Nearly closed a few times. Now they've tarted it up a bit, but is it going to make any difference? Course not. This industry's had it.'

Graham felt as if he had to defend the business. 'That's not necessarily the case. Admissions are rising year on year. If customers can come in to a place like this, have a decent choice of films, comfortable seats and good quality sound and picture, then there's no reason we can't compete.'

John dropped a tea bag into a stained mug. 'Or they can sit at home and watch the same stuff on DVD or Sky.'

It was the old argument. 'Some people prefer to go out,' Graham persisted. 'Teenagers don't want to stay at home with their parents. Older people like to get out of the house and meet up somewhere.' Annalisa had already told him how successful the 'silver screen' showings had been. Reduced prices and the incentive of free refreshments were bringing regular audiences in for morning screenings.

'It's a blip,' John said. 'Wait until this Internet thing takes off. That'll be the final nail in the coffin. Good job I'll be gone by then.'

He met Melvin, the senior projectionist, a few days later. Melvin was tall and thin. The lines on his face were set to permanent misery. Graham guessed he had last laughed in around nineteen-seventy. Melvin made it clear that he was just hanging on in order to draw his final salary pension scheme. He had evidently decided a long time ago that he would do the bare minimum necessary to avoid trouble at work. This basically meant starting the shows at more or less the right time, then leaving them to run until it was time to lace up again. The rest of the time he spent in the staff room, reading vintage car magazines and bemoaning the state of the modern world. Nothing was as good as it had been back in the old days. Modern cars were crap, music was rubbish, and new films were nothing but remakes that had been better the first time round. 'As for this digital sound, it's too bloody loud. Me, I don't use it at all. Who wants all that noise blaring out?'

That had been nearly a month ago. Graham had settled in to his new digs (a room in a converted house, with shared kitchen and bathroom facilities) and had tried to get to grips with the way the cinema was run. He'd already noticed they had no set daily routine. Peter had always started the day by walking round and noting if any of the public areas needed lamping up, so Graham decided to do the same. John didn't seem to mind this – it saved him having to leave the comfort of the staff room.

Graham also took it upon himself to check the film dump daily and carry up the transit cases containing the new films. Both the training manuals and his previous experience had made him aware that it was a good idea to get films made up on the bench as soon as they arrived. If there was a problem, that gave you a better chance of getting a replacement before it was due to be shown. When John saw him winding the reels onto a spool, he chuckled. 'Not seen anyone do it like that for a while,' he commented. 'Me, I do it the easy way. Run it straight onto the platter. Much quicker.'

Graham didn't want to argue with the man who was effectively his boss. 'I've always been shown to do it this way, so if it's all right with you, can I carry on?'

'Go ahead, mate. You do it however you like and I'll do it my way. And I'll be finished at least an hour before you.'

By the end of that first month, he felt as if he was fighting a losing battle. He could see a lot of shortcuts in the way things were being done, but from his position as a trainee, wasn't able to make any changes. All he could hope to achieve was to try and do a good job to the best of his ability and not tread on anyone's toes. Although John and Melvin didn't seem to care what he did, he couldn't be sure how they really felt about their unwanted new trainee.

Others had noticed, however, and that gave him more difficulties. 'Whenever you put the shows on the sound seems a lot better,' Annalisa said to him. 'Why might that be?'

Graham knew exactly why. Melvin didn't use digital out of principal, and John just selected whatever format he felt like at the time. But he didn't feel able to tell her that. "

He shrugged. 'Maybe you should ask John?' he offered. 'He knows a lot more about it than I do.'

'He just says that how it is. And Melvin won't even talk to me most of the time. If there's a problem, I need to get one of the engineers in to sort it out.'

'The equipment's fine,' Graham said, 'As far as I can tell, anyway. Sometimes the film soundtracks don't always play in digital, so I've been told.'

'But they do when you put them on?' She was a bit too perceptive sometimes.

'I need to learn more about it all before I can say for sure.' That was always a good way out of awkward questions.

'Well, you'll have the opportunity soon. I've booked you in to the training centre next week for courses on sound, projection maintenance and presentation.'

The journey up to the training centre was just an hour and a half from London. As soon as Graham opened the train door, the unmistakeable smell of the brewing industry surrounded him. The town was full of tall Victorian warehouses and modern steel cylinders storing millions of gallons of beer. It had an old-fashioned appearance; buildings whose brickwork had long ago been blackened by coal fires and never cleaned. The High Street was full of charity shops, much like his home town. Very large people sprawled on benches eating greasy burgers and doughnuts purchased from the snack vans. He noticed a boarded up old cinema along one of the side streets.

He made his way to the hotel that had been booked and once he'd unpacked, found one of the other new trainees down in the bar. Here was his first chance to compare experiences and find out if he really had been unfortunate in where he'd ended up.

Diego had been sent to one of the central London cinemas. 'My chief, he is really knowledgeable. He has taught me so much in a short time. We use the training manual as a guide, but he also give me lots of practical tips and experience.'

'Sounds great. Mine does as little as possible and just leaves me to get on with things.'

'But how do you know if you are doing things right?'

Graham shrugged. 'Just hope I am. I'm lucky I spent my teenage years helping my Uncle out in projection. Sometimes I have to call him if I'm not sure about something.'

'That's not good, though. You need to tell training advisor about it.'

Graham wasn't sure that would make much difference. 'I suppose I can try. I think the manager was hoping that taking on someone new might inspire the other two. They've basically lost interest in the job.'

'Then they should go.'

'Easier said than done. They've both been in the business forever.'

They sampled the local beer and ordered some food, then chatted about film releases and technology. Diego had been on a visit to Leicester Square the previous week and seen a preview of *Monsters Inc.* 'It is best I think for the animated film which was digitally created. Very clear picture and brilliant colours.'

'Wish I could get a chance to see something like that.'

'You must call me.' They swapped phone numbers and had another beer each. Diego couldn't believe how cheap everything was by comparison to London.

'That's probably one of the reasons they decided to build the training centre here. More or less the middle of the country and if it's not too expensive, the cinemas are more likely to send people.'

The next day they took a taxi to the training centre, which was just out of town, inside yet another Victorian granary building. There were only four trainees present. 'I've had a couple of cancellations,' Simon, the training advisor told them. 'Still, with only a few of you, you should get a lot more hands on training.'

The purpose of the training centre was to enable projectionists of all levels to gain practical experience. On site, there was always a limited amount of time before the cinema's doors opened and unless something actually went wrong with the equipment, no real opportunity for fault finding. Here, they could experiment without time constraints and the worry of not being able to put things right in time.

The morning was spent looking at sound development over the past twenty years, with an overview of all the current sound processors they might encounter out in the field and an opportunity to listen to different sound formats. They ran Dolby tone loops for calibrating the processors to give the best sound reproduction and learned about the three different digital sound formats; Dolby, DTS and Sony SDDS.

In the afternoon, they went on to amplifiers and speakers, then touched on basic fault finding from the projector sound head through to the processor and amps.

'There will be differences at each site. If you're in a multiplex, everything should be fairly similar from screen to screen, but in the older cinemas, there can be a lot of variation. You'll need to ask your chief about specifics.'

Not much chance of that, Graham thought grimly, but didn't say anything.

By the end of the afternoon, his head was bursting with information. He felt as if he'd learned more in a few hours than in the whole previous couple of weeks. If only he could retain it all and use it, there might be some progress.

'Is there a cinema in the town?' asked Eddie, one of the other trainees. 'Might be good to have a bit of a busman's holiday while we're here.'

'There's a fairly new Cineworld on the retail park. There was an independent too, but it closed just a couple of months ago. Pity really; it was a cosy little place and it had some atmosphere about it. But it couldn't compete.'

It was interesting to compare notes with the others at the end of the day. Diego told them he'd already covered most of the basic stuff back at his home cinema. Eddie said his chief wouldn't let him do anything much beyond lacing up and starting shows as yet. 'He's a bit old school. Thinks you need to have done the job for years before you can be let loose on the equipment. Not that the manager agrees. He wants me on shift in four months to save on overtime.'

Janis, the fourth trainee, had another viewpoint. 'My chief's only three years older than me. She got promoted really fast. She's keen for me to learn the proper way of doing things, instead of just being dumped in at the deep end. Apparently, that's how it used to be before they started this scheme.'

'That's how it still is, in some places,' Graham admitted. 'I've just been left to fend for myself. The manager keeps asking me about stuff and I have to try and give answers without putting my foot in it and getting the other two into trouble. It's a bit of an awkward situation.'

'Can't you ask to be moved?'

He sighed. 'That would be like giving up, wouldn't it? And maybe they put me in there because I have some previous experience rather than being a total rookie?'

It was becoming clear to him that although they all worked for the same company, each site still kept its own idiosyncrasies. You couldn't change things overnight, even with a training plan. It was quite a contrast to the way things had been done at the American multiplex where he'd worked during his years at university. There, the projection routine seemed to involve lots of paperwork, which was checked scrupulously by auditors who visited every few months. Everyone got trained in exactly the same way, (or so it had seemed to him), but there were few opportunities for putting your own stamp on things. His prior experience had counted for nothing and he'd had to use their standardised terminology for the equipment and procedures. There were benefits to that way of doing things, but also flaws. All in all, he'd probably end up learning more in a shorter time staying where he was.

The following day, they had the opportunity to learn about the workings of the projector and platter systems. Graham had already encountered the Philips and Cinemeccanica platters, but had never seen a Christie AW3 before. He heard about the Cinemeccanica's tendency for the feed plate to 'creep' in hot weather and how this could lead to a film wrap if it wasn't adjusted. He was also made aware of the common problems encountered on each model.

'It's not that any of them are better or worse than the other. People tend to prefer what they are used to. Me, I learned on Philips, so they'll always be my platter of choice,' Simon told them. 'Main thing is to keep an open mind. Once you've finished your training, you might move on to somewhere that has totally different kit.'

They stripped down a bench mounted projector to see how all the components worked together to provide smooth transit for the film and a steady, well-focussed picture on screen. Various picture faults were demonstrated and corrected. It was stressed at various points during the day that if everything was working properly, it should be left alone. From this, Graham surmised that some people, filled with enthusiasm and new knowledge, had gone back home and messed stuff up.

Eddie confirmed this. 'I reckon that's why my chief is so cautious. One of the blokes he used to work with was always fiddling with the kit, then denying he'd done anything.'

The last day was spent on presentation and provided lots of discussion points regarding what were the definitions of good presentation. Many things had changed over the years, but fundamentally, they should be striving to provide the best quality picture and sound in comfortable surroundings. 'Let's hear about some of the things you can do personally to achieve good presentation.'

Everyone agreed that the basic aspects were to ensure the film was clearly projected and the sound was played in the right format and at the right level.

'Anything that distracts the audience from the story unfolding on screen isn't good. It could be a flickering light in the auditorium ceiling, the heating and ventilation set wrongly, or someone munching popcorn too loudly, not just picture or sound faults.'

'Not much we can do about the last one,' Eddie said. 'My chief's always moaning about the front of house staff these days. They don't employ enough of them to keep an eye on all the screens and they come and go so often. One of his pet hates is when they leave the cleaner's lights on in the screen. If the show starts on the auto timer, it might be five minutes or so before one of us gets there to check and find the lights are still on, washing out the screen.'

'Same thing happens at our place,' Janis confirmed. 'We tell them again and again, but it just goes in one ear and out the other.'

'Plus there's the issue with people using their phones in the screen,' Eddie put in. 'Why do people pay for a ticket, then spend the whole time calling their mates? It's so annoying. We nearly had a punch up last month because of it.'

Diego shook his head. 'That's so bad. We don't get too much of it at our place. The customers come because they are interested in movies.'

'That's London for you,' Eddie said. 'I bet you show a lot of art house stuff.'

He shrugged. 'A mixture, but yes, that's true. And the chief doesn't like us to rely on automation. We have to be there each time to start film manually.'

'In a multi-screen situation, that's not always possible,' Simon pointed out. 'I agree it's best practice, if you can do it. When you're single manning with a lot of screens, the automation is there to help you.' He went into the aspects of setting up automation correctly; placing cues on the film so that each step was triggered at the right time and ensuring the right lengths of film spacing were inserted between parts of the program when it was made up. Graham knew that neither Melvin nor John were so careful and resolved to try and correct some of the errors in programming when he returned.

195

'It's easy to become complacent, or to think it doesn't matter, but every single person who buys a ticket at your cinema deserves the best show they can get. I always used to imagine there might be a projectionist sitting out there; someone who'd really notice any mistakes. It kept me on my toes. You should try to visit other cinemas, whenever you can. Notice the ways in which they might be doing things better – or worse – than at your own site. But bear in mind that because we have such a huge variety of buildings and equipment, there will always be differences in the way things are done. As long as it works, and it doesn't affect the end product, there's no definitive right or wrong way.'

Graham felt both inspired and informed as he travelled back. He'd made some useful new contacts and was looking forward to putting his newly acquired skills into practice. But it was hard to stay motivated when he went back in to work and found the usual chaos. Thursday was always the busiest day of the week – when the old films finished and the new ones were prepared for their first run on a Friday – and John's lack of pre-preparation made it into a mad rush. Normally, Graham sorted out all the trailer packages on a Tuesday or Wednesday, then checked the new week's adverts as soon as they were delivered, but none of that had been done. *Ocean's Eleven* was already on the plate, probably unchecked. The empty cans had been tossed under the bench, leaders and tails spilling out across the floor.

'You'll have to put them lot away,' John said, 'Me back's playing up something awful. I can't hardly bend this week.'

He tried to sympathise as best he could, even though he suspected it was mainly malingering. 'Have you been to the doctor?'

'He's bloody useless. Just tells me to take paracetamol and lose weight. How am I going to lose weight when I can't barely move?' He sank back into the chair. 'Anyway, I can take it easy today now you're here, so that's something.'

Between changing all the programs and keeping the shows running, he had a non-stop day. The good thing about it was that time flew past. John stayed up in the main box, putting on shows and drinking mug after mug of well-sugared tea.

Annalisa caught up with him later in the afternoon, down in the foyer. She was checking the kiosk stock. 'How did the training go?'

'Really good. I've learned loads.' He wished he had the time to stop and talk, but it was just too hectic. 'Tell you all about it later.'

'Well, I won't keep you. I guess you're pretty busy today.'

'Yes. John's got a bad back.'

She sighed. 'He's been on about it all week. Let's hope he doesn't go off sick again. Last time it was nearly eight weeks. It cost me a fortune in relief projectionists.'

Graham wished he could do more to help. 'I can carry a shift on my own if needs be.'

She smiled. 'I know. But it's not fair. You're good, but you're still a trainee. And if anything went wrong, it would be on my head. Just keep doing what you're doing. We'll be fine.'

It was easy to forget there was a life outside of work. He had intended to explore the area on his days off, but there always seemed to be too much else that needed doing. Mundane stuff such as food shopping and trying to keep his room fairly tidy. Having a fairly low tolerance for dirt, he also ended up cleaning the shared bathroom more often than not. He didn't see much of the others who shared the house; they had jobs whose shifts were out of sync with his. Some of them worked all night and slept all day. There wasn't much social life to be had there, so when he had a call from Emilia, one of his university friends, it seemed like a beacon of hope; a step back into a previous, carefree existence.

She had just taken her first step into employment and had recently moved to London, although not particularly close to his area. 'They aren't offering much money,' she said. 'It's a mix of web design and marketing. But it's a start.'

'Look at it this way; the less you're paid, the longer you can put off paying your student loan back.'

'There is that. So how's it going with you?'

'Hard work.' It was good to be able to pour out his frustrations on someone who was outside the business.

'Sounds like a nightmare. Still, at least your manager is sympathetic.' She smiled. 'Sounds like you get on really well with her. Think there might be a chance of anything happening there?'

Graham shook his head. 'She's got a boyfriend in film booking. He took her to Cannes last year. I don't think I could compete with that.'

'Oh well, you'll have to get socialising with the other staff.'

'I don't have time. These days my life seems to be to be work or sleep. Anyway, how about you? Are you still seeing Johan?'

'Not really. He's working in Manchester. We meet up some weekends, but it's not the same. I'm not a big part of his life any more, I guess.' She sighed. 'University feels like something that happened to someone else, a long time ago.'

'Tell me about it.'

As anticipated, John went off sick the following week. Melvin carried on in his usual routine, getting away with as little as possible, and it was a constant challenge to try and fill the rota with relief technicians. Graham found it impossible to attend any more training courses, because he was needed there to keep the cinema running. Three months after he'd started, following an assessment from the training advisor, he was promoted to cinema technician, with the increased pay rates and responsibility this implied. He still didn't feel as if he had enough real experience, but as Annalisa said, he was doing the job, so he might as well have the benefits.

'Melvin might have been in this business for longer than you've been alive, but I've got a lot more confidence in your ability than his,' she said.

Cat: 2003

Cat checked her watch again. Alfie was late this morning. She'd seen his usual bus pull up at the stop outside the kebab shop, but he hadn't got off. And he'd definitely said he'd be along on Tuesday.

She made herself another cup of tea and looked through the timesheets for the coming week. *Johnny English* and *Jungle Book 2* to look forward to. It was nearly Easter and coming up towards the blockbuster season again – not her favourite time of year. January and September tended to be the months there were more likely to be thoughtful, well-scripted and intelligent film releases that she might actually enjoy. Sadly, she often had to go elsewhere to see them; with only five screens, it wasn't often they managed to fit in a non-mainstream film at Fairham. Mind you, it was the same in the multiplexes. Ten screen cinemas often ended up showing the same blockbuster in three or four auditoria, with the times staggered to maximise the number of showings per day. More screens didn't necessarily equal greater variety.

Her phone rang. She fished it out of her bag and recognised Alfie's home number. 'Hello,' she answered.

'Is that you, Cat, dear?' It was Liz, Alfie's wife.

'Yes.'

'Alfie's not going to be able to visit today. He had a bit of a fall last night. No, don't worry, he's not badly hurt. Just a bit shaken up. The doctor told him he should rest.'

'Sorry to hear that.'

'Well, you know what he's like. Still running around as if he was a young man.' She paused. 'I do worry, sometimes, you know.'

'I'm sure. Well, never mind. If he's feeling up to it, I suppose he'll be here next week.'

'I expect so. He looks forward to his cinema visits so much.'

Cat drank her tea. She'd noticed Alfie becoming frailer over the past year. He'd had to give up driving due to his sight problems and his formerly sprightly walk had slowed down considerably. She envisioned a time when he could no longer make it up all the stairs to the top box and the staff room. That would be a pity.

'It comes to us all,' as Phoebe would say. Her landlady was also suffering the constraints of age, although she had a few years on Alfie. Arthritis was her principal mobility issue these days. Cat helped her to stay independent as far as she could, but she sometimes worried what might happen during the long hours while she was away at work.

Today was a short shift, thankfully. She'd be home by six and cook a good meal for them both. Phoebe needed to be encouraged to eat these days; she loved a piece of smoked haddock with peas and mashed potatoes, so that was what it would be today. Sometimes, after supper, they watched television together or just sat talking. Just the other evening, Phoebe had been encouraging her to use her creativity wisely. 'It's a gift,' she'd said. 'I know you do some private commissions now and then, but have you ever thought of teaching?'

'Oh, no. I'd hate to work in a school. Besides, the cinema will always be my main job.'

'I didn't mean that,' Phoebe went on. 'You could teach people artistic techniques. Individually, or in small groups.'

Cat smiled. 'Who'd want me to teach them?'

'Well, there's that friend of yours. The one with the wealthy husband.'

'You mean Amanda? She hasn't the slightest interest in art. Fitness is more her thing.'

Phoebe persisted. 'She probably has lots of friends who are looking for things to fill their day. Why not ask her to ask them?'

Cat had still been hesitant. She had a fear that she couldn't teach anyone anything. All because you had a skill yourself, didn't mean you were able to pass it on. 'I don't think I'm any good at teaching,' she'd said finally.

'Nonsense. You've trained a few people at that cinema of yours, haven't you?'

'Well, yes.' That was a good point. 'It's not quite the same thing, though.'

Phoebe leaned forward slowly and put her hand on Cat's. 'You don't know until you try. And... well, it would give you a second string to your bow. It could become a business of sorts. And I have the perfect room you could use. The one with the bay window on the first floor.'

'I can't take over any more of your house,' Cat protested.

'Don't be silly. I hardly use any of it these days, as well you know. Now promise me, you'll ask a few people. And maybe put a little advert up outside the library as well. You never know where it might take you.'

The conversation had made her think. Maybe it wasn't such a bad idea after all. And the worst that could happen would be that no-one was interested. She'd give it a go.

Tea finished, she went to check the film dump. On the way down, she saw the latest general manager. He looked so young; still with the last vestiges of teenage spottiness, and a scrawny neck with a prominent Adam's apple. Another sign of her own ageing she supposed; managers looked so much like children these days.

He was busy re-stocking the pick and mix hoppers. It was another sign of the times that the retail area had become far more self-service than in the past. Customers picked their own sweets and filled up the drinks cartons themselves, then queued up to pay. The idea was to speed up transactions and (of course) require fewer front of house staff. The customers were also expected to mostly book in advance and collect their tickets from the automated machines, but as Fairham was a suburb with an ageing population, this wasn't always well received. They preferred to come in, have a chat with someone about what was showing, and buy their tickets from a real human being.

'Morning,' she called out, not expecting an answer. He was far too busy to spend time talking to technicians and barely looked up from his task.

She opened the double doors to the long exit. It was gloomy and cold down there and she could hear skittering noises from the flat roof. Squirrels again. They were as bad - no worse - than the pigeons had been at the Gaumont. At least the pigeons fled at your approach. These big, fat greys had some attitude. Marcus, her senior, had said he'd had a stand-off against one, who sat growling in the centre of the passage and didn't want to let him through. 'It's all the popcorn they're eating. It's mutating them. They're becoming vicious beasts.'

'You watch too many horror films,' she'd said. But although he was prone to exaggerate, she felt their beady eyes on her and often wondered what she'd do if they did decide to attack. Swipe them with her walkie-talkie maybe?

Last week's films had been collected and there were a couple of new trailer deliveries in the dump, which she took through to the projection box serving screens two, three and four. Nowadays, she tended to make up most of the programs and features down there as it was more central. Carrying features up and down from the top box was still the worst part of the job as far as she was concerned. It was about the only thing she could think of that was better about working in a multiplex. They had mobile film transport devices, so you could just slide the film onto a wheeled trolley and push it along easily to its new destination. Everything else they could keep – those sterile galleries of identikit equipment, the featureless auditoria, often with no tabs or even masking these days and that relentless film factory approach. It would never feel like real cinema to her. She knew she was a hopeless nostalgia buff and that the things that she loved about the business and the buildings were not what counted in this day and age.

There had been stories in the news that the circuit was about to be sold off again to the highest bidder and that would be bound to lead to more changes. Still, at least Fairham was a leasehold site so it was unlikely to ever be sold off for redevelopment. The land belonged to a local charity and the rent was minimal. She was as safe as you could hope to be, at least from closure.

Engineers brought the usual gossip; head office rumours, people who had been caught fiddling and suchlike. Some of them were convinced their own jobs weren't safe – that the next move would be to contract maintenance out to an external company – but the big unknown was digital projection.

'No-one can say when it's going to happen,' David, the latest service engineer to fill the gap since Bertie's passing, had dropped in a few weeks ago. 'My boss keeps going to various demos by different companies, but there's nothing standardised yet.'

'There's a lot of pressure to convert though. Didn't George Lucas say he wanted the next *Star Wars* episode shown mostly in digital?'

David nodded. 'Yes, but *Star Wars* is just one film out of many. It'll be premiered digitally and there might be a few places around the country you can see it in a digital format, but no-one's going to be the first to spend any real money until there's some kind of incentive to do it.'

'I keep hearing about all this alternative content digital's going to open up. And I guess it wouldn't be a bad thing to be able to show more low budget features shot on video by up and coming directors.'

'We did a cinema premiere of *Jesus the Curry King* a few weeks ago,' he said. 'I expect there'll be a few more like that. And there's all sorts of other stuff in the pipeline. Live gaming sessions, opera, ballet, you name it. Thing is, how are they going to fit it all in? The distributors aren't going to want to cancel a prime evening show, are they?'

'Well, no.'

'It's all experimental right now. Nothing's going to happen for a while. But once it begins, it'll be like a rollercoaster. The only question is when.'

Cat worried about all this. It was in her nature. She'd found herself a niche. She couldn't change the way she felt about cinema and knew that if she had to find another job, it would certainly not be as well paid, or, let's face it, as cushy. Here, she was the boss. She could do things at her own pace, in her own way. But maybe if Phoebe's idea came to fruition, she'd have something else to fall back on. Just in case.

Graham: 2005

'I'm pleased to say we'd like to offer you the position,' the general manager finished. 'How do you feel about that?'

Graham couldn't wipe the smile off his face. After all the pre-interview preparation; the revision of technical topics and searching for the right answers to those difficult interview questions that always gave him more trouble, he'd finally done something right and would be moving on. The eight screen multiplex was still under construction, so the move wouldn't happen right away, which gave him the opportunity to hand over the reins gracefully to his successor, whoever that might be.

'Brilliant. Thanks for the opportunity.'

'I'll have all the paperwork emailed over later, okay? Look forward to meeting you again soon.'

The phone went dead. Graham slipped it back in his pocket. This was the best part, he knew; the euphoric moment when you heard you had been accepted for a new job. Later would come the hard graft and stress of opening a new cinema for business, but he wasn't afraid of that. It was all a part of his plan for the future. A couple of years at a multiplex, more experience under his belt, then next time they took on more projection engineers, he'd be in with a good chance.

Spencer, his technician, bounded up the stairs into the box and took one look at Graham's expression. 'Good news, I'm guessing?'

'The best, mate. I've got the job.'

'Hey, congrats. Not that we want to lose you and all that, but well done.' He took a can of Pepsi from the fridge and opened it. '*Batman Begins* is in. I'll make it up later.'

'Excellent. I'll check with Annalisa and see if we can do a run through for the staff. Maybe Wednesday night as we've got previews on Thursday.'

'Great stuff. Been looking forward to that one.' He drained the can, belched loudly and dropped it in the bin. 'Right, I'll be getting on.'

It was hard to believe this was the same site he'd started in as a trainee just three years ago. Once John and Melvin had finally gone, the gloom and despair had lifted. He'd been effectively promoted to chief within a year. Graham didn't kid himself that this was due to any kind of superpowers on his account, just that these days it was hard to fill vacancies at smaller sites. But he'd coped, and had taken on new, keen staff like Spencer who were willing to learn. The training centre had been a help too. Pity it was closed now; victim of the latest round of sell-offs.

It didn't seem to matter who you worked for these days. There were mergers and acquisitions going on everywhere. The industry was growing and the larger companies were taking their pick of smaller chains. Uncle Peter's cinema had recently been rebranded yet again. 'Can you believe it,' he'd said. 'When I started here, it was a Cannon, then we went to MGM, then Virgin, then UGC. Now they're gone and it's all change again. The shop fitters and sign makers must be coining it in. You had word of anything happening at your place yet?'

'Not really. Since the sale went through they're closing down all the London offices except for booking and moving it all up to Manchester. The managers are getting lots of info about procedural changes, but so far they've left us alone in the box.'

'And they'll keep it like that if they know what's good for 'em,' Peter sniffed. 'If it works, why break it?'

'Unions,' Graham said. 'You know how it is. The American chains never signed up to the union agreement. That's why we've always had better terms and conditions. Plus they work longer hours, don't get premium overtime payments and their manning levels are totally different. The chiefs are more like managers, sitting in an office doing paperwork most of the time.'

'Don't worry. They can't change things overnight.' Peter was an eternal optimist. 'In ten years we'll still be around. Probably with yet another different name over the canopy, but that's how it goes.'

Graham wasn't so sure. He liked to keep up with what was happening in the industry and he very much doubted things would stay the same. *Revenge of the Sith* might not have opened on as many digital screens as George Lucas would have liked, but technology was moving on inexorably.

He devoured articles in the trade magazines and researched online. Just recently it had been reported that the UK Film Council planned to install a digital film network across the country, enabling both large chains and independent cinemas to screen a wider variety of British made films and documentaries. These projectors would be compliant to the latest specifications with 2k resolution and encryption. 3D systems were also being developed and rolled out. Things were definitely on the move.

There were lots of conflicting viewpoints. Conventional wisdom said that there would always be a need for skilled technical people on site. As well as all the film and projection related work, Graham and his colleagues looked after the technical aspects of the whole building. They kept an eye on the heating and ventilation, changing drive belts when necessary, or calling in engineers if there was a problem they couldn't deal with. They maintained the primary and secondary lighting systems. They ensured the tabs and masking worked correctly and sometimes even had to carefully remove tomato ketchup and other debris from the screens. Nowadays the less civilised members of the audience had found another game too. They chewed up the paper wrappings from the straws provided to slurp their super-sized soft drinks, then spat out the tiny missiles, making little black dots over the screen which needed brushing off regularly.

Whether the film was shown on 35mm or digitally, all of this would still be necessary. He doubted very much that maintenance work would be contracted out; why would the cinema industry, always reluctant to spend money, choose to pay hundreds of pounds for an electrical company to come in and replace dud light bulbs when a technician did the same job for a couple of hours of overtime?

But most of the digital cinema hype ignored all of this. The holy grail seemed to be that once you replaced your 35mm projection equipment, then you no longer needed anyone to operate the new digital kit. Automation would control everything, putting shows on at the right time in the right screen. If things went wrong, engineers could simply connect remotely and fix it.

Of course, this was an over simplification, designed to sell equipment. You couldn't dial in to replace a blown speaker or amplifier, or to check if a cable had worked loose, or a breaker had tripped out. It stood to reason that without the time needed to make up and pack off thousands of feet of film each week, you could make do with fewer technical staff, but there would still have to be someone present in case things went wrong. Let's face it, digital cinema was a lot more complex than the electro-mechanical machinery it would eventually replace. It would be a different skillset – one that he was comfortable with too – but common sense had to prevail.

In any case, all of that was still a long way off. He had a new multiplex to open up. His career plan was going just the way he wanted it.

Cat: 2007

Cat went in to fetch the breakfast tray. Phoebe hadn't had much of the cereal, and the toast was limp and soggy on the plate.

'Can't you try and eat a little bit more?' she cajoled.

Phoebe looked up. 'I don't really feel like it, dear. But don't worry. I've had what I want.'

'Shall I get you some more tea?'

'Please.'

She took the tray back downstairs to the kitchen. How much longer would this go on? Despite her increasing frailty, Phoebe was a fighter. Medication took care of her pain and doctors and care workers visited regularly. She was determined to spend her last weeks in the house she had lived all her life. 'I don't want to die in some hospital corridor on a trolley,' she'd said so many times to Cat. 'Spare me that indignity.'

Cat felt she owed it to the old lady, who had provided her with a pleasant home and company for so many years now. It was tough, though. The nights were long and she dozed fitfully, ever alert for any sign that Phoebe needed something. On the days she had to go to work, she worried constantly. She'd tried asking the manager for some compassionate leave, but he was unsympathetic. 'You're not even a relative.'

'She doesn't have any. Her parents died long ago and she was an only child.'

'Surely the NHS can do something. Or social workers?'

'Not what she wants, though.' It was useless. She did her shifts like a robot. Fortunately, her colleagues knew and appreciated what she was doing and covered for her.

Alfie was another worry. He still came to the cinema; another bone of contention with the latest manager. 'We're not open yet,' he'd shouted through the doors when Alfie had been tapping to come in one morning. 'Go away.'

Cat had explained that he was the former chief and that he was now suffering with memory loss problems. 'He's always visited us,' she'd told him.

'This is a business, not an old folk's home.'

After that, she had to try and ask Liz not to let him come in on the days the general manager would be on duty, but it was difficult. 'I can't keep an eye on him all the time. He likes to get out and about and the cinema's one of the places he can still get to.'

It was strange how the mind worked. Alfie still had a clear recall of the films he'd shown over the years and could name the director, distributor and ratio for most of them when asked. But his grasp of the present was fading and she tried to keep him from the areas of the cinema that had suffered the most changes, as they seemed to distress him.

'What's going to happen to him?' she asked Liz one day when she had come to take him home.

'I don't know. I want to keep him with me as long as I can, but it's so hard sometimes.'

Cat could empathise with that.

'He gets up during the night, forgetting what time it is. If I wasn't around, he'd turn on the kettle with no water in it or leave the taps running. I worry about him wandering off, but I can't keep him a prisoner in the house, can I?'

'No, of course not.'

'The children don't understand, either. I know they want me to get him into a home. But I'm not going to do that unless I have to.'

'I know, I know,' she sympathised. Getting old was tough. Either your mind stayed sharp while your body failed, like poor Phoebe, or it went the other way. Given the choice, she didn't know how she'd rather end up.

The spring days lengthened towards summer. Another blockbuster season beckoned. The staff were cajoled to up-sell food and beverages. Poster frames were changed to advertise combo food and drinks packages rather than upcoming films.

Phoebe faded as the buds broke and leaves burgeoned. 'I've had a good life, all in all,' she said to Cat. 'I don't regret leaving it.'

'You're not going anywhere yet.'

'Don't be silly. I know when my time's up. You know, last night I dreamed I was walking along a beautiful pathway through the woods. And right down at the far end, there was Ronald, holding out his hand to me. I know I'm going to be with him soon.'

Cat felt her eyes begin to prickle.

'You make sure you do all the things you want to do, young lady. I know you love that cinema, but there's more to life. Get out, meet people, have experiences.'

'Seize the day, you mean?' She had always remembered that quote from *Dead Poets Society*.

Phoebe held her hand surprisingly tightly. 'Yes, that's it. Don't have any regrets.'

Over the next few days, she spent more time sleeping than awake. Cat gave in and took some annual leave as the doctor had told her it wouldn't be long. One sunny afternoon, just as she was having a respite break, the carer from the local hospice gently shook her awake. 'It's time. She's slipping away.'

She went through. Phoebe was barely breathing now. They sat and waited as the shadow patterns of beech leaves flickered across the walls of the room. Cat wondered if she had finally managed to reach Ronald; if somewhere in her last vestiges of conscious thought, she would be reunited with the man she'd loved and lost.

Afterwards came all the processes; the doctor, the undertakers, registering the death. She was not entirely surprised to discover that Phoebe had made all the necessary arrangements; after all she had been an intelligent and organised woman. She was shocked to find out that she'd been left the house and enough money and investments to keep herself in comfort. It gave her a welcome sense of security in a world that seemed to be on the edge of change.

Graham: 2008

In the two and a half years since the cinema opened, Graham had seen some changes. His job title for one thing. He was no longer a Chief Technician, but a Technical Manager, paid a salary rather than an hourly rate with overtime. It wasn't a problem for him, but had raised the predictable grumbles from some of his colleagues who were used to claiming large amounts of overtime whenever they could get away with it. All of the technical team now worked a basic forty-hour week rather than the old thirty-five hours. Again, nothing to complain about as it boosted the basic wage.

The merger had brought in some new ways of working. More paperwork, as he'd foreseen, but that wasn't really a problem either. He'd always kept maintenance records; now he just did it the way the company wanted. No-one had come to check anything so far, but if they did, they wouldn't find any issues.

He had a good team; two full-timers who had been with him since opening and a recently recruited part-timer. And there lay another bone of contention for some of the old guys to moan about. Part-timers worked some of their weekly hours front of house and some in projection.

'I'm not having no sausage turner in my box,' one old chief had stated at a recent meeting. 'It's not right.'

Graham had tried to point out that quite a few full-time projectionists had started their cinema careers working downstairs.

'I've got no objection to them who are properly promoted. I just don't hold with this. Nor should the Union.'

'Union's useless these days,' someone else commented. 'They don't fight for us anymore.'

Be that as it may, Graham's part-timer Ayaz had learned the necessary skills quickly and had become a useful member of the team. And there was no doubt that they needed the extra pair of hands at times, particularly during the blockbuster season when five or six prints might come in the day before a film was due to open.

As the cinema had fallen into a routine, so had his home life. Just over a year ago, there had been some management issues, necessitating one or two relief managers for a couple of months. One of them was Maria. They'd got talking in the office one evening, found they had a lot of shared interests, including a love for cinema, and had started seeing each other outside of work soon afterwards. Now they were sharing a flat together.

'So when are we going to hear wedding bells,' his mum had said during one of his home visits.

'Give us a chance, mum.' He loved Maria, but he wasn't going to go jumping into commitment just like that. She and his dad had got together in a different era. People married younger back then. They could afford to buy a house too.

'It'll never work; a manager and a projectionist,' Uncle Peter put in. 'Two different species, lad.'

Graham tried not to smile. His uncle could be so old-fashioned some times. 'She's still a woman, not some creature from the Black Lagoon.'

Peter shook his head. 'I used to work with this old guy. He'd been a projectionist all his life and he'd got this idea in his head that one day the aliens would visit our planet.'

'Sounds like a crackpot,' Graham's dad commented.

'Well, maybe. But anyway, he said that when they did, they'd grab the first human they met and they'd ask him – or her – various questions regarding life, the universe and everything. And here's the scary bit. If that one human being gave them the wrong answers, they'd exterminate all of us.'

'That's a bit harsh.' Graham said.

'Maybe. But do you know what his main fear was?' Peter paused for dramatic effect. 'That the first person the aliens met might be a cinema manager. "And if that's the case, we're all doomed," he told me.'

Graham laughed. 'Good job Maria's intelligent, then. Plus she can do karate, so she'd have no bother subduing the aliens if they grabbed her in the first place.'

'Still, be careful, lad.'

'Always am. How's things at your workplace, then?'

Peter was still working at the multiplex. 'It'll see me out until I retire.'

Graham did a quick calculation in his head. Peter would be due to retire in about four years. The day that digital projection came in might be a bit closer than that.

'I went to visit a totally digital show the other week,' he said. 'Ten screens, no film at all. It's a bit of an experiment at the moment, but it was interesting to see how it's run.'

Peter made a disparaging gesture. 'If there's no film, it's not a cinema.'

'The audience don't know the difference. In fact, if you asked an average person, they probably think it's been that way for years. But it's a total change for the projectionists.'

He'd taken notes of all the new terminology. 'You get your film on a hard drive. It still comes in one of the big transit cases, but it's light as a feather. And the process of loading it onto the server is called "ingesting".'

'Sounds like something a monster does once it's reduced its victim to sludge. Like *The Fly*.'

'Then you make up a playlist. It's not that different from assembling a programme on the bench, except that instead of joining pieces of film together, you're creating an order for the content to play in.'

'So you need to know about computers, then?'

'Well, yes. But it's not hard to learn.'

'Not for you young ones, maybe.' Peter sounded doubtful. 'We're supposed to be getting some of that stuff put in soon. It worries me.'

'Thing is, it's going to happen. We're all going to have to face quite a lot of changes in the next few years.' He didn't like scaring his uncle, but the truth had to be told. 'I'm sure they'll give you any training you need. I can help you out myself, when I'm home, if you like.'

Peter smiled. 'I'll learn what I have to. Doesn't mean I like it, though.'

'Come on. Get up to the table,' mum interrupted. 'Tea's ready.'

Some things never changed.

Reel 5

The Digital Rollout

Bill: 2009 - 2010

Bill took his seat in the roomy auditorium. He'd been looking forward to this demonstration of the Real-D 3D system ever since he'd seen it advertised. Not that he was under the illusion that 3D was going to be the next big thing. During his career, various 3D processes had been hailed as a step forward for cinema technology; another way to immerse the audience in the on-screen action, but to be honest, if a film had a good enough story, it didn't need the gimmicks. Besides, audiences had never like wearing the glasses needed to appreciate the visual effects and after the first few shocks, got bored of things popping out of the screen at them.

This time was a bit different though. The initial installs of digital projection equipment had already begun in several cinemas and he'd recently found out the date for their first conversion. In June they would be getting a digital projector alongside the 35mm machine in Screen Two. It would enable them to show some of the 3D releases that were scheduled for later in the year, as well as 2D digital versions of available films. If 3D showings were an incentive to get more people through the doors, he was all in favour of it.

Glasses had been handed out on the way in. They were made from robust plastic and a lot more comfortable than the old-style cardboard type. He noticed that those in the audience who wore their own glasses still had a few problems making them fit over the top. The lenses were slightly tinted, making the auditorium seem darker, too.

Real-D used polarised light to differentiate between the left and right eye images, which meant that the normal screen had to be replaced by a silver screen prior to the installation. Bill wasn't all that keen on silver screens; it was difficult to avoid hotspots and get an even light across the full width. Plus they were expensive to replace. Good job smoking had been banned in cinemas a long time ago. Still, you were bound to get the inevitable marks when the audience threw objects at the screen, or parents let their children trail sticky fingers over it.

The auditorium lights dimmed, and the demonstration began with a couple of 3D promotional titles. Not too much of the 'in your face' stuff, he was glad to see, but with a pleasant feeling of depth to the picture. This was followed by ten minutes of footage from *Monsters V Aliens,* which he'd already shown on 35mm earlier in the year. It was a lot better than he'd expected.

After the demo, they all visited the projection room to see the hardware. The Real-D polarising filter slid easily in front of the regular projection lens on rails. 'They can be a bugger to line up,' said one of the engineers, 'But once it's done, it's fine.'

'Bet you lose a lot of light though,' Bill commented.

'A fair amount, yes, but that's 3D for you.'

Bill took his turn to look over the projector, a blue box mounted on top of a substantial base, which held the other essential components of digital projection; a server, power supplies and a shelf holding the keyboard and mouse.

'When we got ours installed, one of the staff said it looked like a coffee machine,' someone said. 'Look, it's even got cup holders on the back.'

It was true; the indentations had obviously been designed for placing the feet of a larger sized projector, but they did look like cup holders.

'So this button's for cappuccino?' someone else joked, pointing at the side panel.

Bill glanced at the server screen, displaying the playlist that had just been run. It was fortunate he'd kept up with the times and that computers held no fear for him. Some of his colleagues weren't so comfortable with technology. His senior, Jim, had only recently bought himself a mobile phone and still hadn't really got the hang of text messages.

The technical manager explained the process of loading content onto the server. 'Trailers come on one of those memory sticks; you just plug 'em in here. The features are on hard drives and they slot in the front. It takes an hour or so for it to ingest the whole lot; about the same time as making up a print, except you don't need to be there while it's happening. But you can't play it until you load the KDM and that's usually sent by email to the office. You need to chase 'em up sometimes, they don't always rush to get them to you.'

'What about problems? I've heard they crash a lot.'

He shrugged. 'Sometimes there's a glitch when the lamp strikes and you have to reboot the machine. It takes about five minutes. But that only happens a few times a week.'

Well, it was good to know that technology had its own problems. All the more reason to need a competent person around the place. It was exciting too; whenever new kit arrived, there was always something to be learned. He picked up one of the glossy brochures explaining all the acronyms and terminology of D-cinema to take back home with him.

The day ended in the usual way with a couple of drinks in a nearby pub. It was here that the less glossy information was circulated via some of the Union negotiators. 'The company's being very cagey about manning levels. So far, all that's been mentioned is that anyone who leaves or retires won't get replaced. But some of the head office bigwigs hate us lot. I overheard one of 'em say he's longing for the day when they can get rid of every last projectionist.'

Meanwhile, the normal work carried on. Bill and Jim spent a sweltering day standing at the rewind bench when five copies of *Harry Potter and the Half-Blood Prince* arrived the day before the preview showings. Outside, the July sunshine beat down on the cinema, and as the day wore on, the projection room became hotter and hotter. They'd been told that digital projection equipment was less tolerant of heat than human beings, so once the installations began, air-conditioning would be retro-fitted to stop the servers from shutting down.

'Typical,' said Jim. 'No-one cares about us poor buggers sweating our balls off, but when it comes to keeping the shows running it's a different story.'

More rumours circulated. It was said that at some sites, technicians were being forced to wear the same uniform as front of house staff; those awful, ill-fitting T-shirts and baseball caps. 'That'll be another way of making people so fed up they want to leave,' Jim commented. 'Like all this bloody paperwork they want us to do. I've nothing against record keeping, but when it takes longer to write up what you've done than to do the job, that's where I draw the line.'

'It's the same in the office, you know. Look at the pressure the managers are under nowadays. It's all about retail spend and selling loyalty cards, not promoting films any more. Let's just keep our heads down and see what happens, eh?'

Hardly a week went by without an engineer visiting to take more measurements for the next phase of the digital rollout. Following the initial install, more projectors would be replaced in the New Year, the difference being that the 35mm equipment would be removed instead of staying alongside.

'When all this is finished you'll only have the two dual screens,' Bill was told. 'Just in case there's still a few releases on 35mm.'

Christmas came and went. *Avatar* was a huge success, proving that people would pay extra to see a 3D film. It didn't run totally without issues though. Several times, Bill had frantic calls on the walkie-talkie that the picture and sound had frozen, although whenever he got to the porthole, everything was working again. He felt a sense of frustration at not being able to diagnose the fault himself and it was only after two visits from the engineers that the cause was found to be a failing hard drive.

A couple of sites had already transitioned to full digital projection and Bill spent hours on the phone to colleagues trying to discover what had happened to manning levels. He knew that his position was relatively safe; it had been announced that technical managers would be unaffected, but Jim and Karl were naturally worried about their own job security.

'So far, there haven't been any cuts, but there's going to be a review in a few months,' he heard. 'Mostly, they're cutting down on part-timers hours and trying to keep the full time staff employed. It doesn't seem too bad at the moment.'

People who had come in to see *Avatar* were disappointed when their next helping of 3D turned out to be *Clash of the Titans*. Filmed in 2D, the 3D post production was poor. If it had been his first introduction to the format, Bill would have been decidedly unimpressed.

The new equipment arrived. The squat rectangular bases were assembled first and as he walked from one end of the box to the other, they loomed in his peripheral vision like lurking black shadows. He cleaned the platters in Screens One and Five for the last time, noting it on the maintenance chart. Their next destination would most likely be a skip. Sad really; the equipment was fewer than fifteen years old and would have lasted another twenty at least. That was the wonderful thing about 35mm projection equipment – the basic working principles hadn't really changed in a hundred years and it was infinitely upgradeable as technology progressed. Digital equipment would become obsolete in around ten years, even if it still worked, just like everything else these days.

The initial expense of changing over to digital projection was being partly funded by the film distribution companies. Bill had read a lot about this process and tried to explain it to Maureen.

'It's the film distributors who stand to make the biggest saving long term. Think of how much it costs them to have film prints made for a major release right now. There's the cost of the film stock, having prints run off at the labs, getting it all packaged and delivered to sites in good time. Once they can distribute copies on hard drives their costs will go right down.'

223

'So it's in their interest as much as anyone to make sure as many cinemas as possible go digital?'

'Exactly. So someone came up with this clever financial idea called a virtual print fee. Basically, the distributors pay a percentage every time one of their products gets shown digitally.'

'What, to the cinema?' Maureen asked.

'Not exactly. It's a bit more complicated than that. They pay the money to someone called an integrator and these third parties provide the finance to the cinema companies to purchase the digital equipment, and use the virtual print fee to pay off the capital.'

'That sounds complicated.'

'It is. But it means a big saving for the cinemas on having the kit installed and everyone's happy.'

'Everyone except the ones who lose their jobs,' she commented.

'Don't worry, love. It's not going to be as bad as people are saying. Remember, we've been down this road a few times before and everything's been fine.' All through his career there had been times when everyday practices turned to history. Carbon arcs had given way to xenon lamps, changeovers to platter systems. Increasing automation and numbers of screens to manage had forced changes to be made to ways of working.

'Yes, but you're not as young as you were.'

'I've still got a brain. I can adapt. It's the people who are scared of change that'll suffer.'

'Like poor old Jim, you mean?'

Jim had been getting increasingly agitated as the rumour mill ground on. He'd recently heard there might be a voluntary redundancy package on offer. 'It won't be much, I'll be bound,' he'd said.

'He's wittling on about what's going to happen. You know what it was like when him and Jean split up. He's got no savings to fall back on.'

'What about young Karl?'

'He's thinking about moving across to management. It's another way to stay in the business. But I keep telling them both, it might not come to that.'

'And if it does?'

'Then we'll cross that bridge too.' He smiled. 'Imagine me as a duty manager. I'd make those lazy so and so's get their feet off the seats.'

Graham: 2010

Graham had gone to visit his parents during a weekend off. It was strange how the town where he had grown up no longer really felt like 'home'. Many of his old school friends had stayed there and settled down. They would probably spend their whole lives in the same place. A bit like Uncle Peter, really.

He parked his car and walked up to the multiplex. Peter was on duty today and he'd said he'd drop in for a chat. The colour scheme and signage had changed, but the building was still much the same; like stepping back into his teenage years.

He made his way up to the projection staff room. Peter was making tea. He looked a little thinner, his hair slightly whiter and with a bit less of it on top, but in every other way, he too was just the same. Blue shirt, grey trousers and his sandals, which he always put on once he was in work for the day. 'Much healthier to let your feet breathe,' he said.

'So, how's it going,' Graham asked, once tea and biscuits were served.

Peter shrugged. 'We've had two of the beasts fitted already. Horrible things. All you can hear when they're running is air blowing out of the extracts.'

'When's the next stage?'

'After Christmas, we've been told. And by this time next year, the whole lot will be gone.' He sighed. 'I never thought it would happen so quickly.'

Graham took a sip of tea. 'What are you going to do?'

'Whatever I can. They've said we can "retrain" if we want. Like I need training to shovel popcorn for minimum wage on a zero hours contract.'

'There'll be some sort of redundancy package, won't there? That's what's happening with our company.'

Peter crunched a ginger nut. 'No details as yet. I suppose if I get enough to tide me over for a few months I might find a job somewhere else. Remember my mate, Les? He works at B&Q. Says it's not bad.'

'The DIY stores take on quite a few older people, don't they?'

Peter nodded. 'So I've heard. Us oldies have a lot more common sense and experience when it comes to home improvements. But... well, it's not cinema, is it?'

'No.' There wasn't much else to say.

'Last week, after one of the senior shows, this man and his wife asked if they could have a look round the box. Lovely couple, they were. He used to be a projectionist at an independent cinema, years ago. Couldn't believe all the changes.'

Graham nodded.

'Anyway, he was telling me about one of the old school managers he used to work with. You know; the real showman type. Lived, breathed and ate cincma. Knew everything about all the films coming out, always organising publicity stunts. He'd been there donkey's years. Anyway, when the place finally closed down, all he could find was a job in an office, nine to five. He didn't have much choice; he had a family to support. And you know what happened?'

'No?'

'He lasted three months, had a heart attack. Dropped dead. More like a broken heart.'

Graham didn't know quite how to react. 'That's sad,' he commented.

'It's like all these blokes who retire from the business and pop their clogs two months later. Their reason for living's just... gone.'

'That happens in other industries too. Some men devote their lives to their job and don't have any hobbies outside.' Kind of like his own dad, Graham thought. 'Once they retire, they've no idea what to do with themselves. But you're not like that. You've always been interested in other stuff as well.'

'I suppose. Anyway, what's your news?'

'Well, I've applied to be a projection engineer. The interview's in two weeks.'

'You're bound to get it, son. With your degree and all.'

Graham shook his head. 'It's not quite that clear cut. There's been a lot of applicants. I know I'd be good at it, but there's a lot more out there equally as capable.'

'You'll do just fine,' Peter assured him.

'I hope so. I've been working on it all week. We have to do a twenty-minute presentation on what we can bring to the role, then there's a written exam afterwards.'

'I'll be thinking of you.'

They spent the afternoon reminiscing about old times. Graham watched parts of the programme from the viewing port, remembering all the films he'd seen from that same vantage point back when he'd been too young to see them from inside the screen.

At two-thirty Peter said. 'Nearly changeover time in screen three. Who'd have thought we'd recover that lost art in this day and age?' The trailers and feature were showing in digital, but so far, the adverts still came in on 35mm film, which entailed running the old and the new side by side.

Peter had timed it seamlessly. 'There you go. The audience won't even know it's changed,' he said, as the tail of the adverts ran through the Kinoton projector. 'Unlike when it comes to the lens change from wide to scope on this piece of junk and the screen goes black for fifteen seconds. That's what they call progress?'

He left the cinema as it was getting dark and drove back to the family home. Dad was slumped in his usual chair watching the football. Mum was busy cooking. He joined her in the kitchen. 'How's Peter today?' she asked.

'He seemed a bit down.' But wasn't everyone in the business these days?

'I hope he's looking after himself.'

'You'll have to ask him round for dinner to fatten him up. I think he's lost some weight.'

She looked at him. 'He didn't tell you, then?'

'What about?'

'He's been having tests at the hospital.' She paused. 'Maybe I shouldn't say, if he doesn't want you to know.'

'I'm a grown up now, mum. What's up with him?'

'Well, he's been diagnosed with prostate cancer.'

Graham sighed. 'Shit! Sorry, mum. Is he... will he be okay?'

She strained the beans, looking up though a cloud of fragrant steam. 'Hopefully. They've caught it early. But he'll have a lot to go through in the next few months.'

Not what anyone needed when their job security was also on the line. 'Why couldn't he have told me?'

'He probably didn't want to worry you. You know how he is.'

The following day, he set off in the morning before the Sunday rush hour back to London got under way. If all went well, in the next few months, he'd be out on the road most of the time.

Back at the flat, he put in a bit more work on his presentation. He wasn't looking forward to that part. It was all the corporate-speak and bullshit. Did anyone really believe in it? Or did they just play the game to land the job? He knew he would.

Maria finished her shift at seven and arrived home shortly afterwards. 'How was the frozen north?' she asked.

'It's only the midlands,' he said, as always.

'Same thing, isn't it. North of here, anyway.'

'It was okay. The parents are fine. My uncle Peter's got cancer, but he didn't tell me that. Mum let me know.'

'How bad?'

'Well, he's going to be starting treatment soon. But what with all the rest of what's going on at work, it's not the best time, is it?'

'Don't worry,' she reassured him. 'If someone's genuinely sick no company is going to give them any hassle.'

'Let's hope not.'

It seemed like no time at all until the appointed interview day came around. Graham spent his spare time poring over projector and server manuals, making sure he could roll off facts and figures about digital with the same ease and confidence as when referring to 35mm sound and projection equipment. He carefully planned the route to Manchester and left in plenty of time in case of accidents on the M6, wearing his usual interview suit and tie. He double checked everything. A copy of his presentation both on his laptop and on a memory stick; printed notes; spare pens. He knew he couldn't be better prepared.

The interview part was slightly nerve wracking, but he thought he said the right things, in the right order. Then he went through to the written test room. There were three people already seated, busily writing. It reminded him of exams at school, that same frantic scribbling, interspersed with sighs. One man sat with his head in his hands, as if he was about to give in to despair.

Graham briefly skimmed through the questions first. One thing in his favour was that he'd had more recent experience of sitting exams than some of the older candidates. It was always a good idea to estimate how long each section of a test might take, otherwise you could waste a lot of time giving a detailed answer to one part before realising you hadn't left long enough for the rest. Then he started, determined to give it his best shot.

The two hours sped past, but he'd planned well and still had time to check and review all that he'd written. There were a couple of questions he wasn't sure about; there had been nothing in any of the manuals he'd read suggesting what a 'marriage tamper' might be, but he thought it sounded like some kind of digital security issue so wrote that down. It was also difficult to describe exactly how to do a disk clean up on a server, take off an error log and check the drives. If he had been sitting in front of the monitor it would have been a piece of cake, but recalling the steps blind wasn't quite the same. Still, he thought he'd done as well as he could and all he could hope was that, together with his reputation, it would be good enough. Otherwise, Plan B, whatever that might be, beckoned.

Three days later, he had his answer. 'We'd like to offer you a position. Unfortunately, it's only temporary at present. You'd be seconded from your current role, with the option to go back if it ends.'

Go back to what, Graham thought. He wondered how he'd explain that to Maria, then banished the thought.

'However, with the digital rollout starting in the New Year, there's going to be plenty of work for everyone and once the project is underway, there will definitely be more permanent vacancies arising. How do you feel about that?'

'Well, great. I mean, thanks. I accept.'

'Excellent. Good to have you on board. You'll be starting in a month or so, once everything's been through HR. Well done.'

Cat: 2011

Cat went through to the main box and started the show. If you could call it that; selecting a playlist and clicking play. She waited for the projector to go through its start-up sequence, just in case the lamp didn't strike again, or it opened in the wrong ratio. As she was standing right beside it, everything worked as it should and the picture sprang into life; crisp, clear yet somehow sterile, on the distant screen.

Marcus had left her a note in the diary; the previous evening two power drops in a row had necessitated re-booting projectors and servers. Twenty–two customers had been given refunds, unwilling to wait for their film to resume. The manager had asked Cat questions about why it should take so long to get back on screen. She told him that no-one could have done any better – it wasn't like 35mm where you just re-set and re-started in an instant.

Up here, the 35mm equipment had been dragged to one side on installation day, left in a huddled mess against the back wall of the projection box. Cut cables were loosely draped around the bases. The three shiny platters were forced together by the weight of the rectifier, which had made deep scratches in their formerly pristine surface. It was a good job, she reflected, that Alfie would never see this desecration.

Three screens down, two to go. The last would be converted in March. She'd seen the writing on the wall; the list of cinemas and the dates when they would be going digital. She had also read the letter from HR, hot off the press that week. It invited people to apply for voluntary redundancy, giving details of the enhanced package that would only be available for a short while and on a 'first come, first served' basis. A few facts and figures were mentioned; about half the sites owned by the company might be affected and the job losses could amount to around sixty out of three hundred.

'That's not so bad,' Marcus had said, last time they worked together. 'It'll be mostly the old blokes who want to go, won't it?'

'I'm not so sure about that. When I went up to the Christmas party I found out loads of people have left already. Some of the union guys were offered special terms if they went quietly. I got the feeling they want all the experienced negotiators gone so they can do what they like with the rest of us.'

'But it says here...' he tapped the document.

'I know, I know. But that doesn't tally with some of the other stuff I've been hearing. The sites that've gone fully digital already have had their hours budget cut drastically. One place went down from a hundred and fifty hours a week to just eighty-five. That's only enough work for two people and they had four previously.'

'So what are you going to do?'

'Stay, for now. I'm not just going to abandon the place. I can't.' She owed it to Alfie, to all her predecessors. 'Even if they cut the hours, there should be enough to keep the two of us going. Good job we didn't get around to replacing Jasmine after all.'

'Won't be no overtime any more though.'

'Probably not,' she agreed. 'Mr Skinflint downstairs will love that.'

She carried on with her daily routine; checking the boilers were turned up high enough to cope with the bitter January weather, lamping up the emergency lights in the exits and fixing a toilet cistern whose handle had been pulled off the previous evening. As she often did, these days, she wondered if she would still be doing all this in a year's time. Even if she didn't go for the voluntary package, who could say what might happen further down the line. Would the company leave things as they were, or review the situation and nibble away some more hours at a later date?

She was in a far better position than a lot of others. If she lost her job, she wouldn't be struggling to survive. The new painting courses she'd started up last summer were beginning to take off and she had regular students visiting the house these days. It wasn't quite a fully-fledged business, but it could become one. The cinema was something different, though. Something special. She couldn't let it go without a fight.

The following day, she was off. She did some food shopping, changed her books at the library, then drove over to the care home to visit Alfie. Liz had been reluctant to give up caring for him, but had finally given in just over a year ago when it became clear she couldn't manage his condition at home any more. Cat wondered how Liz coped; watching the man she'd married losing himself piece by piece. She found it difficult enough herself, but a sense of duty and the feeling that somewhere, deep down, a part of him was still intact, kept her going. There were times he seemed to understand who she was and what she was talking about. There were also times when he seemed lost and unreachable.

Today, he was in his room. The bland magnolia walls had been covered by a multitude of pictures that summed up his life and career. A much younger Alfie and Liz beamed at their wedding, posed in various sunlit holiday locations and celebrated with groups of friends. The cinema wasn't forgotten either. In Cat's favourite picture, Alfie was lacing up the old Victoria 8 projector which had so recently been junked in favour of the squat, black box.

A large TV and DVD player stood on one of the tables, together with a selection of his favourite films. Because he could no longer operate the controls, it was up to the staff to put these on for him and most of the time they attempted to comply.

Alfie was propped up in bed, facing the screen. She could see as soon as she went in that he was agitated and it only took a few moments to work out the reason. *My Fair Lady* was playing, but not in the right screen ratio. She picked up the remote and corrected it.

234

'There you go, Alfie. That's better, isn't it? You just can't get the staff these days, can you?'

She'd tried explaining to them that as an ex-projectionist, he couldn't bear to see a film shown wrongly, but the girls seemed oblivious. 'Surely you can see that's not how it's supposed to look, can't you? Everyone looks short and fat. It's really easy to change, though.'

Oh well, it was marginally better than having to watch Jeremy Kyle with the folk in the lounge, she supposed.

She talked mostly about the past. 'Remember that time Bertie Arkwright came in ranting about a sound problem he'd been called out to fix?' She recounted one of the familiar tales, miming Bertie's rage at the sort of idiots he was being forced to deal with. Sometimes it raised a smile; not today.

One of the staff brought in some lunch and she helped him to eat it. Like Phoebe in her last days, Alfie was eating less and less. She wondered how long his body could keep going like this. In the year she'd been visiting, his decline had been steady; something like the way the cinema business was being eroded away, piece by piece. How long could it – or Alfie for that matter – stay alive?

Graham: 2011

Graham had been doing the job for nearly five months and was just beginning to feel useful. It had been the steepest learning curve of his career so far. On the day he started, he'd picked up a car, a bag of tools, a company BlackBerry and various spare parts and manuals. He'd spent a few hours training with one of the experienced engineers, scribbling notes frantically as they upgraded software and set up screen files on a projector. As a newbie, with mainly 35mm experience, he had been told that initially, he would be spending most of his time keeping the existing equipment running until the time came for its replacement. He was allocated an area, which covered a large part of the South East and would be expected to provide emergency cover for one weekend in three. 'Don't worry,' he was told. 'There's always help at the end of the phone. Don't be afraid to ask questions. We're all learning at the moment.'

He'd also had to fill in the forms applying for voluntary redundancy to cover the worst-case scenario. 'It's just a formality,' they said. 'If anything, we're going to need more engineers rather than less.' But the knowledge that he didn't have anywhere to return made him a little bit uneasy. Maria didn't like it either.

'Why can't they just make a decision one way or another? It's not fair on you.'

'It's just the way it is. No-one knows what's going to happen over the next few months.'

The digital rollout moved inexorably onward like an unstoppable juggernaut. A different team was in charge of the installations, so he wasn't involved in the actual changeover days. They started early; at four or five in the morning, ripping out the old and setting up the new, until by mid-afternoon yet another cinema was ready for the brave new digital world. The old equipment piled up in boxes and exit ways, waiting until the day came when it would be collected and taken off for recycling.

The digital cinemas were sad places. It took a few days for reality to sink in and for the on-site technicians to realise that things had changed forever. 'It's only been ten weeks since we changed over,' one told Graham. 'But it feels like forever. Yesterday I had to carry a film down to the dump and I couldn't believe how heavy it was. I used to do that all the time!'

Problems often arose in the first few days after an install. Boards and plugs tended to work loose and needed re-seating. Sometimes if one of the side panels had become slightly bent in transit, they didn't always make a good contact with the security micro switches and the projector would refuse to play content. Lamp power supplies – the digital equivalent to a rectifier – failed surprisingly often, but could be changed in less than half an hour once a replacement was shipped from the factory.

Like his colleagues, Graham learned quickly to leave plenty of time for software upgrades. They sometimes got stuck half way, rendering the projector unusable. If you were lucky, a second try solved the problem. If not, the ICP board needed swapping out; another wait for delivery if you had already used your own spare and not received a replacement yet.

He attended courses at the factory where the projectors were assembled. It reminded him of the long-gone training centre; a place where you could take your time and do things properly without the stress of being on-site. Without some of the inevitable problems caused by lack of space too. Changing his first light engine at the factory was a doddle; it was quite different when he had to do the same job at an old cinema where the projector sat on a four-foot high wooden plinth. The top was only a short distance from the low ceiling and he had to balance on a step ladder to gingerly remove the expensive heart of the digital projection system from its casing. Just to make things worse, many of the cinemas had used the conversion as an excuse to remove everything from the projection rooms. Rewind benches might not be needed to make up film any more, but it would have been useful to be able to work on equipment at bench level. Much of the time, the only available flat surface was the floor.

Now that he was seeing the whole picture, rather than just having knowledge of his own and a few surrounding sites, it was clear that a lot more people had accepted the redundancy payments rather than opting to stay. Already, a few sites were running with no technical staff in place at all, and with no plan to replace them. Another couple of cinemas had retained their technical managers, but they were expected to work some of their shifts each week as front of house management too.

'This is all supposed to be top secret,' someone told Graham. 'It's even got a codename; Operation Tinkerbell. The ultimate plan is to run cinemas with no technical staff at all, just team leaders in charge of day to day running. The duty management will have to do everything else; chase up hard drives and KDM's, ingest content, report faults and the like.'

'They're going to love that.'

'Can't you just see it? I almost feel sorry for the poor buggers. No extra money and a lot more hassle. Now when something breaks down, they won't just have to deal with the angry mob, but try to fix it at the same time.'

Graham dreaded calls from the sites where no one was left running projection. He'd spent two hours digging through a tiny storeroom where all the projection spares had been hurled together with spare seats and poster frames, looking for a power amp to replace one that had failed. The first he found had been damaged from its impact with the floor, entailing yet more rummaging before he finally uncovered one that had kept its protective polystyrene casing. He managed to fit it in time for the next show.

'Couldn't you just have left them in the spares cupboard?' he asked.

The team leader shrugged. 'They told us to get rid of everything,' he said. 'How am I to know what's good from what's not?'

Other engineers had similar experiences. 'I got an emergency call to say a sound processor had failed. "Dead as a dodo," they told me. They were due on screen in less than an hour. So I picked up my spare, raced across town and when I got there, guess what? It wasn't the processor that had died at all. The whole bloody sound rack had tripped. Guess no-one told whatever numpty was on duty that day you need to switch the power amps on one by one to avoid that happening.'

It wasn't just projection equipment that was causing problems. Graham met one of the heating and ventilation engineers at a site and was told a similar story of a mad dash half way across the country to an unfamiliar cinema where the heating had failed. 'This manager came up to me and said, "I hope you know where the boilers are, because I don't have a clue."

'It took him an hour to find the key to the door once we'd worked out where the place was, and when I finally got in there, all I needed to do was hit the reset button. My boss is loving it. He's sending out invoices left, right and centre. Money for nothing, mate.'

It was a hectic life. Instead of regular hours and pre-scheduled shifts, Graham became used to five o'clock starts to avoid traffic jams. It wasn't unusual to spend several hours a day in the car, much of it on the hands-free phone. He noticed he was putting on some weight around the waist; unavoidable when proper meals were replaced by grab and go snacks from petrol stations. You never really knew when you would finish. There'd been a few times when he'd been almost home when yet another call came in and he felt obliged to divert.

Maria didn't like it much either. 'We hardly see each other these days,' she complained.

'It'll settle down once the installs finish.'

'You said that a couple of months ago. Do you really want to carry on like this?'

'What choice do I have?'

'Get out of this stupid business before it's too late.' She had started looking for alternative employment herself, not liking the way things were going. 'We could both find regular jobs with sensible hours and decent pay.'

'But… It wouldn't be cinema, would it.'

'It wouldn't. But maybe what we both enjoyed about the business is slipping away. It looks that way from my end, anyway. Think about it. Remember, they still haven't made you permanent. It's as well to have a contingency plan.'

Bill: 2011

Bill ran the last ever 35mm show later that autumn, three months after digital day had come and gone. Everything about the experience was both nostalgic and mundane. Cleaning down the machine, lacing up as he had done so many thousands of times before. Checking that the film was seated properly on all the rollers. How many millions of feet had he shown through all the years he'd been working, he wondered, as he waited for the appointed time? The film trembled slightly in the breeze from the supply fans, light reflected from its shiny black surface.

He pushed the auto start button. After a second or two, the warning buzzer sounded and the projector motor began to run up to speed. The leader counted down, lights dimmed slowly in the auditorium, perfectly timed so that the dowser opened exactly as they faded to black. He checked the focus, had another look to see all the rollers were turning as they should, just as if this print would run a hundred times more. There were only a handful of people in the auditorium; some lads wearing baseball caps with their huge trainers rested on the backs of the row in front, a couple both engrossed in the glowing screens of their mobile phones. They didn't know and neither would they care that they were witnessing the passing of an era.

There was no-one in projection to share the moment. Jim had gone three weeks previously, having opted for the redundancy package. 'If this hadn't happened, I'd have been getting my forty years' service certificate in November,' he'd said sadly during his last shift. One of the staff had made him a cake, shaped like the Titanic. They'd ceremoniously cut it in half on the rewind bench then shared out the pieces with the manager and a couple of other invited guests.

The platters turned gently, feeding out film to the projector's demand, and winding it back again. He watched for a while, then went back to the theatre management system workstation to make up some more playlists for the coming week. But he couldn't settle. Every few minutes, he found himself drawn back to Screen Two, where the film progressed steadily. He recorded the sound of a join going through the gate on his phone even though he knew it wouldn't sound quite right when he played it back.

Time passed. Joins clicked through the gate as each reel came to its end. Eventually the credits were rolling, reflected back from the porthole glass onto the wall behind. Then the final pulse triggered the end sequence, whose shrill whistle would never be heard again. The loose end of the feature clattered over the sprockets and the projector motor sighed to a halt.

It was only when he went over to the platter and caught sight of the words 'FOOT…END' on the tail of the film that it sunk in. He had showed his last reel.

Reel 6

The End of an Era

Graham: 2012

Graham sat in the car at the side of the cinema, next to the wheelie bins. It was after nine o'clock, but no-one was there yet; an increasingly common situation these days. It made his job harder with less time before opening to get things done, but he couldn't blame the managers for not wanting to come in earlier than they had to. They'd be working until late in the evening. Mind you, so might he, depending on what went wrong and where today.

Some of the other engineers had got around the problem by obtaining keys to let themselves in to some of their cinemas. Graham was reluctant to go down that road; he had worries about the Health and Safety implications of working alone in a building. If an accident happened, you could lie there for hours. There were also security issues. What if you turned off the alarm and then someone broke in and stole a load of stuff? You might be accused of colluding with the criminals, or they might just clobber you and leave you bleeding.

This was one of the good sites; a place where people cared and still tried to keep up standards of presentation and showmanship. Gavin, the TM, had stayed on and still ran his domain as he had always done, in addition to working shifts as a duty manager. The projection rooms were tidy and clean. If you needed anything, it was easily found. There was even – a miracle in this day and age – a working kettle.

It was a routine visit. A couple of the fire triggers hadn't worked when the alarm was tested the previous week. He expected it would be down to the usual macro problems and it would be a fairly quick fix. Gavin would find him a few other bits and pieces to do and it would almost be like old times, with the benefit of some social contact. Too often these days, he'd be given the projection keys, left to get on with his work, then speak to no-one until it was time to hand them back and leave the building.

Gavin's car pulled up next to his. He grabbed his tools and laptop bag from the boot and they went inside, to the main projection room where the TMS had been installed. Next to its black bulk, the polished desk held neatly labelled box files. On the wall above, the whiteboard was filled in with lists of features to come in, KDM's to be received and maintenance notes.

'So, how's it going?' Graham asked.

Gavin filled the kettle. He seemed a little tense today. 'Not brilliant, to be honest. I guess you've heard about these trials they're starting.'

Graham hadn't. The latest news had been that all the projectionists left in Ireland had been made redundant in one fell swoop, as if a modern-day St Patrick had decided to rid the country of these anachronisms along with all the snakes. There were so many rumours these days, you never quite knew who was privy to actual information and who was just speculating.

'More trials, eh?' he said, hoping to hear more.

'They told me before I went on holiday, but I was sworn to secrecy.'

This sounded interesting. Could it be something to do with 'Operation Tinkerbell'?

'Plus they've brought it all forward by two weeks. I'm not happy about that.'

'Right, right.'

'Then there's what they've done to poor Chris.'

Chris was the technician; a quietly spoken young man. Graham had always found him unfailingly polite and efficient. He had been trained up by Gavin and took his duties seriously.

Gavin handed Graham his mug of tea and sat down. 'He was devastated when I had to tell him yesterday. Still, better hear it from me than from HR, I suppose.' He sighed. 'They said he could work

246

front of house during the three month trial, but he doesn't want that. So they've sent him off on "gardening leave". Full pay, but that's no compensation when your job's just been wiped out. From what I've heard, once the three months is up, there's no going back anyway. So Chris has done his last shift already.'

'Wow. That's brutal.' Graham needed more information. 'So this is starting, when?'

'Friday. I've got four days to train up the other managers, then I go onto shift with them and there's no-one left solely in charge of projection any more. Four days to teach them everything about the procedures and maintenance and during normal shifts too. Mind you, it's worse at the other trial site. There's going to be no-one technical working there at all, just to see what happens.'

'For three months, eh?' Graham anticipated lots of callouts. He'd need to find out where the other site was. Hopefully, not on his patch.

'They'll be assessing the situation as it progresses, then make a decision about the way forward. It's a cost saving exercise, obviously. But they'll take into account all the lost shows, breakdowns, wrong films being put on and suchlike.'

'If there's no-one technical on site, things are bound to go wrong.'

'I'll have their guts for garters if they mess up my shows.' Gavin took a drink of tea. 'To be honest, they're not that bad here. They know my routine and things are well organised. But when you're trying to concentrate on two different jobs, it's not always that easy. I can appreciate that since I've been doing shifts front of house. Some of the guests are animals. I had a really rough lot in a couple of weeks ago. They'd bought a big box of popcorn and eaten most of it, then came out to complain it tasted funny. I told them it couldn't have been that bad if they'd managed to eat so much of it. I wouldn't give them a refund, so one of the lads stuck his fingers down his throat and vomited all over the retail counter. We had to close it down and sterilise everything.'

'Yuck.' Graham had heard similar stories from Maria and was thankful he didn't have much contact with the film-going public.

'Well, I suppose I'd better get on checking these fire triggers. How long until you're on screen?'

'The first one's at eleven-fifty. Can you have a look at the light in screen eight while you're here. The lamp's started to flicker even though it's only done just over four hundred hours.'

'Will do.'

'I've got a delivery to bring in, so I'll be in the stock room if you need anything.'

By afternoon, news had travelled fast. Graham had quite a few calls from the other engineers who had also heard about the trials. Later on, an official email came through to inform them of what they already knew. He also called Maria.

'So this is the next stage,' she said. 'Our TM is going mad about it. He's wishing he'd put in for the redundancy while the terms were good. He feels betrayed and I don't blame him.'

'It's a mess,' Graham agreed.

'Will I be seeing you later?'

'Hopefully.' Once he'd finished, it was only a short drive home; fewer than eighty miles.

'Get something from Sainsbury's on your way. I fancy a really hot curry tonight. And a decent bottle of red. No, make that two.'

Bill: 2012

Bill sat in the office, reading through the latest paperwork. It seemed he was going to have to re-apply for his job in the near future. The roles were changing again. Following some trials, it had been decided that every cinema with over five screens would have one dedicated Digital Manager in place. It wasn't a solely technical role; you would also be expected to work some of your weekly hours in the cinema office, or front of house. He wasn't too worried about this. Unlike some of the old school chiefs, for whom the divide between management and projection had been an unbridgeable gulf, he had always taken an interest in both sides of the business. And, to be honest, learning some new skills would keep his mind sharp.

'So how do you feel about all this?' Felicity asked.

'If it's what I need to do, I'll do it. If you think I'm up to it, that is.'

She smiled. 'Of course you're up to it. I'm glad you feel that way. Some of my colleagues are really worried about being left in the lurch without any technical support on site. If they've got less than five screens, they've no choice in the matter anyway, but from what I'm hearing, quite a few of the TM's aren't intending to re-apply for these new roles.'

'The company will have to offer some sort of training and support when it gets under way.'

'You'd hope so, wouldn't you? I don't mind switching things on and off, ingesting films and so on, but I'm always glad you're on the end of the phone if I need some quick help. And if I had to set up for one of those live satellite broadcasts without any support, I'd be having kittens.'

'There's always the NOC.' The Network Operations Centre was supposed to be the first line of support in case of problems. Based in Sweden, the operators spoke perfect English and could dial in to the projectors and servers if there was a problem. If they couldn't track it down, they would talk the manager through some diagnostics and if the problem still couldn't be fixed, would make contact with an emergency engineer to turn up on site.

'It's not easy trying to re-boot a projector and hand out re-admission tickets at the same time. Wait until you have to do it.'

Bill smiled. 'I can imagine.'

Later that evening, he showed the proposals to Maureen.

'You know, you don't have to do this,' she said. 'You could take the redundancy. It would tide us over until your pension comes through. We could start doing some of those things we always promised ourselves.'

'True. But I've only got another year anyway. I don't want to leave them in the lurch. It wouldn't be fair.'

'You've got a life too, Bill. Look at how many of our friends have left it too late. By the time they retire, their health isn't so good and they're limited in what they can do. Remember that engineer you used to know, who didn't even make it to retirement?'

'Bertie Arkwright. Now there was a character. I wonder what he'd think of all this?'

'From what you told me about him, it wouldn't be complementary.' She laughed. 'More likely to turn the air blue.'

Bill put his hand on her arm. 'Listen. I'm fit and well. So are you. Look at us, out walking ten miles last weekend and not even getting out of breath climbing Thorpe Cloud. Sixty-four isn't old these days.'

'I suppose not.'

'I just don't like leaving a job half done. It doesn't feel like I've finished yet.'

'Well, if that's how you see it, I'm not going to argue. Once you set your mind on something, I know how you can be. And as long as you're happy, then so am I. But promise me this. If you stop enjoying work, don't hang on just because you feel you owe them something.'

'Of course not, love.'

She turned the volume up on the TV again and resumed watching *Casualty*. Bill opened up Facebook on his tablet. He'd been invited to join another group of ex-projectionists. All the usual suspects were there and it was somewhere to reminisce about the good old days. Some of the posts were tinged with bitterness, but you couldn't blame them for that.

As he still worked for the company, he was always careful to keep his comments neutral, or to only like and reply to posts that were safely set in the past. One of today's posts raised a smile – a picture of a cinema canopy back in the nineteen eighties with three film titles on display; Screen 1 – *Big*, Screen Two – *Frantic*, Screen Three – *Shag*. Harmless fun, and a reminder of happier times.

So here he was, about to handle yet more changes. You couldn't deny that it wasn't the same job he'd started in; but this was just another in a long line of alterations that the industry had gone through. It all boiled down to the same thing really. All you could do was your best. Even if he wasn't up in projection full time, he could still ensure his show – in his mind it would always be his show – held on to the highest possible presentation standards. There would be no complaints at Saxfield about poor light on screen because people couldn't be bothered to slide the 3D XL unit out of the way when playing a 2D film. The auditoria would remain well-lit and inviting, the heating and ventilation controls set correctly and the sound levels checked. And he'd make sure that by the time he was ready to retire, those who were left to carry on would subscribe to the same standards. It would be a fitting end to his long career.

Cat: 2012

More rain. The second week of it; skies mourning for the end of the cinema industry, if you wanted to think that way. Cat unlocked the door to the void, turned on the ancient brass light switch and shone her torch up the vertical wooden steps that led up to the roof space over Screen One. As she climbed, she could hear the rain hammering on the corrugated asbestos above her head. The air was damp, chilly and had a slightly musty smell. Catwalks stretched the length of the auditorium, disappearing into the gloom. Dust motes whirled around the hundred-watt light bulbs like planets in orbit. Another few weeks and this space would be filled with the cries of swallows, whose last-year mud nests still lurked under the eaves.

This was probably the last time she would set foot up here. She carried a bucket of lamps, ready to replace any downlights that had failed. It was hard to imagine the manager doing this type of work in future, or indeed any of the other tasks that kept the old place shipshape and well-maintained. Already she had heard of other sites where the screen masking had been turned off so that no-one needed to worry about checking and tensioning cables, or what to do if it failed. Decorative lighting inside the auditoriums would go the same way; as long as there was sufficient illumination for the customers to find their seats, no-one would care about lining up colour washes on the walls. It was only presentation; not essential for the business, they would think.

Now that she knew the plans, she had resigned herself to what was going to happen. Her career in the cinema business was about to end.

The final blow had come from HR the previous week, when she had been called down to Mr Skinflint's office to discuss her options.

He had given her five minutes to read through the paperwork, twiddling his thumbs at the other side of the desk as she took in the contents. Any cinema with five screens or under would lose all their technical staff. That meant both Marcus and herself would no longer be needed. She stared numbly at the page.

'Well?' he asked at last. 'Any questions?'

'When?'

'Within the next two months. As you can see, the company are still offering generous redundancy terms, so with your years of service, you'll do well from it. Unless...'

'Unless what?'

He twiddled his thumbs again. 'I'm no happier about this than you are. I appreciate it's a sound business decision, but I'm also a realist. I know how much you do to keep this cinema running and I'm not sure any of us in the management team would be able to do it as well. Or even if we had the knowledge, whether we'd have the time. We're only being allocated forty hours a week for projection, after all.'

'That's not much,' she acknowledged.

'No. Plus we've got our own responsibilities and my regional manager is setting tougher targets all the time. I've been wondering if there might be a way round the problem.'

A flicker of hope stirred inside. 'Like what?'

'Well, I can't offer you a management position, but you could become a team leader.'

She started to protest, but he held up his hand. 'Listen up for a minute. I'm thinking you'd spend most of your time on maintenance and projection duties. You'd have to do a few shifts front of house, naturally, just to make things legit, but it wouldn't be all that different to how things operate now.'

Cat considered the offer. Would it really turn out as he said? Would the company actually allow him to do it? And would she want to go back to serving the public again, especially in this day and age? Back when she'd last worked front of house, there'd still been an element of fun about the job. Nowadays, the staff were in competition to see who could sell the most, with their figures emblazoned on boards in the office and gold stars for the top seller of the month. Only last week, someone had been sacked for giving out a larger portion of salsa than what was considered acceptable. 'I'm not sure...' she said cautiously.

'You need some time to think, naturally. Well, you can have a few days to let me know one way or another.'

Those few days had passed and the more she considered the offer, the less attractive it seemed. When she'd talked about it with Marcus, he'd picked out the flaws right away.

'Team leaders get just above minimum wage. That'd be a big drop in money. And I bet if you accept it, the redundancy package melts away.'

'If I don't want to take it, what about you?'

He shook his head. 'Nah. I'm not going to work my guts out for less than what I'm getting now. Anyway, who's to say it'll last? They might move the goalposts again in another six months.'

It wasn't as if she needed the cinema any more. With the redundancy package and her growing business, she would survive. Thrive, even. It was a no brainer.

Except for her long ago promise to Alfie, to keep the cinema going when he retired. But Alfie wasn't around anymore either. He had outlasted 35mm by just over four months. The funeral had been well attended. She'd used up the last trailer reels she'd kept back to make a unique wreath of coiled and woven film, admired by many of the former colleagues she'd met at the crematorium. It rustled and shimmered in the spring sunshine. Liz had insisted it had pride of place next to the family's floral arrangement.

'What a beautiful thing to do,' Liz had said. 'Alfie would have loved it.'

'I hope so.'

After the service, the former projectionists had adjourned to the nearest pub, as was customary. She soon discovered she was one of the last to still be in the business.

'Not for much longer though,' she'd told them. 'It's all change again.'

They had all adapted in different ways. Some were retired, some had moved on to other careers. 'Would you believe I'm working for my son now. Who'd have thought I'd be a plumber's mate at my age?'

'I've started a gardening business. Always loved being outdoors, on me allotment, so thought I might as well do it full time. All those years I spent stuck inside a stuffy projection box in the summer. I must have been mad.'

She told Mr Skinflint of her decision. 'I'm disappointed, of course,' he said. 'But if that's what you want...'

Strange that *Titanic* was showing again during her final days; the hundredth anniversary of the disaster and nearly fourteen years since its first release. They'd played it for sixteen weeks back in nineteen ninety-eight and neither of the prints had looked any the worse on the day they were plated off than on the first showing. Of course, back then, there were projectionists who cared about presentation and film handling working in most cinemas. And none of them, herself included, had thought that their way of life was as doomed as that of the passengers aboard the ill-fated liner.

She recalled a photograph that summed up those last few peaceful Edwardian summers. *Heavy Roses, Voulangis, France, 1914*, it was called; a monochrome picture of old- fashioned roses at the height of flowering. You could almost smell them.

The photographer had suffered in the Great War, as had so many young men of his era. Afterwards he came back to Voulangis and burned all his pictures. *Heavy Roses* was etched on her memory. What other image symbolised so well the fragility of life itself? It could also stand for the transition from film to digital, she realised. Film – tactile and easily damaged, yet capable of such powerful imagery - versus the new media, always perfect, yet intangibly lacking in the magic of cinema. An old rose's time was fleeting; the bloom lasted at best for one or two days. The soft, blowsy petals browned and fell fast. The bushes themselves were susceptible to attack by pests and diseases. Modern varieties were better in so many ways; they flowered repeatedly rather than having a short, sweet season and were resistant to many of the common blights. Yet their impeccable blooms had no scent at all.

During those last few days, she found herself remembering the end of her first cinema career; the final lingering days of the old Gaumont. Fairham would still be open, but no-one would lovingly tend these new machines, or care for the building as she had done; the last in a long line of custodians whose skills and knowledge has been passed down over the years. Not for the love of the company, but for the satisfaction of a job well done and the feeling of pride in presenting a show to the people sitting out there beyond the porthole. All over now.

As the credits rolled, she looked around the projection box for the last time. In her mind's eye, the squat black rectangle of the NEC projector was replaced by the pair of Victoria 8's that had been there on the first day she walked in. She remembered the comforting sound of their running; the spill of light from the old President lamphouse conversions onto the red tile painted floor, the slow turning of shiny platters, the hum of the rectifier and the snap of a join going through the gate. All gone now to a scrap yard somewhere in Milton Keynes. Only the ghostly outline of their bases remained etched on the floor to show where they had served well for forty odd years. This was the future, and much joy may those who remained have of it.

Cat powered down the projector then took one last look around. 'Goodnight,' she said, for the last time. She turned out the light, locked the door behind her and trod softly down the stairs, never to return.

Graham: 2012 and beyond

Traffic on the M40 was bad this afternoon. As the line of cars stopped yet again, Graham had time to admire the slowly turning circles of the red kites in the air above. They were majestic birds and could usually be seen somewhere along this section. If he wasn't in such a hurry, he could have enjoyed the sight more.

The emergency call had come through over an hour ago. He'd got out of London fairly fast, only to get stuck in this jam. All he could do was to call the cinema and reassure them that he was on the way. If it had been a multiplex it wouldn't be so urgent, but for a three screen cinema to lose two of its available auditoria wasn't a good thing.

The traffic began moving again. He wondered why some drivers immediately speeded up, got too close to the slower moving traffic in front, then had to slam on the brakes again. In situations like this, he played the smooth driving game; accelerating as slowly as possible, then trying to avoid stopping at all. It was one way to deal with the stress of jams.

His BlackBerry chimed. Another email. Another problem somewhere. He checked it quickly. It was up beyond Birmingham; the northern half of the country, so thankfully not his. There had been a few times when so many calls had come through, you had to try and prioritise, even though you could only get to one place at a time. Not being able to help everyone was another cause of stress; he didn't like to think of cinemas losing shows.

'That job is going to kill you,' Maria had warned, yet again. 'If not in some motorway smash, then you'll end up with an early heart attack.'

'I'm fine,' he'd protested.

One of his colleagues had recently been diagnosed with high blood pressure. His GP had fitted him with a twenty-four hour monitor so that they could find out when were the worst times of day. 'When I checked the data against my phone, guess what? The times my blood pressure sky-rocketed were when I got a call from the NOC.'

They were moving more quickly now; up to twenty-five miles an hour. His sat nav gave him an ETA of forty minutes. Not too bad, considering. He rummaged in his bag for a snack, but there was nothing left, not even the emergency Twix. The phone rang, the number prefixed with +46. Sweden. Damn.

He answered on the hands free. 'Hello. Graham Cooper.'

'Yes, Graham. Are you busy?'

'I'm on the way to Headley. Two screens off, remember.'

'You couldn't pop in to Mineford on the way?'

'That's a hundred miles further along.' He often wondered if they even had a map of Great Britain on the wall in their office. How often had he been asked if he could 'pop' to somewhere that was the opposite end of the country. 'What's their problem?'

'They are saying they have an electrical problem in Screen Four. I can't connect to anything there. Could you give them a call?'

'Okay.' Certain that his own blood pressure must have ratcheted up a couple of notches, he found the number and dialled.

The phone rang but no-one answered. 'Come on, come on.' Eventually, someone picked it up.

'Graham Cooper,' he said, 'I'm calling about your problem in screen four. Can I speak to the technician?'

'Who?'

'Whoever's in projection.'

'Oh, we don't have no-one there anymore.'

'Well, your manager then.'

'I'll see if I can find her. But she's busy. Something's gone wrong.'

'Yes, I know.' Bloody idiot, he thought. 'That's why I'm calling.'

He was put on hold, listening to a crackly and distorted version of *Greensleeves*. The traffic was crawling again. He changed down to second gear, keeping a good distance from the car in front.

'Hello.' A female voice came on to the line at last. 'I'm the duty manager.'

'Great. I've been told you've got a problem in screen four.' He'd not been to Mineford for several months; it wasn't one of his regular sites. It was an old cinema; a conversion. Screen Four was somewhere down near the stage end, as he recalled.

'Yes, nothing's working.'

'Nothing?'

'No, the projector is totally dead. It won't switch on at all.'

'Okay. Are you in there now?'

'Yes.'

'So, there's no lights on anywhere on the projector, right?' He thought quickly. 'Is anything else in there working? The sound rack, for example?'

'Yes, that's all on.'

'Okay. Now, I need you to look around the box for me. If you look at the front of the projector, you can probably see a thick cable running from it to somewhere on the wall. Can you find that?'

'I can see a black cable, yes. It goes to a blue and grey switch.'

'Is it plugged in securely? And is the switch turned on?'

There was a long pause. 'I think so. Er, yes.'

'Okay.' So that wasn't it. Unless the connections inside the plug had burned out. 'Can you smell burning? Does anything in that area look like it might have overheated?'

'No,' she said.

Probably not the plug then. 'Now, somewhere in the projection box, up on the wall, there'll be a big distribution board, with a flap you can open. It might be grey, or black. Hopefully it will have a label somewhere on it so you can identify it. Can you look for that?'

They were speeding up again. He changed gear. ETA was now twenty-five minutes to Headley. If he was really unlucky, once he'd sorted them out, he'd be heading west for another hundred miles.

'I've found something here behind the sound rack. Shall I open the front?'

'Please. You should see a lot of circuit breakers. They look like little switches.'

'Yes.'

'Now, you should be able to see which ones are on and which ones are off. Some of them might be deliberately turned off because they aren't in use any more. But if you look carefully, see if you can see one labelled "projector" and if it's off, turn it back on.'

There was another long pause as she searched. Then, even before she spoke, he heard the welcome bleep of a digital projector booting up. 'It's back on!' she said. 'Everything's working.'

'Wonderful. Now, I don't know why it tripped. But if it happens again, you'll probably need an electrician to come in and check the circuit.'

'Thank you so much.'

'No problem.'

Another one solved. He might get home by seven tonight. Not that it would make any difference to Maria; she was on a late shift, so wouldn't be back herself until nearly midnight. By which time, he'd be out like a light, ready for another early start tomorrow.

Twenty minutes later, he walked in to the foyer at Headley. A sign on the front doors apologised for the technical problems in Screens One and Three. The manager was hovering around the kiosk, passing the time by fluffing up bags of popcorn.

'Thank goodness you're here. Do you think we'll get the next show on, at five?'

It was just gone four. 'Maybe. Depends on how serious it is.'

'Upstairs went off first. We had a full house of seniors in there waiting to see *The Iron Lady*. The film just wouldn't play. I tried re-booting it, then I called the NOC. Meanwhile, we sent them all downstairs thinking we could play it there instead, but the projector kept showing an error. And there's a warning message up on the server too.'

It turned out to be a combination of problems, most of them preventable. Screen One's server was nearly ninety-five percent full. A lot of cinemas forgot to delete old content on a regular basis, or thought to save themselves time by leaving it in place. To make matters worse, another drive had been inserted to ingest a new feature. No wonder it couldn't play anything.

He stopped the ingest, cleaned up the server and re-booted it. Bingo. Content played first time.

Screen Three was in much the same condition. Once they'd swapped the audience over, they'd started to transfer *The Iron Lady* from the TMS to the server down there, but because it too had insufficient room, it had slowed the process right down. The projector error turned out to be a simple lamp strike fault, but he guessed that by then, the cinema staff had been so panicked, they must have just given up trying. He couldn't blame them. They weren't technically minded people and they'd had a load of disgruntled pensioners to handle as well.

'There you go. All sorted.' He leaned on the kiosk. 'Make sure you clean up those servers every few weeks to stop it happening again, okay?'

'You're a miracle worker. Can I get you a coffee before you go?'

'Please.'

Later that evening, he sat watching the TV. It was hard to believe he'd been doing this job for almost two years and was still officially employed on a 'temporary' basis. He knew he did a good job and worked hard, so felt fairly safe. But with all the other cuts that were happening and some of those that were rumoured, he wondered if that would be enough. There had been a few news items lately on the Internet indicating that the private equity company might be angling for a sale soon and that could mean all sorts of changes.

Maria still hadn't found anything else. She'd applied for a several vacancies outside the cinema business and even got on to the shortlist for one or two of them. But when it came to the crunch, they had decided to play it safe and take someone on who had prior experience in a similar industry.

'They're all the same when it comes down to it,' she'd fumed. 'I was perfect for that last job.'

'It was probably someone's cousin they took on. Or someone the boss had already worked with. That's how it goes.' If Maria was finding it difficult, with all her management skills and qualifications, what sort of chance would he have?

Still, he was better off than Uncle Peter. He'd responded well to the cancer treatment, but just after he was pronounced fit to return to work, all the projection jobs in his company had been wiped out. Nowadays, he spent most of his time posting on Facebook, ranting about the cinema companies and their policies with others of his generation, while simultaneously trying to jump through the hoops necessary to claim his Jobseeker's Allowance. 'It's no fun looking for a job these days. You spend hours filling in forms online. Someone my age doesn't stand a cat's chance in hell of getting anywhere.'

Just before he went to bed, his BlackBerry chimed with a message about some playback issues at one of his sites. Not too far away either, so even better. He called the cinema and told them he would be along in the morning. As expected, no-one would be in until nine, but at least they still had a dedicated technical person to meet him. Someone who could give him the exact info he needed and be of some use.

Next morning, Graham dragged over a chair and positioned it so that he could see out of the porthole. He'd re-seated the Dolphin board in the server and hoped it might solve the playback issues, but the only way to be sure was to run some content.

As the adverts played, each one in sparkling, pristine condition, he couldn't help but remember the days – only two years ago, but seeming much longer – when each week he'd checked every 35mm advert on the bench, ticking it off against the list provided. Back then, he'd have known these ads by heart. He'd have examined them when making up the program and then viewed them on screen just to make doubly sure nothing was back to front or upside down, or the wrong certificate for the feature. Now as each ad ended, the next began instantly, whereas in film days there would have been a foot or so of black spacing between each one and the evocative sound of the spliced join going through the gate. There was something about digital that was a bit too perfect, a bit too slick; like watching an extra-large TV screen rather than real cinema.

No glitches so far. That was the trouble with intermittent faults. Everything might run fine for a couple of hours before it started to play up again. All you could do was replace the potentially faulty boards, one by one. At least with 35mm, you could get around lots of problems, whereas this stuff played perfectly or not at all. Plus audiences seemed less tolerant of faults in a digital programme. Maybe that was just because they resented the amount they were being charged to see a show these days, so felt more inclined to complain if things weren't right. Less people were opting to watch the 3D version of films too, presumably objecting to the extra cost. Mind you, some of the stuff coming out in 3D these days was rubbish. The latest release was *Piranha 3DD*, the second in the series. The storyline was minimal and the attraction seemed to be based on scenes in which bikini-clad busty girls were ripped apart by the savage fish.

The door opened, and Byron returned with two steaming mugs of tea. 'Here you are. No sugar, wasn't it?'

'That's right.' He took a swig. These days, tea was a welcome bonus.

'How's it looking so far?' Byron asked.

'Behaving itself for now. I'll keep an eye on it for a bit longer, see the feature goes on.'

'You've not got anywhere else to go, then?'

'Not at the moment.' Graham glanced at his BlackBerry. No new emails or messages. Maybe this would be an easy day.

'You guys must get around a bit.' Byron set his mug down on the empty bench, its vacant holes showing where the rewind heads had once been bolted in place.

'I did over a thousand miles last week. Had to go to the wilds of Wales to swap an amplifier.'

'An amp? Couldn't the techie have done that?'

'No techies. Everyone at the site took VR and walked. The managers don't want to spend any time in the box. They've got their own jobs to do and as they said, "We're not getting paid any extra." And there's the techno fear element.'

'That's the thing. My GM said, "If I'd wanted to work back there in the dark, never seeing a soul, I'd have become a projectionist." He doesn't want to do it and I don't much care for working on the floor. Can't stand the general public, me. They're all right on the other side of the glass,' he gestured towards the porthole, 'But face to face? No way.'

'So you won't be staying then?'

'No. I've been with this company for nineteen years. The redundancy package is pretty good. Might not be so generous once the suckers who fall for this reprieve have taught everything they know to the managers. I reckon this whole project is just temporary. Another year or so, maybe less, and they'll cull us again. Anyone who stays will get screwed royally.'

The feature began. If there were going to be any problems due to security issues, now would be the time. Everything continued playing as it should.

'So, what are your plans for work, afterwards?' Graham asked.

'I've had my own photography business for a few years now. In fact, sometimes I have to turn down work because of being here.'

'That sounds good. Weddings and such, is it?'

'That's how I started out. But recently I've gone into a more... specialist market,' Byron continued, clearly enthusiastic about his new career. 'This friend of the wife asked if I could take some glamour shots for her profile on a dating site. Then a friend of hers saw the photos and asked if I could do the same for her. Word of mouth's the best advertising you can have. Plus a lot of the guys doing that sort of work are dirty old men. They just want to ogle the women or even feel them up. I'm strictly professional. I get couples too, wanting to dress up in outfits, if you know what I mean.'

'I can imagine.' Graham wasn't sure he wanted to hear any more, even if it was good to know that for at least one old-school projectionist, there was life after cinema.

'No-one has a job for life, these days,' Byron said. 'You've got to keep sharp and keep your options open.'

'They'll always need people to fix stuff.'

'That's true. What is it they say? "If they replace you with a black box, learn how to fix the black boxes".'

'Something like that. It's worked for me so far.'

The summer blockbuster season began and once the school holidays started there was even less time to get any work done before the doors opened. Nowadays, blockbusters were shown every half hour on multiple screens, meaning that no matter what time people turned up, a show would be starting soon. The down side was that it was rare for an auditorium to fill up. Graham had always liked the atmosphere of a packed cinema. Watching a film surrounded by people made the whole experience more intense. Laughter surrounded you. Tension was palpable. People jumped or gasped at the scary parts. It just wasn't the same when there were lots of empty seats.

The new regime began. Some of the projection rooms were still well maintained, but in many cases they began to look untidy and uncared for. Graham went on a scheduled visit to one of his smaller sites. Here, with no technical presence and minimal management, he needed to service the site monthly.

'You know where to go,' said the manager. 'I've turned everything on already. You know, I can't believe how long it used to take the projectionists to do that. I was in and out in five minutes this morning.'

'Any problems since my last visit?'

'Not that I can think of.'

Film transit cases were scattered over a wide area of the box floor. He stacked them together purely so as not to fall over them and to give himself room to sit in front of the TMS to check its function and content. Following this, he visited each screen in turn to play some content and to test picture and sound quality.

Something was definitely not right in Screen Two. The dialogue was barely audible. In fact, it was coming out of the surround channels. He opened up the back of the sound rack and soon found out the reason. They had obviously needed to change an amplifier, but hadn't plugged the inputs and outputs into the right places. Left and right were okay, but the centre and surround channels were swapped around. He corrected it and went to find the manager, who was busily stocking up the retail area.

'Did you know there was a sound problem in two?'

He shrugged. 'No-one's said anything.'

'Who changed the amplifier?'

'No idea. It wasn't me, so it must have been one of the team leaders.'

'Well, they connected it up wrongly. Shall I show you how it should be done for future reference?'

'Later, maybe. I've got tons to do before opening and only one member of staff to help.'

Graham went back upstairs again, carrying on with his checks. He found a xenon lamp that had been removed from the projector in Screen Three. The quartz envelope had gone totally black and the end caps were discoloured, indicating that it had overheated. When he looked at the replacement, he found the new lamp's connections had been done up so loosely, it would soon have gone the same way.

He made a note on his paperwork, feeling frustrated. You couldn't totally blame the manager; he was obviously overstretched already and yet it was clear that a cinema like this needed much more than a monthly visit to keep on top of things. Trouble was, he didn't have the time either; what with all the rushing round to keep cinemas on screen and the reduction in technical hours and people at all the sites.

He talked about it with Maria. 'I feel like there's only so much I can do to help. They keep telling us that part of our support role is to provide training, and I don't mind doing that, but there's just no time.'

'Tell me about it,' she said. 'If I'd have known how this business would end up, I'd never have gone into it in the first place.'

'Maybe it'll get better, once it settles down.'

'And maybe it won't. Trouble is, you're always looking on the bright side.'

When he visited one of the new sites under construction, he began to realise that she might be right. Now that there were no technicians on site, the latest idea was to reduce the amount of space necessary for equipment, so that extra seats could be added at the back of an auditorium. The new rooms were called 'machine rooms' rather than projection rooms, implying that little or no human intervention would ever be required.

Mind you, the next innovation touted in all the industry publications seemed to be 'boothless projection'. This entailed mounting the projectors from platforms built into the auditorium ceiling, accessible via lifts or ladders 'for the occasional times that they need maintenance or servicing'.

'We'll be hanging in the air soon, like Spider-Man,' one of his colleagues joked. 'With all the yobs chucking popcorn at us as we try to get it back on screen.'

That was the trouble with the hype. It promised the kind of reliability that could never be delivered in a real-world scenario. Yes, the old projection equipment could be temperamental and mechanical systems broke down too, but often the projectionists could keep it running one way or another until parts and professional help arrived. Digital equipment was only as reliable as any computerised system and of course, totally inaccessible to anyone on site due to the security issues. All they could really do was turn it off and back on again to see if that cleared the fault.

Graham was shocked at the size of some of the machine rooms. There was barely enough space to get around the projector console and he foresaw some interesting problems in the future getting at some of the parts. Plus, there was nowhere to work on equipment if you took it out of the rack. All this for the sake of seven or eight extra seats in the auditorium.

'You're lucky there's even any lights in those boxes, mate,' one of the contractors told him. 'On the original plans they'd not put any in, 'cos it's all unmanned these days.'

Routine visits to cinemas became increasingly solitary affairs. The manager would give him the keys and he'd let himself into the empty projection rooms. At one of his regular sites, they'd turned the air conditioning down so low the place was cold as a tomb, emphasising its inimical nature to mere humankind. There were often poignant reminders of the vanished projection staff; calendars that had been left turned to the last date anyone had occupied the space, dried out kettles and mugs left on the draining board, never to be used again. In one room, someone had altered a film poster – *Will the last ~~one~~ projectionist to die please turn out the lights.*

The service work he did was tedious; a never-ending Groundhog Day of checking each screen's projection and sound equipment, filling in the obligatory paperwork and racing against the clock to finish before the doors opened. Once his work was complete, he handed back the keys and left, having only spoken a few words to anyone on site. He talked more often to other engineers on the phone than he did face to face.

As the last of the summer blockbusters tailed off, the news came that numbers were going to be reduced yet again. Every cinema would need to lose at least one person from their management team; this could be the current Digital Manager if their skill set wasn't seen as being right for the business.

Maria had already been included in the discussions at her site. Two people would need to go, she'd been told. One would be the DM, as his customer service skills weren't up to scratch. The other would be chosen either by a selection process, or through voluntary redundancy.

'My GM said he'd like me to accept the new offer,' Maria told Graham that evening, as they ate together. 'So I'm safe again, if I want to stay.'

'Well, that's good news for you.' He had recently been given a permanent contract, which had vastly increased his sense of job security. It was good that Maria was in the same boat.

'It's just…' she paused. 'I'm not sure I really want to. I've had enough.'

'But…'

'No buts. This isn't the business I started in. Back then, there was good career progression and the prospects of a decent wage by the time you got to manage your own cinema. Now they want to pay as little as they can and work you into the ground. We don't have enough front of house staff most of the time, so we're out on the floor, but they still expect all the office work to get done too. Plus there's the projection stuff on top of it. If the redundancy package on offer is good enough, I think I'm going to take it.'

'So what will you do?'

'Who knows. I'll find something. It's time for a change.' She sipped from her glass. 'And what about you? Do you really enjoy driving all those miles a week like a mad thing?'

Graham sighed. 'It can be overwhelming some days. But I still get a sense of satisfaction when something's fixed and back on screen. I feel as if what I'm doing is worthwhile.'

'At least your lot get some kind of appreciation,' Maria said. 'When we know an engineer's on the way it's like in those old cowboy films, when they're down to their last bullets and suddenly the US cavalry appears over the hill.'

He laughed. 'I like the idea of that.'

It made up for all the early starts and the frustration of waiting in traffic jams. Graham thought about how his life had changed along with the industry. With the accelerating pace of technology, there would always be work for people like him. New innovations meant new opportunities and the necessity to improve and extend your knowledge – all of the things he was good at.

'You know that I want to keep on doing this job, don't you,' he said to Maria. 'I can see why you're disillusioned. Lots of the management teams I meet feel the same and I can understand why. Whatever you decide, I'll do what I can to help.'

She smiled. They curled up next to each other on the sofa. 'Maybe I was wrong about cinema,' she said. 'Maybe there's a future for it after all.'

'I think there is,' he said. 'It won't be the same as it was, but nothing stays the same, does it? I mean, when we were kids, hardly anyone had mobile phones and now most people couldn't live without them.'

'A bit like you, checking your BlackBerry every time it makes a noise.'

'Well, that's work, isn't it? And if I don't, the emails and messages just pile up, so it takes longer to go through them later.'

'I know. Mind you, I'm just as bad with my Facebook notifications.' She took another sip of wine. 'We'll manage, won't we? Even if I don't get a job right away?'

'Of course we will. Now I've got a permanent contract, I'm on a better salary. There are going to be so many new builds and improvements over the next few years, I'm in a good position to progress. My last appraisal went well too.'

He was up early again the next morning, leaving Maria sleeping peacefully. It was bright and sunny; the sort of day that made you feel optimistic. He was glad they had talked so freely the night before and that she could see why he still wanted to remain in the business. Once she got out of the situation she was in; once the pressure and the stress had gone, he had no doubt that she would make a success in her new career.

There would always be ups and downs; it was the same with any job or relationship. You had to deal with them as best you could. Just as his parents had done before him, even though the pace of life had been slower back then.

Much as he appreciated that he had the skills to hold down a job in his chosen field, it didn't stop him thinking about those who hadn't been so lucky. Uncle Peter, for example, made redundant before his time from the only career he'd ever wanted. All of the countless others, who had attempted to adapt and jump through new hoops, but who had ultimately been forced out.

It always hit him harder at the old sites; the places where once there had been friendly faces, chatter and welcoming cups of tea waiting for him. He could hardly bear to enter some of the staff rooms, often still packed with film memorabilia collected through the years by projectionists. They were reminders of a time that had passed into history in what seemed like the blink of an eye, just as earlier eras had brought the demise of silent films, the cinema organist and huge, single-screen cinemas.

In these places, you felt an absence. Something was missing in this brave new world. Not just the sound of film running through projectors and the click as a join passed through the gate. In those unmanned projection rooms, he sometimes caught sight of a shadow out of the corner of his eye, as if some long-vanished projectionist was about to fade into view.

Sometimes, he felt obliged to reassure these unseen ghosts, even though it felt a little strange.

'Don't worry,' he'd say. 'I'm still here. I'll look after your legacy as best I can.'

In a time of endless change, it was all you could do.

Author Biography

Ben Dowell worked in the cinema business for almost thirty years, as a projectionist, trainer and engineer. Last Reels is an affectionate evocation of the changes in the industry from the 1960's to 2014 and the final transition from film to digital which brought in the end of an era

Ben's next book is a supernatural mystery set in an old cinema during the 1980's.

The Dark Behind the Screen

Eastgrave cinema was built on cursed ground. Now, a misguided experiment has stirred up vengeful ghosts.

Tess Draper's mother, Betty dies in a mysterious car accident, years after she worked in the cinema as a teenager. Tess is determined to find out what happened and in the process unearths more mysteries concerning Betty's past and her own parentage.

Mark Patterson, the new Chief Projectionist at Eastgrave, has his own secrets. Will the malign influences of the cinema allow him to escape unscathed?

Together, Tess and Mark must find a way to defuse the growing powers under the building before it is too late.

Visit www.mawgrim.co.uk for more information.
Email:bdowell@mawgrim.co.uk

Printed in Great Britain
by Amazon